STAY

ASH KNIGHT

Author's Note:

This is a work of fiction. Autism Spectrum Disorder (ASD) is real. Over 200,000 new cases are diagnosed each year and there is no cure. Every person diagnosed is unique. Every individual has their own story. Joe's story does not depict a specific person, nor is Joe meant to categorize the disorder. His character is completely fictional.

This story takes place in Oregon, near Corvalis, in a city that is fictional. None of the buildings, streets, or businesses are real. Any resemblances are entirely coincidental.

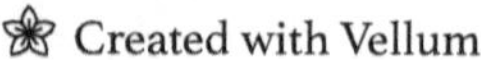 Created with Vellum

1

———

Bird–Age 7

My dresser is right under my window. When no one knows I'm awake, I pull out my drawer and stand on my jeans to get to the top so I can sit and look at the stars. Someday, I'm going to be an astronaut. Someday, I'm going to reach out my hand and touch the stars. Someday. But not today.

Today is a bad day. Again. Mom made me stay in my room and close the door. Then she opened and closed the front door seventeen times. Next, she's going to open each kitchen cabinet door twenty-two times. Then she'll open and close the bathroom door. I always lose count. I know I got to eleventy-seven once and then I couldn't keep going. I'm not very good with math.

"Not again, Lucy. Are you kidding me? Don't you have anything better to do than count every fucking thing in this house?"

That's Venom. He's the bad guy. He's my father.

When my mom starts counting, he gets so mad. Madder. He

spits when he screams. One time he spat from the countertop all the way to the fridge. After that I started watching better. I think that was the farthest he's ever spat, though.

"I'm sorry. Fourteen. Fifteen. I'm almost done and dinner's... nineteen. Twenty... almost ready. Just go get... twenty-six. Twenty-seven. Twenty-eight...changed from work and every-thing will be fine—"

I heard the bedroom door shut with a strangled click. It sticks. It's like the door knows it doesn't want him in the room and tries not to close.

I really don't want to eat dinner if he's home. I'm going to sit behind my bed and hope he doesn't look for me.

"You worthless waste of skin!" He yells from his room and I can hear his feet on the carpet.

One, two—

One, two—

One, two—

One, and he's here.

I try to make myself as small as I can.

I can fit my legs up under my shirt and Bunny is resting inside. He's my friend.

He knows me.

"Get over here now, boy." He means it.

I start shaking.

"I can hear you over there. You better get over here before I count to three or you'll see what mad looks like, Bird." He's turning into Venom now. I bet he's trying to get as much spit in his mouth as he can. It's his weapon. Well, one of them.

I slowly pull my legs out of my shirt.

One.

I tuck in my shirt so Bunny can't see. He doesn't like Venom.

Two.

I stand up.

"Get over here." He points his finger at his feet, and his face is red—I didn't even leave my room today—I didn't *do* anything.

As I walk over, he takes Bunny by the ear and yanks. "No!" I grab his wrist and try to stop him, but I can't do anything. I wish my hands were big.

As he pulls Bunny out of my shirt by the ear, he takes his other hand and grabs *my* ear and pulls. "Ow. Please. *Please.*" I know I should just stop, but he has Bunny. Bunny hates Venom.

"'Please, please, please.' You sound pathetic. You make me sick. Begging for some stupid baby toy." His head shakes and Bunny is flopping in the air in his hand. He likes playing astronaut but not with Venom. Never with Venom. This isn't fun.

"I just want Bunny back." I bite my tongue as hard as I can to keep the tears back.

"You listen to me. This is my doll. It's in my house. You have nothing. You hear me, boy?" He tugs hard on my ear. "You have nothing. Everything you think is yours, isn't. It's all mine. I can do whatever I want with it because it's all mine." He starts to turn like he's going to leave me here without Bunny.

"Please give him back. I'll do anything." My ears are ringing and my face is so hot you could heat up bacon on my cheeks.

"You want this pathetic doll back? Here, take it."

Just when I think he's going to give Bunny back, he rips his ears off and throws them at me. They bounce off my wet face and onto the floor. As I bend down, he rips off his legs, then chucks them at me, the body comes last. Once he's finally turning to leave, I let out a sob.

I will do anything it takes to get to the stars. I'll sit up there and shoot lightning at him.

2

____

Joe-Age 22

"I can do this. No one is looking at m-m-me," I chanted, taking in a gulp of air. As I pulled open the huge glass door to Pump It Up, the local sweatbox of death, I adjusted my cloak of invisibility and prayed for the best. Well, that's a lie. I didn't pray. I didn't get religion at all. But that was personal, and I didn't do personal. Swiping my card under the tiny red laser beam, I waited for the brash sounding chirp that signified that I had paid for my membership for another month and the manager didn't just take my cash and pocket it. It had happened before, so I had plenty of reasons to be suspicious.

Finding my way two steps past the curving countertop, I heard a loud voice yell, "Hey, Joe, don't forget we close at eight tonight for the holiday," Penny, the automaton that sat at the front desk seven days a week, said. I'd only ever witnessed her wearing booty shorts and skin-tight tank tops whilst dutifully ignoring anyone who wasn't a muscle god. If you *were* a muscle god, she found a reason to touch the goods, each and every time. The only reason she spoke to me was that I had been known to help her out from time to time fixing things when the members got upset that the equipment wasn't working. Otherwise, I was sure I'd be a pariah.

"Got it, t-t-thanks," I replied, briskly walking to the changing rooms, wincing. After opening my locker (lucky #34), I pulled out my shower basket and towel and threw in my backpack.

Sometimes, I regretted my life. Not today, though. Today I had work. A guy I knew from a few months back, Mitch, said he needed extra help at a job site because one of his guys called in sick and the framing inspection was tomorrow. I'd done my share of odd jobs and helped enough with construction that I could be helpful and not a disaster. I'd always been a hard worker. I just needed a chance to prove it. Anyway, I'd made a bit of cash today so on the way here I'd stopped at McDonald's and bought myself two Big Macs and a Coke. I didn't think I'd ever had food taste that good. Or at least, I couldn't remember the last time I had the money to pay for something freshly wrapped and untouched. It was heaven. Or it would have been if I believed in that. But I don't.

Once I'd showered and shaved, I pulled my laundry out of my locker and started washing it in the shower. One important tip I'd learned is that if you kept the shower curtain closed, no one bothered you about washing your laundry at the gym. And really, I had bigger issues to deal with.

I'd also learned that it was important to take care of your belongings. I'd only ever truly cared about something once. And then I understood that caring was a liability. Anything could be taken away. Used against me. Since I was a kid, I'd vowed never to find myself in a situation like that again. Nothing was worth feeling like your heart could stop beating at any moment. Like each second it was gone you'd inch closer to self-destruction. No. I'd had that once. Never again.

Who was I kidding? I owned 4 shirts, 1 pair of jeans, 1 pair of boots, 3 days worth of underpants and 1 good pair of socks. With flamingos. The other pair of socks had a hole where a nail caught along the side when I hauled ass out of the abandoned building on Trent Street two weeks ago. Those were my unicorn socks. Now I only wore those in case of emergencies. The point was, even if I'd wanted something to care about, I couldn't have it. If it didn't fit in my bag, I didn't need it.

After running the hair dryer over my wet clothes for a while, they started smelling like burnt toast, so I knew the cotton had had enough and I gave the weave a break. I rolled everything up, stuffed them back in my backpack, threw my basket into the locker and pulled the key from the lock.

Passing the cardio equipment, I could see it ended up being a busy night, which meant there would be lots of activity in the parking lot for awhile; I'd need to walk around until it calmed. As I passed the southern corner of the gym building, I could see the dumpster and Phantom. He roamed around as usual, taking in the last vestiges of light before the sun set. Phantom loved the sun and would stretch out for hours, inching across the parking lot as its rays lazed fluidly across the concrete.

I'd met him about four months ago, when I first found myself in this town in Oregon, a week after I had started coming here. He had scared the shit out of me in the night, rubbing against the cardboard and purring like a motorboat. I had never heard a cat purr so loudly in my life and now I found I couldn't sleep without the sound of him. Phantom was comforting to me in ways that I couldn't even think about. I couldn't allow myself to go there.

As I strode over to him, he stretched his legs up, up, up until he was directly on the edge of the building's shadow, then gave up. I could see the moment he'd resigned that it was getting dark, signaling his time to hunt. He'd usually be gone for most of the night, but he'd be back to slay the demons in my nightmares later. After crouching down and giving him a nice neck scratch, I wandered behind the dumpster, behind the old pallet boards lined up against the fence and unpacked my still damp clothing. It would most likely take all night to get everything dry, so now was a good time to start.

After laying everything out across the wooden boards, I threw my bag into the tent that I'd rigged up between the pallets and the chain link fencing. It could have been worse. I could have nothing. I'd been there and lived that life already. I'd learned from that experience as well...don't ever let yourself be vulnerable, physically or mentally. If you had to be alone, make sure you had somewhere to hide.

After a few hours of walking around the area, I headed back home. The gym should've been empty by then and I was exhausted. As soon as I had turned my clothes over to dry the bottom side, I got into the tent, pulled my boots off and lay down on the cool sleeping bag. I told myself I would not think of her. I would not think of him. Venom. I couldn't. Every night it was the same. *Don't go down that rabbit hole.*

Sometime during the early morning hours, Phantom joined me and curled up around my neck, purring into my ear, regaling me with his debauchery and antics while I had been fighting with my prefrontal cortex. I wished I could dream of the night sky. I'd be a star, twinkling in the dark, shining on only the people I'd want to see me.

~

It was Sunday and Sundays were the worst days. There were less people on the roads, but more were out wandering around, aimlessly peering into windows and sitting around people watching. I understood it, though. I had once sat on a bench in the park on Edgar Street for eight hours watching people pass. I'd met two kids named Ethan that day. Both Ethans had jam hands. Kids have this peculiar knack for seeing invisible people. You can't hide anything from them. I wondered at what age that ability went away. Most adults looked right through me. Of course, that was the way I liked it.

My mind kept going back to the Big Macs from McDonald's. I had a few bucks in my pocket, but I couldn't buy food today. I needed to get myself a jacket and a pocket knife. Life on the streets had turned me into a scavenger. And now that I had money for it, I needed a knife. For protection as well as for useful things. Like opening cans. Cutting through boxes.

Going to the Goodwill in town was always a nerve-wracking struggle for me. On a good day, I could tolerate a few people milling around. When there was more of a crowd, I'd get itchy. My eyes burned, my face grew hot. My skin got too tight. I felt like I was being ripped apart. But I had some money today, so I needed to take my chances that everyone would be praising Jesus and hailing to their God while I looked for the necessities of life.

After twenty minutes and about twelve death stares, I had a jacket, a knife, and a couple of pairs of socks. This was one of my better trips. On the downside, I now only had a couple of dollars to last me until I found another job. Phantom would be waiting for me when I got home, so that gave me purpose, and I stepped lively.

3

____

Madden-Age 27

After hip-checking Adam away from the computer, I finally had ten minutes to log my last case of the day into the new computer system that all the nursing staff was required to learn this year. With the rainstorms we'd had the last few days the ED had been hammered with car and bike accident patients, and I'd been on doubles since Tuesday. I could have used a break and about thirty-six hours of sleep. I didn't even remember my last name at that point, let alone what day it was. Fortunately, I had Adam. He'd been on the same shifts for the past few days, and it had meant the difference between sanity and my soul being claimed by some powerful forces of evil.

"Hey, Mads, let's grab a coffee before we take off," Adam said, handing me my raincoat and umbrella. Apparently, he was in as much of a hurry as I was to get the hell out of that place. We'd both gotten a day off and I, for one, had planned on doing nothing. I took my proffered rain gear and saluted the on-call nurse wiping off the patient board. "So long, loves!" I yelled, as I tipped my invisible hat and bowed dramatically. "We'll see you on Saturday!"

Adam and I practically raced out, knowing that any trauma call before we stepped off the hospital grounds could be assigned to us. The second our feet landed on the other side of Grant Street we both high fived, and he gave me an evil smirk.

"Dude, I'm so fucking done. Stick a fork in me. Hell, I doubt I would even notice at this point." He lead the way to Spill the Beans, the local coffee shop and deli and said, "I'm sure I have nothing edible in my house, so I'm grabbing a coffee and a sandwich and I am willing to bet your kitchen isn't any better stocked, am I right?"

I laughed as he opened the door, and I shook my umbrella out on him.

"Hey, that was uncalled for," he yelled, brushing the water down his jacket. "Don't mess with me, Mads. I've been up for days, and I haven't had a decent coffee for longer than that."

"I'll grab a table, you get us sandwiches and drinks," I told him, grabbing at his wet jacket. He made a pinwheel turn while he untangled his arms, I laughed at the way he was not so subtly unstable on his feet. After laying both our jackets across the back of the chairs, I took a seat and looked around. I'd always felt at home in this café, with its rich wood paneling and floors. It always smelled like cinnamon and chocolate, the way my parent's house used to around the holidays. I'd never tell a soul, but I had once run to the bathroom, worried I'd cry after thinking about how my mom would have loved it here. Walking into the place felt as though you were being embraced by outstretched arms. It was the closest I'd ever get to my mom again, so it was comforting.

Adam and I had been coming here for years. It was literally around the corner from the Twin Oaks Medical Center where we both worked as triage nurses. I met him in nursing school a million years ago. He was this super geeky twink that sat in the front row with his laptop and notebook with highlighters, I figured he'd be the perfect one to befriend as both an ally and study partner. It was the best decision I'd ever made. We'd been best friends since and I relied on him daily, for both personal and professional problems, though I preferred his professional side. He tended to make me cringe with tales of his many encounters with professors, daddies, and bears that he met at the gay clubs in town. I quite enjoyed my life of solitude, thank you.

I wasn't completely alone, though. I had my sister, Anna, and her seven-year-old son, David, who I saw on a regular basis. Anna's husband, Dawson, was a commercial airline pilot and was away a lot, so David, Anna, and I had weekly 'dates'. Sometimes, David spent the night at my place. We'd stay up late playing video games and eating ice cream until we couldn't even roll ourselves off the couch. It gave me the opportunity to read him a story before bed. If I had to pick one thing in my life that I couldn't live without it would be reading to David at night, him all curled up in his bed, pajamas on, breath smelling of mint toothpaste. He got this super dreamy look in his eye when we'd get to a romantic part of the story. When I made silly voices, he had a giggle that could light up the Empire State Building. I would literally do anything for that kid, and I couldn't imagine my life any different.

Adam walked over with two steaming mugs and shook his head at me when he set them down. "You'll never believe what Lulu said to me, man," he whispered as he pulled out his chair and folded himself onto it. "She had another one of her premonitions, and she thinks that a change is coming. Something about the weather and the elements being shaken up."

"Elements, huh?" I asked, skeptically. "Well, hopefully Lulu has a plan for emergencies because I do not want her changing anything about this place. It's my fortress of solitude. I'm positive I'd melt, turn to smoke or be molded in carbonite if something happened to it."

Adam laughed. "Well, Lulu isn't usually wrong about these things so maybe you should figure out your Achilles heel and plan for the worst." He took a sip of his coffee and winked at me over the rim. "I am so fucking in love with this cup right now. I want to take it home and curl up with it and never let it go."

"Well, as long as you don't call it Daddy I don't care what you do with your cup."

4

———

Joe

The weather gods had found me offensive and had taken it personally, I was sure of it. Some sort of vendetta against me. My tent had been dripping for two days, meaning there was nowhere to hide from the wetness creeping in. There was little relief outside, what with the pouring rain, but I chose to walk a bit anyway. I wasn't going to get any drier in my soaked tent.

There was a park not far from the gym that I often spent time in. It's where I'd met the jam-handed Ethans. It had these fun all-weather statues and slides for kids to climb on, and in the rain, it was just perfect. The bright colors of the play equipment against the dulled gray sky was beautiful. As I sat raptured, lightning lit up the sky and thunderous booms and cracks played a beat above my head. Then it started. The downpour. Just up ahead around the corner was a café that had a few lights on still, so I made my way over as quickly as I could in hopes of sitting out the worst of it.

Yanking the door open, the smells of fresh coffee and pastries assaulted my senses, making it damn difficult to ignore the roaring sounds from my stomach. I turned just in time, narrowly missing bashing into a woman with a bright yellow raincoat pushing on the door to leave.

"Sorry, I..." I hadn't even finished my thought before she made her way outside. My boots squeaked beneath me, and I looked to see how much of a wet mess I'd made.

As I got my bearings, I noticed that there were about ten small tables scattered around the large room with a couch and a couple of wingback chairs close to the rear. To the right stood a long, wooden counter with two glass cases filled with plates of assorted sizes, shapes, and colors, mostly just crumbs remaining on each surface. A square red dish held a black and white cookie and what looked to be the remnants of a lemon cookie on a tray below.

When a short woman emerged from a doorway behind the counter, she smiled at me and said, "I'm so sorry, but we are closing now." Her hair was mousy brown with grey streaks that were twisted up in some sort of clip. There was something about her eyes, a deep blue that was bright and cheerful, despite the day. Her mouth was bracketed by laugh lines that disarmed me. It was obvious she had happiness around her. It shone like an aura. The way she looked at me made me feel like she could see my secrets and interpret my thoughts. Like she could somehow see through me to what was buried deep inside. In a single moment I was unnerved. The last thing I'd ever wanted was for someone to see me.

I turned, realizing that I was the only one here, still dripping on the shiny wooden floors. All the tables were empty, the previous patrons hastily making their way home before the storm, I assumed.

Swallowing, I managed to squeak, "S-s-sorry." As I turned towards the door, I glanced back and added, "H-h-have a nice n-n-night."

Before I reached the handle, I heard her sigh, tossing a rag on the counter as she cocked her head.

"Wait a minute." Surprise rippled through me as she eyed me. *Really* looked at me, as if, again, seeing something below the surface. "You seem like you could use a warm coffee and a treat. Just give me a minute and I'll grab you something." She sounded nonchalant as she wiped her hands on the towel she'd just thrown onto the counter. I felt so twisted up inside. Of course, I wanted a hot coffee and something to eat, but I didn't want to owe her. I had no way of paying her back and I couldn't just let that go. Not with her. Somehow, she was different. Kind. Not a person to take advantage of.

"N-no." I refused, raising my hand, feeling anxious and vulnerable. "That's t-t-too much," I continued, my hand waiving through the air as if I was directing landing planes.

"Nonsense. How do you take your coffee? Sugar, cream?" She pulled a ceramic mug from the cabinet and I realized that meant she was inviting me to stay.

"Uh, honestly, you don't have to," I mumbled, as my face heated. When I looked up, she smiled. Shit. She was being so thoughtful, and I had no idea why. I had nothing to offer her. As much as I wanted to, I couldn't accept. "I can't. I don't have money to pay for anything." Of course, my stomach chose that moment to let out a thunderous growl to rival the storm.

Blowing out her cheeks with a knowing smile, she said, "Okay. I'll make you a deal. If you stay and help me wipe down the tables and chairs, you can have the coffee, on me. What do you say?"

My mouth dropped open. "Why?" The word came out and I instantly knew I sounded like a fool. I shook my head as I snapped my mouth shut. So much for making a good impression.

She had that look on her face that I'd seen before. It was a look that I'd grown used to. *Pity.* I didn't need her to feel sorry for me and I was going to tell her just that. But then she smiled at me and it was gone. Replaced by something else. Something I couldn't quite name.

"You look like you could use a cup of something warm and I could use the help," she sighed. "One of my employees had a midterm this evening and he's usually the one who does the tables. So, you'd be helping me out, too." She made her way around the counter and through the café and held out her hand. "I'm Lulu and this is my café. And I'm pleased that you walked through the door tonight."

I looked at it, bile rising in my throat at the thought of someone's hands on me. Panicking, I wiped my hands on my pants. With a sheepish look, I croaked, "They're d-d-dirty." I could feel the flush run down my cheeks and into my neck.

Lulu smiled. "No bother. There's a restroom right there. Why don't you go ahead and I'll get you that coffee and something sweet to go with it." She turned and sauntered off behind the counter, then through the doorway, which I assume led to the kitchen area.

I was paralyzed. Why would someone offer so much to me? I couldn't even believe this was happening. I must have glossed over because suddenly she was standing right next to me and said, "Hey," her hand reaching out and landing on my arm. I flinched automatically and then felt a sick feeling in my gut. "You look like someone who's been hurt and could use a break." Squeezing my arm lightly, she explained, "I just get this feeling from you. I'm not usually wrong about these things and I don't think I'm wrong this time. Just, give me a chance, okay?" Her deep blue eyes crinkled, and I wondered if anyone had ever been this nice. No, I knew the answer to that.

"Okay," I whispered with barely a voice.

I found it cathartic to clean. It was something I could do alone and feel instant gratification. Mopping was exactly what I needed to calm my racing heart. I'd seen the industrial yellow bucket and mop in the hallway, so I went ahead and proceeded with my chore. It felt satisfying to do something with my hands, to be useful. I had barely gotten the hang of the water wringing contraption attached to the bucket when Lulu walked over with a cup of hot coffee. Setting the mop in the bucket, I accepted my reward and thanked her with a smile. Before I could say anything, she waved me off and started cleaning out the display cases and wiping down the machines.

We worked in silence for a while, and it was calming, not awkward. I'd never had this. This sense of presence. Of being okay with where I was in the moment. I felt secure with Lulu somehow. Not safe, just... like my heart could take a beat and then rest before starting again. I wasn't *worried.*

About forty minutes had passed with us working around each other when she said, "You don't have to do anything you don't want to do, but I could use some help around here a couple of days a week. I mostly have college kids on, and they sometimes have crazy schedules. Would you be interested in helping me out?"

My mouth hung open in shock. "Are you... I mean, are you... offering me a job?"

Reaching her hand out, I took a step back. I didn't miss how her eyes widened in surprise, but she quickly recovered, replying, "I am. It wouldn't be too many hours at first, but if you like it and we get along like I think we will," she winked, "there will probably be an opportunity for more."

No one was this nice. No one. *Nothing comes without a price.* I wondered idly what the price would be for this. I could possibly earn enough money to keep paying for the gym and have some for food. I'd have somewhere to go. I would be useful. I could *belong*. No. NO. Shaking my head, I tried to erase that thought like a child's Etch-A-Sketch. "I...I would really like that," I croaked out.

Lulu held out her hand and I shook it. "Now that we have that settled, how about you tell me your name?"

For fucks sake. I really was an awful person. "Joe. Joe Calloway." I was pretty sure that was the first time I'd said my name in weeks. Maybe even months. But it was absolutely the second time I'd blushed and humiliated myself in front of this woman in under an hour.

"Well, Joe. I'm pleased to meet you and I'm glad to have you on board. Why don't you stop by tomorrow around four o'clock and we can show you the ropes."

As I WALKED through the park that night, I couldn't hide the smile that rose in my cheeks. This could be the start of something. The twinkle of a beginning after so many ends. I tried not to think about that as the chill of the night bit into me.

That night I had the same dream that I usually have when I allow myself to start feeling happy.

I'm in my brown corduroy overalls, and a blue striped shirt. Bunny is sandwiched between the bib of the denim and my chest, his head poking out to see. I can hear Mom counting. Always counting. Walking down the hallway of the only home I've ever known, the walls turn black and slimy. It's like tar is being poured down from the ceiling to the floor. If I don't hurry, I'm going to get stuck, but Mom is counting my steps. If I go too fast, she'll lose track, and we'll have to start over.

Eighteen.

The tar creeps into the center of the hallway from both walls, and there are only a couple of inches of carpet lining the center like a track. The tar is steaming hot, I'm scared. My hands shake as I pinch Bunny's ears between my thumb and forefinger.

Twenty-three.

I look up to see how much further she is, and the hallway is suddenly narrowed and lengthened like some sort of awful illusion. Mom is standing at the end of the hallway crying, counting, waving her arms over her head, begging me to hurry.

Thirty-one.

I can't hurry. She'll lose track.

The hallway is closing up. She's further and further away.

Thirty-nine.

I'll never make it. I'm sweating now. I have to turn around. When I do, I see Venom. He's at the end of the hallway behind me, rocking back and forth in a chair, a disgusting sneer on his face. I can see his finger tapping on his knee. He's just waiting for me, so he can take everything away.

Forty-one.

I've stopped. I try to lift my foot from the floor, but the tar has me now. It's grabbed onto my foot and won't let go. Venom stands and laughs his maniacal laugh. I know I have nothing left. When he's directly in front of me, he rips Bunny from my embrace.

And then I woke up. Just like I always did.

Sometimes, I wondered if it was my own brain trying to save me from seeing Bunny ripped away from me one more time. But then, my brain probably isn't that keen on saving me from anything. It's seen bad things so many times over. What would be the point now?

I'd awoken sweaty and cold, needing to wash my clothing in the gym bathroom quickly to ensure it was dry for my shift at the café. Damn, that sounded nice in my head. *I have somewhere I need to be today.* I needed to shut out the overwhelming urge to preen. That would mean hope, another thing on my list that I couldn't allow myself. I used to be able to feel it, see it, and smell it. It was green and blue and wonderful, like the ocean at sunset. I had once tried to keep it safe. I had wrapped bubble wrap around it and kept it out of sight, but it still broke. No matter how much I tried, I couldn't keep it.

5

———

Madden

Adam had taken a patient down to X-ray right as my shift ended, so I patted him on the back and bid him adieu, grateful it was him instead of me. Yeah, I was an asshole, but I couldn't handle one more hour of work today. I'd been bled on, peed on, thrown up on and had to deal with an old, wrinkled man who'd taken two blue pills thinking they were aspirin. So, yeah, sticking a needle in his shriveled junk to relieve the boner on a guy who looked like he'd seen Jesus himself was not something to put in the memory bank. This was a day to forget.

I walked across the street and passed a cute couple pushing a baby stroller with a tiny baby bundled up beneath a pillow of blankets. Heat swarmed into my chest like fireflies buzzing. I wanted that someday; a family. Being gay these days still held a ton of stigma, but having a family was a real possibility. Ever since David was born, I cherished the time I spent with him. I still fondly remembered how tiny he was the first time I held him at the hospital. He smelled perfect. His scrunched-up face and puffed-up lips tugged at my heart from the beginning and never let go. Even at his worst he was the best thing in the world. Love can be a fickle thing and it can be difficult and wrong and unyielding but there's something so right, so *perfect* about the love you feel for a child. There was no doubt in my mind that I would lay down my life for his. I'd donate my heart if he needed it. And he wasn't even mine. So yeah, I wanted that someday.

Before letting my somber mood get to me, I pulled out my phone and opened my text messages. Anna had sent me the daily horoscope again, to which I just rolled my eyes and responded,

{M}: **you know I never read those** and added a winky face emoji. She was the perfect example of a Phoenix, rising from the ashes. Our parents passed when Anna was a junior at Oregon State and I was a senior in high school. They left for a weekend getaway to celebrate their anniversary and never made it back. Some idiot thought drinking until the sun came up and then driving to work was a good idea. Now she was living the dream—A perfect family and a perfect life.

Anna and I were always close. Even with the age difference, we just fit together somehow. Having her away at school was difficult for me. It was like the sun stopped shining and the clouds rolled in and never left. I felt lonely, barren, and realized how much I relied on her. We shared everything afterwards. There were no secrets between us. She was the first person I told that I was gay. I remember being nervous, but not worried. Somehow, I knew she'd be okay with it, and she was. She just said, "Well, duh. Thanks for telling me. Now can we talk about hot men, because I've been dying to do this with you for months!" And that was that. If anything, my coming out strengthened the bond between us.

Months after our parents died, I noticed a change. She was somber, mopey, and obviously depressed. She just kept saying that she wanted to come home, but I wouldn't let her. She was attending college, working to get her degree in veterinary science and I was damn proud of her. I told her I'd be fine. It hurt like hell not having her at home, but it was only for a few months, until I graduated high school and ended up moving to Corvallis to attend OSU as well. Our parents had life insurance policies that paid for our schooling, but with enough left over to ensure we never wanted for anything so long as we didn't go crazy. As much as I'd struggled without them, Anna had always been the solid presence in my life. My rock. And I am constantly amazed at how she's able to balance her husband, her child, and work as well as me. I only wish she would worry less about my love life, or lack thereof.

I let out a sigh and reached for the door to my second home, the café. Sadly, I spend more awake time here than I do at my apartment, but it's lonely there and this place fills me up, both physically and emotionally. I love the peace that I feel when I relax into one of the chairs, letting the day wash away from me with every sip of rich coffee. It smelled like what a home should smell like, too. The bold cinnamon of the sweets paired with the coffee beans and sometimes a hint of bacon. I am a sucker for bacon and of the opinion that everything is better with bacon, so yeah, this place gives me the warm comfort of an embrace. And it's close to work and home, so Adam and I spend a lot of time here on breaks or after a stressful shift.

Today, I felt a change in the air. It was subtle, but lingering. I casually looked towards my regular table, checking if it was available. I was in luck. There were a couple of abandoned coffee mugs and crumpled napkins on the table, but it was otherwise empty, so I headed over. Throwing my bag on the extra seat, I leaned back in my chair and let my legs stretch under the table. It felt good to just let the events of the day roll off me like water off a duck. I could feel my muscles loosen and it was heavenly. The sound of footsteps and the feeling of someone watching me had me opening my eyes. I instantly sat up straight, knocking my knee into the table in the process. I bit my lip in pain.

The stranger squeaked out a quick, "S-sorry," and fled for the kitchen.

I had no idea what just happened. In the years that I'd been consuming coffee here, I'd never seen this guy. Tall and rangy with a shock of blond hair falling around his face. His voice was deep and cautious. After only a single word, I wanted to hear him recite the Declaration of Independence just so it lingered in my ear. I wondered who this guy was and where he'd been hiding.

Heading to the counter to order, Lulu greeted me with a wink and glanced over at my table. "Oh, Madden, so sorry about the mess over there. I'll have Joe run over and clean it up for you."

Before she could turn around, I caught her arm across the counter and asked her, "Joe?"

She smiled. Her lips were higher on one side, like she had some secret she'd been hiding, or she was about to ask me to bury a body. I hoped it was the former.

"Yeah, Joe. He's new, going to be helping around here. Today is his first day so cut him some slack. He needs it." Before I had a chance to respond, she leaned in to me, eyes soft and warm. "He just really needs some good things in his life right now." The way she spoke made me shudder like a strong breeze whipped through me. I nodded, curiosity coursing through me, then placed my regular coffee order with Sloan, the raven-haired punk emo kid who'd been there for months and had never once made eye contact with me. Figuring I'd lingered at the counter long enough, I made my way back to my table, sighing loudly as I sat and dug my phone from my pocket. Before I could even swipe past the home screen, Joe was back, a gray bucket balanced between the table and his slim thigh. He tossed the dishes in with a clunk then wiped down the table quickly with a towel.

Before I could think, my hand flew across the table and grabbed his wrist. My grip was loose enough that it wasn't threatening, but tight enough he would have to pull hard to get away. *What was I doing?* I'd never reacted like this.

"Sorry I spooked you earlier. It wasn't your fault I wasn't paying attention." I smiled, but he wasn't looking at my face. He kept his head down and said nothing. When he didn't respond after a while, I let go. He resumed wiping the table, then turned his head back to me, eyes wide and full of something—like wonder, maybe?

He said, "Sorry if you hurt your leg. I didn't mean to scare you." I had barely blinked before he was gone.

THE NEXT WEEK flew in a blur of patients and ambulance sirens. I couldn't get my head on right. My thoughts were invaded by my run in with Joe at the café. There was something in the way he spoke, or rather didn't speak, that haunted me. I felt like I was missing some vital sign or key component of him. Something I'd glazed over. It was a puzzle I couldn't solve, and it had me on edge. I'd been to the café a handful of times since and I hadn't seen him once. And not for lack of looking. I'm sure I resembled a prairie dog in the way I popped up every time the kitchen door opened. I annoyed myself, but I couldn't get a hold of it. It was silly, really. I'd spent less than a full minute in his presence. Why was he taking over my thoughts? A flash of movement ran across my face and I blinked to see Adam peering at me from behind the counter at the nurse's station.

He smiled. "Man, I don't know where you were but that smile on your face is going to devastate some lucky guy." Rolling a stool over, he sat, knees against mine, arms crossed. "Okay, spill. Who is he and when do I get to meet him?"

I laughed and shook my head. That was why I loved Adam. He cut through the bullshit and got to the meat of the issue every time, whether I wanted to spill or not. There really wasn't any point in dodging his inquisition because he wouldn't stop until I told him everything anyway.

"I went to the café, and there was a new guy working there," I started, then held up a hand to shut Adam up before he could ask me anything else. "I don't know anything about him, just his name. Joe."

"Oh, my God. Look at you!" Adam exclaimed excitedly, like a total dick.

As my face heated, I second-guessed my reaction. My smile fell, then my hands mirrored the action. Staring ahead for a few beats, I turned and looked Adam in the eye.

"Man, I don't know how, but he's in my head. I can't stop thinking about him. I want to know every detail of what he's been through, why he's here and what he wants in life." I shook my head because even I was aware of how stupid I sounded. Like a teenager with a crush. "Man, this isn't me. I've literally spent less than a minute with him. I don't get like this," I said, waiving my hand up and down. "What the fuck is wrong with me?"

It was a rhetorical question, but Adam being Adam, responded anyway. Laying his hand on my shoulder he said, "Dude. You sound a little scared," then squeezed once, twice, three times. "I think you need a breather and a minute to wrap your head around what's got you all weirded out and moody, then go and see him again."

There was no point in responding, because he was right. I needed to figure out what my motivation was here. Why I'd gotten so worked up about someone that I didn't know anything about. Other than the fact that I wanted to hear him speak again, to me. I felt like I needed to get to know him and I had no idea why. Maybe it was my need to take care of others. I'd always had this innate desire to comfort and support the people around me. That was the appeal of a nursing career. Being a doctor never interested me because, even though fixing people was noble, I wanted more to be there for them. To exist in their space and time and hold their hand, both metaphorically and physically. I'd accept that was the answer I was searching for with Joe. I had picked up on something from him. Maybe he just needed a friend.

BEFORE I CAME to my senses and retreated home, I was standing in front of the café praying that Joe would not be there. In my next breath I was praying he would. He wouldn't. He would. Over and over, ad infinitum. Until a lovely young woman jerked the door open roughly and barreled out right into me.

"Excuse me," she said pertly, giving me a look of disdain. Maybe I should have just gone home after all. As the door shut, I looked up to see Joe standing at a table a few feet away. My heart lurched for no reason whatsoever. This was madness. And yet, there was something deep inside of me, primal almost, that needed this. Breathing through my nose a few times, I tried to collect my thoughts. And that's when it hit me, full force. I didn't have a choice. It was a *need*. I couldn't bring myself to get any farther away from him than I already was, so I grasped the door handle and pulled.

The smell of coffee and buttery pastries filled my senses as I made my way to the counter. I was surprised to see Lulu, as it was just after the mad morning rush and she usually came in later. She'd mentioned watching her grandchildren at her home a few mornings a week so that her daughter could go back to work. She was some sort of editor or journalist, but I couldn't remember. All I could think about was finding Joe and ordering a cup of coffee and a chocolate croissant.

Having luck on my side, I found my table empty. Thrilled to have a minute to check myself, I set my phone down and took in my surroundings. There were quite a few people standing, and two groups of women with small children in the opposite corner of the door. With about eight adults in their party, they'd moved a couple of round tables together, forming a large triangle with the kids herded between them. A few other tables were littered with single adults on phones or tablets, trying to waste a few minutes before they had someplace more important to be. Me, I was just here to catch a fleeting glimpse of the new guy and hoped for clues for my ongoing investigation into, well, *him*.

Opportunity knocked swiftly when I heard footsteps approach and saw Joe. He carried my cup of coffee, a plate with a croissant, the napkin tucked between the yellow ceramic dish and his fingers. After setting it down without making eye contact, he was on the move again, turning towards the kitchen. I almost fell out of my chair reaching for him and encircling his wrist with my fingers for the second time. The instant my skin connected with his, he froze as if he'd been shocked. He stood still, a statue in front of me. I wasn't sure if he was waiting for me to move, let go, or say something. Maybe I'd freaked him the fuck out and he was deciding whether to fight or flee. I let go, but stood, diminishing the distance between our bodies. He was only about 2 inches shorter than my six feet, one inch, but I probably had fifty pounds of muscle and bulk against his smaller frame. He looked delicate where I looked like I lifted weights, which I did. "I'm sorry," I said, hoping he'd turn around and acknowledge me.

I got one of those requests.

"Sorry for what?" he asked, barely a whisper as he faced the busy counter and kitchen. I could see the kids getting restless and the group of mothers finishing their snacks. Joe probably didn't have much time before he'd need to get to work bussing the tables.

"For grabbing you again," I admitted, not sure what else to say.

"Then why did you?" he asked, rotating slowing until he looked right at me.

"Instinct?"

"What?" he asked, his head cocked to the left. The innocent gesture warmed my chest.

"I wanted to talk to you," I said, taking in his face. His jawline was so sharp it could cut granite. *Focus, Mads.* I cleared my throat. "I wanted to introduce myself. I am something of a regular, so I thought I'd say hello." I sounded like a three-year-old. I might as well have gone to hang out with the yoga moms, for crying out loud.

"What is it?"

"What is what?" I asked, confused.

I watched as his eyes took me in, starting with my feet. When he moved up my body, I felt myself stiffen, as if he was seeing too much.

"Your name. You said you wanted to introduce yourself." His face remained totally expressionless.

Oh. Right. "Yes. My name is Madden," I replied, holding out my hand. He looked at it like it was the first time he'd seen one, then slowly raised a hand to meet it.

"Madden." He repeated it slowly, as if trying to memorize it. To learn it. It sounded amazing emerging from his lips. Like a song. "Joe," he said quietly, pumping my hand with his, a slow, but firm grip.

With a smile I couldn't hide if I tried, I said, "It's nice to meet you, Joe."

6

—————

Joe

I hated being touched. I never allowed it at all. It was too personal. Like each touch gave something of yourself away, and I hardly had anything left to give. I understood that shaking hands was a common courtesy, though I didn't know why. It made my skin crawl. As if allowing a handshake somehow also gave permission for someone to touch you freely. I once woke up on the streets with fire ants haphazardly making trails over my skin, communicating with one another, searching for food or anything useful to take home, I assumed. That experience was similar to skin on skin contact for me. My entire body shivered and convulsed at the thought. It wasn't a tactile disorder. It was limited to people. Animals were fine. Madden was fine.

Madden was fine. Madden could touch me.

The first time he put his hand on my wrist, instinct took over, and I forced myself not to vomit, but to breathe. In and out. I waited for the darkness. For the tightening. For the sound of sandpaper. I waited.

Nothing.

As I stood there facing this man, this *stranger*, I couldn't understand. I swallowed. Again. Why? Who is this guy? He was obviously attractive, if you liked a straight, sloping nose, firm jaw, and green eyes the color of sea glass. Okay, he was hot. His raven hair was long on top and kind of floppy around his face, softening the slick line of his jaw. He had stubble on his chin today where he hadn't previously. That made me pause. He'd lived an entire life since the last time I'd seen him. He'd gone to work and home, spoken to various people. *Touched* various people. He'd eaten. Slept. My face heated as I wondered if he'd slept alone or if he'd had company. I worried that my face was heating on the outside as well. Everything was wrong. But everything *felt* right.

"I have to go," I said to Madden, registering too late that his hand still cradled mine. He startled as I ended up pulling him with me a step, his tennis shoes squeaking their protest on the wood as they dragged a few inches. I let go like his hand was a pulsing flame of fire, ignited in mine. Quickly moving towards the kitchen, I almost tripped over one of the small children attempting to put his shoes on. I couldn't stop. I didn't stop until I pushed through the kitchen door, then through the back door to the alley. I never went out there because Sloan constantly smoked during his breaks or on the phone with various people discussing hookups. All inhibitions went out the window because I needed air so badly my lungs were heaving. Never had my body reacted like this and I was genuinely confused. Why did his touch feel like satin instead of sandpaper? Why did looking at him cause my body temperature to rise? I felt like I couldn't breathe or speak in the same room as him. But I had. I had spoken to him and then he'd touched me.

"You okay, man?" I turned sharply to find Sloan standing in the doorway, his arm propping it open. He'd never been shy around me, but him looking out for me was a surprise!

"Oh, yeah, yeah," I replied, like an idiot. "S-s-sorry, just needed air. I'm coming back in now." I slipped by him, careful to keep a few inches between our bodies as I passed.

OVER THE NEXT couple of days, I fell into a routine. I spent mornings with Phantom, washed my laundry, and showered at the gym where I sometimes worked out now. On days that I had more time I headed over to the quaint, brick-faced used book-store over on Tarrant Street and sat in an oversized chair and read. I'd been reading there for months, taking up space in the far back corner, sometimes in a chair, other times sitting propped up against a shelf of books. Reading had never been much of a pleasure for me. Honestly, I'm not very good at it and I hadn't felt safe trying until recently.

Since I'd met Madden, he had consumed my thoughts. His glowing eyes heated my skin. The way his hand felt wrapped around my wrist caused my face to blush. I'd even imagined him taking that hand and running it over my body. How warm and soft it would feel.

My mind would take me to a certain point, then the image of Devin would pop into my head. Devin and his roaming hands. Devin, my father's buddy, who waited until Venom gave him a drunken nod one night at our home. Shuddering, I could envision that night so clearly in my head.

Bird-Age 12

"Now, come on, son. Your dad said it was okay. I just want to see your bedroom is all. It's no big deal."

Devin's yellowing front teeth had me thinking of an over-ripe banana peel. "Please leave me alone. I just want you to go."

"Just show me something of yours and I'll leave." He took a few steps into my room and ran his finger against the edge of the dresser. "What do you do in here when you're all alone?"

"Nothing." My heart was starting to beat out of my chest as I climbed higher on my bed.

"Well, I'm sure you aren't doing nothing. Why don't you invite me in? Hmmm? We can talk for a few minutes. I just want to get to know you better."

"P-p-please leave." My hands were fisted by my side, shaking.

I watched as he moved clumsily across the worn carpet, almost falling over next to me on the bed. He looked up at me with a sneer and said, "Now, this is better. This way I can touch you."

I froze, knowing what was coming. He wasn't the first guy Venom had let into my room. I was positive he wouldn't be the last.

"Just g-g-go!" I cried, my hands covering my face.

"Shhhhhh," he whispered, his hand snaking around my thigh. "We're friends now, aren't we?"

That was the first time Devin touched me.

I WAS SCHEDULED four days a week, mostly evening shifts. Lately, worry had been sinking into my chest at the thought of Lulu putting trust in me. I wasn't like Sloan or any of the other college students she had working here. They were friendly with customers. I didn't possess that gene. Eye contact was extremely difficult for me. Always had been. Living in the home that I had growing up didn't help matters. If I'd looked Venom in the eye, he'd have blackened it without remorse.

When Lulu came to me with my paycheck, she must have sensed that I had no idea what I was going to do with it.

"Joe, if you don't have a bank account, I'll help you get one. They'll need me to sign up with you, if you don't mind, but after a few months of deposits we can remove my name from your account." She stepped closer and waited for me to look up at her. "We can use my home address if we need to." She said it so matter-of-factly that I couldn't help the warmth bloom in my chest. I nodded, giving her a wide grin.

MADDEN HAD MADE a daily appearance at the café, his order the same each time. My favorite part of the day had become seeing him look around the room until his eyes met mine, then I'd see the slight upturn of his lip. Never a full smile, though. I needed to work for that.

I couldn't overlook how my rules went out the window with him. He was like the Tasmanian Devil, getting too close and breaking down all my barriers. My skin heated when he touched me, but not like I was covered in bugs. Instead, it was warm and bright; the color of the sun. When his eyes searched for mine, I let them, and it wasn't terrifying, more comforting. The rest of the room melted away as his gaze burned me from the inside out.

When Madden walked in with a woman and a child one Thursday evening, I blanched and headed for the kitchen. With sweaty palms, I tried to put some of the mixing bowls away, close to dropping one. It caught on the lip of the sink when Lulu pushed through the door and caught me.

"You doing okay, Joe? You look a little pale."

I nodded, wiping my hand on my jeans.

"So, it wouldn't matter to you if I told you Madden just came in with his sister and her son?"

I looked up to find her smirking at me. I let out a relieved sigh, making my entire body shudder.

"That's what I thought." The knowing smile hadn't left her face. "Why don't you wash your hands and take them their order." It wasn't a question.

She laughed at my wide-eyed expression. "I see things," she said as wagged her finger at me and walked back into the café.

Chanting my mantra, (*you won't trip and fall, you won't trip and fall*) I forced my way through the crowded tables, full tray in my hand. When Madden spotted me, I had to look away. I hadn't done anything to deserve the smile on his face.

"Here," he said, taking the tray. "Let me help you." After setting it on the table, everyone picked up their items and Madden's sister started sipping her coffee.

With nothing in my hands, the awkwardness doubled. Until Madden stepped around his nephew's chair and put his hand on my shoulder, pressing gently. I felt anchored, no longer adrift in a sea of unease.

"Anna, David," he nodded at each while saying their names, "this is Joe."

I had three sets of eyes looking at me and my mouth felt as though I'd swallowed cement. "H-h-hi," I croaked out, my palms slick once again.

"Madden, why don't you grab Joe a chair so he can join us. I'm sure you can spare a couple of minutes, right?" Anna's smile was charming, just like her brother's.

"Oh, um. Well, I d-d-do need to get back to work." I saw Madden's face fall. "B-b-b-but I could probably m-m-manage a f-f-few minutes, if you don't mind." I practically fell into the chair I was offered, somehow in between Anna and David.

David was paying no attention to me at all. He was drawing extremely detailed dinosaurs with crayons. With his head bobbing back and forth and his foot bouncing wildly underneath him, I smiled. He was a content, happy child. That told me a lot about his mom. And his uncle.

"David." I waited, but he didn't turn his head. Moving my face in front of his, I tried again. When he looked up at me, I leaned back and waved at him. He waved back, pointed at his sheet and started rambling incoherently about dinosaurs. I picked up every 8th word and just smiled as he told me whatever was in his head. When I realized Anna and Madden were staring, I thought maybe I'd done something wrong. "Sorry. Is it okay that I talked to him? I'm not good meeting new people and I either can't get words out or I just keep talking and talking and try to stop myself. Like now. Sorry. Sorry." I looked down at my hands that were balled into fists on my lap.

"Thank you, Joe. No one ever knows how to speak to David, so they just don't bother." I smiled wide enough to show teeth. "So, Joe, tell us about yourself. How long have you worked here? Are you in school?"

"Joe just started here a few weeks ago, right?" Madden answered for me.

"Um, yes. R-r-right." My attention went back to David's drawings and the ease with which he moved from one dinosaur to the next, never looking back. I was zoned out, watching the colors take flight, jumping when a hand touched my arm.

"Sorry," Anna winced. "Do you know Madden from here, or —" she trailed off, voice lilting.

My gaze still on the paper, I nodded. There was silence at the table for a while, then Anna broke it. "David doesn't usually talk to strangers."

I peered up at her through my lashes and asked, "Why?"

"Because he's autistic. It's difficult for him to break through and focus on someone and identify what they're saying." Her eyes narrowed.

Taking a deep breath, I responded. "Saying he's autistic is

considered derogatory. You should say he's on the Spectrum. Saying he's autistic sounds like there isn't anything left. B-b-but there is. And he can hear you. When you say things like that. He may not look at you or show you he's listening, b-b-but he is. It's just stored in a separate p-p-place. But it's there. He knows."

I put my hand out next to David's coloring. When he noticed, I waved. He waved back. "I have to get back to work." I stood up then turned to Madden, nodded and walked away.

MADDEN WALKED in out of the rain like some kind of superhero. With his dark hair slicked back and a red tinge to his cheeks, I had to look away. Looking at him made my skin feel like I was out there in the storm but covered in the softest fur, so even though I could feel each individual water droplet splash my skin, I wasn't cold or wet.

Turning away from the noisy café, my forehead against the wall, I took a couple of deep, calming breaths. How was he unnerving me like this? How was he able to see past my defenses to me when I'd worked so hard at being invisible?

"Hey, Joe, order ready for table 9." Turning around, Sloan handed me a tray with a coffee and a croissant and winked at me. No way I would let him see my blush. I recited my mantra and darted through the crowd to Madden's favorite table.

"Um, hi," I said to the side of his head. He surprised me by pulling a chair out and pointing to it.

"Hey, Joe, you're just the man I wanted to see." His grin did something to my insides.

"Oh. Why?" I asked.

He laughed. I think one side of my mouth turned up in response, but I couldn't be sure why.

"Well, I wanted to tell you how sorry I was that my sister

gave you the third-degree before. She meant well, but can be socially inept on her best days." When his eyes widened and his face pinked, I thought about his words.

"Oh. R-r-right. Well, I'm on the spectrum so I have my own issues, but I am quite proud of myself. You can't apologize for your sister anyway. She would have to apologize, or the effort is meaningless."

Madden's head tilted back in laughter. "That's true. But she isn't here, and I am, so I thought I'd put it out there. She didn't mean to be rude, she's usually inquisitive in general, but especially when it has anything to do with me."

"Did it?"

His eyes narrowed. "Did it what?"

"Did it have anything to do with you?"

"In a roundabout way, yes."

"I don't understand what that means." My shoulders slumped as I felt as though I was missing some vital piece of information.

Madden ran a hand through his hair and let out a giant breath of air. With his hands interlocked on the table, he said, "I told Anna that I wanted her to meet me here because I had told her about you." When I looked up in shock, he raised a hand and continued. "No, not like... I don't know. I don't really know anything about you, Joe, so there wasn't much for me to tell her, but I mentioned you in passing and how I wanted to see you again—I wanted to spend more time with you. So, that's why she was trying to interrogate you." He chuckled. "Actually, what you said to her about David was interesting. And that's why she wanted to apologize. She didn't mean to be rude or ignorant. Honestly."

I nodded. "I wasn't o-o-offended, Madden." I looked up at him and hooked a thumb over my shoulder. "I should probably get back to work."

"When is your next break? You get breaks, right?" he asked, fingering the lip of his coffee cup.

"Um. Yeah. Yes. At seven o'clock." We both immediately looked up at the clock by the door. Six thirty-eight.

"If I wait, can you come back over for your break?"

I could scarcely hear him over the beating bass drum in my chest. "Oh. Y-y-yeah. If you like."

His hand reached mine over the table. "I'd love to spend some more time with you. I'll be here when you're ready."

When he lifted his hand from mine, I felt the loss of heat and pressure like nothing I'd ever known.

7

————————

Madden

When Anna had asked me for coffee the other day, I had jumped at the chance for an excuse to see Joe. Obviously, she'd heard something in my voice because she wouldn't let it go.

"Why are you so excited to go to *that* coffee shop? There are a million around the city."

"No reason."

"Mads, I've known you your entire life. Don't bullshit me. I can hear the smile in your voice. Just tell me."

Fuck. Leaning back on my sofa I threw my arm over my eyes. "Fine. There's a new guy working and he's fun to look at, okay? Just don't ask me anything else cause I don't know anything about him. Just—he has this furrowed brow that does something to me. And his skin is so—"

"Okay, okay. You can stop now. You have a crush on a

barista. Fine. I'll meet you there in an hour. I'm bringing David. His Physical Therapist cancelled last minute on us."

As SOON AS we were out of the building, Anna grabbed my forearm and sighed heavily. "Look, he seems really nice, but—"

"Okay, no. You aren't going to spend five minutes with him and form an opinion. I won't listen to it."

"I just want to say my piece and be done. Okay?"

Looking down the street, I focused back on her and said, "Yeah, fine. Go."

"He's *on the spectrum*, Mads," she said, widening her eyes to emphasize her point.

"Are you serious, right now? Anna, I can't believe you'd use that as a reason to stay away from someone." My tone was harsh, but I couldn't help myself.

"Look at how much work David is, Madden. I love him to death, but it isn't easy. He doesn't see the world like we do."

"I can't fucking believe you, right now. First of all, you can't put David and Joe in the same box just because they are both on the spectrum," I said, using finger quotes. "Secondly, are you going to give this same advice to someone who has feelings for David in the future?"

Her face dropped and her arms fell to her side. "Oh. I didn't realize."

"Realize what?" I quipped.

"You already have feelings for him?" Her arm reached out to me, but I stepped back.

"Well... Yeah, I do. Pre-feelings maybe. I don't know, honestly. I do want to get to know him more. Talk to him more. He talks to me. He was distracted today by David, but he talks to me."

After a moment, her eyes softened and she said, "Yeah, Madden. Okay. I'm sorry."

I shook my head. She leaned in for a hug and I let her, wrapping my arms around her slim waist. "I love you. I don't want you to get hurt. By anyone, okay? Just be careful."

I grunted. "Don't worry about me. I've probably scared him off already anyway." She laughed and I grunted. "But thank you."

I WAITED at the table for Joe to take his break, alternating between looking at the clock, looking for Joe, and reading the news on my phone. I wondered for the twenty-fourth time what I was doing here. Did I want to try to start up something with him?

I caught a glimpse of him wiping down a table and I couldn't help but stare. His ropey forearms caused a heat in my belly. I wondered how much of him he'd let me touch. If he'd ever let anyone touch him like that before. Yeah, there was no way I would let this go without a fight.

When he walked up to the table a few minutes later, he looked unsure. So, I stood up and pulled the other chair out for him to sit in. After staring at it for a beat, he looked at me and asked if I wanted anything to eat or drink. I had already finished my coffee and sandwich, so I was fine, and I told him so.

"S-s-so, hi," he said, then looked away.

I laughed, then gently rested my hand on his over the table. That got him to look at me. "Hey, Joe. How's your day going?"

"Yeah, fine."

"Tell me your favorite part of the job."

"Why? Does it matter?" His hand slid off the table and onto his lap.

"It matters to me," I replied. He shot me a look then folded his arms across his chest.

"I don't understand w-w-why you ask me questions. No one asks m-m-me questions unless they have motive. What's your motive, Madden?"

I leaned back and held my hands up in surrender. "Whoa, man. Not trying to take you off balance. I just want to know you better. I like you. I want to find out more about you to see if we have things in common. There's not a dark mystery here. Not with me. I wouldn't do that."

Looking at the floor, I figured he was done. He'd get up and leave and that would be that. He surprised me, though. And fuck if I didn't smile at that.

He said, "I enjoy organizing the kitchen. It helps to calm me. And I feel like everyone isn't watching me when I'm in the kitchen. Everyone is too busy."

"That's great. I'm glad you have time at work that you can take a break from everything and still be productive." He nodded.

"I also like stacking all of the plates and cups after they're washed. They are all different colors and Lulu doesn't care if I make patterns with them. I don't have to, I just like to. I'm not an idiot." He looked up from the table at me. "I might not always know what to say or how to say it, but I'm not stupid. I have my GED. I studied the last two years of h-h-high school at the l-l-library and aced the test. I want to go to college."

"Joe, I don't think you're stupid. At all. I think it's awesome you want to go to college. Why did you get your GED instead of finishing at school?"

His head whipped around, gaze darting at the door, then the front windows before he turned back and leaned into the table. "If I tell you, I might have to kill you," he whispered.

My eyebrows shot up in shock, but the smirk on his face

had me laughing so hard, the men at the table next to us looked over and scowled.

"You really want to get to know me?" Joe's voice was close to a whisper.

"Yeah, I really do. I like you. You are fun to be around. I need more people in my life that make me laugh. And you do that quite well." I smiled at him and he rewarded me with one of his own.

We spent the next twenty minutes talking about nursing, the hospital, and Adam. I told him about some of my responsibilities at work and was surprised at how fascinated he was by the medical equipment and terminology that I had vast amounts of experience with.

I found myself relaxing in the hard, wooden chair, not even noticing the spindles sticking into my spine. It wasn't until he needed to go back to work that I felt it. He thanked me for 'an enjoyable time', making his way back to the kitchen and I realized that I felt detached from everything else while in Joe's presence. And I loved it.

8

____

Joe

Two days later, I met Adam. He reminded me of a hummingbird, both flighty and free, quick-moving, but effortless. He radiated light through his perfect pale coloring. After watching him flit about Madden for a few minutes, I felt an ache in my gut. They had a shared language that I couldn't understand. Full sentences and explanations weren't necessary between them. I was mesmerized by watching them interact with each other, so easily. Effortlessly. Jealously clawed at me and I startled in my seat.

Madden noticed, immediately asking if I was okay. I nodded and tried for a smile, but it was obvious he knew I was lying. He cleared his throat and Adam stood up to grab a to-go cup for home. On his way out, he pulled Madden into an embrace that was all about tight squeezes and back slaps. Then he made his way over to me and I froze, my eyes widening in horror.

"Sorry, man. I'm not used to being hands-off. I'll get better the more we're together. It was really nice meeting you." Adam gave me a quick salute and walked out. He'd taken my aversion to touch well, I thought.

When Madden had introduced us, he'd grabbed my forearm and I almost screamed. Thankfully, through their bro-language, they silently discussed the ins and outs of my issue through facial ticks and hand manipulations. I wasn't sure if I should be upset or not, so I let it go for now.

"Sorry about Adam. He means well, but he can be excessively tactile. I should have warned both of you before bringing him here, but we just finished shift and it was a last minute decision."

"It's fine," I replied to the table.

"Obviously, you are upset about something. I saw you flinch earlier. Tell me what it was." His hand lifted quickly and surely from his lap and rested on my forearm, right where Adam had grabbed me. His touch didn't burn my flesh, instead felt warm and soft.

"I-I-I I am not like other people." My hand went to a divot in the table and my thumb traced back and forth over it.

"Right. Which is why I want to spend more time with you."

"I still don't understand. Adam is easy. Y-y-you are effortless together. I can't be like that. I don't know h-h-how to be like that."

Madden leaned forward in his chair and put his arm around the back of my shoulders. My body leant towards him without my permission.

"Hey," he said, his forehead touching my temple. When I didn't look up, his hand captured my nape and squeezed lightly. I turned and side-eyed him. "Adam is fun and crazy and a very sweet guy, but I don't want to spend more time with him than I already do. As for us being easy around each other, I've known him and spent most of my time with him for the last 7 years. He's like a brother." Another squeeze to my neck. "Okay?"

I nodded. All I could do was nod. I had a lot of things going on in my head that I needed time to unpack and process. Alone.

His face was still close, but no longer touching mine. I whispered, "I have to go."

He leaned back and his face fell. "Okay," he responded, nodding back. "Joe, wait." His hand reached out and grabbed ahold of the arm I used to push in my chair. "Are we okay?"

I paused. "Sure, we are," I told him, my eyebrows lowering.

"I mean it, Joe. It's important to me that we are. If I've done something, I—"

"You haven't. I just need time to think about e-e-e-everything that just happened."

Removing his arm from mine, he sighed. "Fair enough. I'll give you time, but I'll be back."

I nodded and went back to work.

"I'M SO pleased with how well you're doing here, Joe. I had a feeling about you when you walked in here that night," Lulu gushed as I finished cleaning up the baking pans in the sink.

I couldn't help the blush that heated my cheeks at her words. "Yeah, thanks," I responded, more to my shoulder than to her.

I saw her reach her hand up to touch me, and it seemed like it was suspended in a vacuum of air between us. As if she'd just realized what she was about to do. I sighed, knowing I had caused her to censor her actions around me. It wasn't what I wanted, but what I needed. That didn't make it any easier.

"I'm sorry."

"You don't have anything to apologize for. We all have our quirks and it's just part of what makes us all unique." Her hand stirred the air between us, accentuating her thought. "Can I ask you a personal question, Joe?"

So many people were asking the very same question. Having connections with other people was not something I was used to. After escaping the only home I'd ever known, I moved around a lot. I had no choice; I had to watch my back. No ties, clean breaks. But lately, that had all changed. This was a different person standing here, possibly one with friends. I had people who asked me questions, wanted to get to know me. Before I could finish my thoughts and panic, Lulu stepped into my space and caught my gaze.

"Honey, I know you have had a hard time of it, and I want you to know that I want to help you. Now that you have some money and a bank account, maybe we can find you a place to stay? What do you think?"

"Oh. N-n-no, I'm ok-k-kay." I panicked, turning to look at the door to the alley behind the building.

"I see things, Joe. I know you aren't living somewhere safe and taking care of yourself. I want you to know that I will help you in any way I can. You've shown me what a good, honest person you are. Just remember that I'm here for you, okay?"

When I didn't respond, she stepped even closer. "Joe?"

"Yes. Okay, yes. T-t-thank you."

Lulu left and I opened the back door, catching the bite of cigarette smell left from Sloan's break. Leaning against the brick, my shirt stuck to the rough texture taking my mind off the smell. I counted to 168 before I had to step away. I had started breathing heavily at 79, but 156 was my previous record, so I beat it.

I needed to figure out what to do. Now that I knew people here, they were starting to get to know me. Was it safe? Could I really stay here much longer? What if—NO. I couldn't even go there. It was too much to think about. I would just watch my back better this time. Take no chances. As much as I wanted to ask for Lulu's help, I couldn't get my own place. I couldn't put my name on a lease. No paperwork attached to my name. I needed to be smarter this time.

9

———

Madden

Adam had a Cheshire Cat grin on his face when he walked into the nurse's station on Thursday afternoon. I groaned, knowing it was one of two things. He'd either gotten laid or he thought I did.

"Dude," Adam said smugly, stretching the word a few beats. "I was just on my way in and stopped for coffee." The smug leer and wink he aimed at me was unnerving.

I pulled him to me by his bicep and harshly whispered, "What did you do?"

Adam fucking cackled, pulling his arm out of my grip. He saw my face and bent over with laughter, which had me so confused. I stood with my arms crossed while he got a hold of himself enough to find words.

"You should see yourself right now. You are so into this guy." I smacked away the finger that was pointed at me.

"Fuck, man. I know," I said, a hand raking over my hair. "I

don't know what it is, but—"

Adam cut me off, gripping my arm. "You don't know what it is? Are you kidding me right now? Man, if I had to draw a picture of your type of guy it would be Joe." Adam snorted then turned towards the counter.

I sat on a stool, my knee furiously bobbing under the counter as he continued.

"Yeah, he's kind, gentle, passionate about things he cares about, and he has that stutter. Like, I want to push my finger in his dimple when he does it. But most of all, he needs you."

I started to argue but he cut me off with a hand in the air. "He does. He is kind of lost and sad and you are just the type of guy he needs to protect him and help him get unlost." He shook his head and said, "I think I'd be honored if he looked at me like he looks at you, man."

And with that, I choked on my cold coffee, slamming my fist into my chest. Adam just laughed. The shithead.

JOE and I had settled into a good place for the last few weeks after our first conversation with Adam. I found myself smiling like an idiot when he was lost in speech about something he cared about. He spoke like a bullet train, fast and wordy, not stopping until he lost steam, took a giant breath and started all over again. Other times, he stuttered out a few words and then stayed silent. I found it utterly charming and I was enraptured by his quirks. I may not have gleaned a lot from his long-winded answers, but I learned some interesting things about the man. Like, when I asked him a question that was personal, a glazed look would transform his face while he took the time to think about his answer. Or when he was thinking about how to ask me a question, he'd sometimes tap his dimple, forcing my chest to tighten, my neck to blaze with warmth. Or when he said my name it was like the first time I'd ever heard it.

"Someone's got that lovesick puppy look in his eye," Adam sing-songed at me. We were outside the ED in the ambulance bay waiting on a burn victim from a house fire. "Brother, you need to get this moving. Why haven't you asked him out yet?" He asked me, smirking as he leaned back, resting the sole of his shoe against the brick wall.

"Stop. Jesus." I didn't want to admit how lit up inside he made me when I thought of him. Of his long, slender, tan fingers playing at the edge of my coffee cup. Hearing him stutter out my name. Fuck, that sound had a direct line to my cock, and I had to bite my cheek to hold in a moan when he said it. "He's not like other guys. He's special." Even I had to roll my eyes at my words, but they were truer than I'd realized.

"Holy fuck, Mads." Adam was full on laughing and I didn't care at all. Before he could continue the harassment, the sounds of sirens blazed around us.

IN A MATTER of a few weeks Joe had chipped away at something in me. The wall I'd managed to erect around my heart after Charlie, my cheating ex, had been reinforced and sturdy. Unbreakable. Until one day a blue-eyed, blond-whirling dervish of a man stammered into my life, annihilating my hard work, and began tearing down bricks one at a time. The crux of it though, was knowing that I wanted to let him in.

After three more rounds of ambulances and restocking the shelves in the emergency bays, Adam and I grabbed our gear to go home. It'd been a long twelve-hour shift. I was exhausted and in no mood to deal with my stray thoughts or Adam's. When he brought up Joe again, I shut him down quickly. "Please, man. Just let me have a night to myself. I'm exhausted and I can't get into a deep conversation with you. Please."

"Yeah, I got you. Okay, man. I'm going to go to Red's anyway. He'd been texting me all shift and I told him I'd stop by for some dessert." His wink made me smile.

Shaking my head, I responded, "See you Friday. Have a good day off."

~

THE WEEKEND WAS cold and rainy. I spent most of it at work dealing with lacerations, fevers, car accident victims, and kids swallowing things they should never have had access to. By Sunday night, I had worked three back to back nights, and was ready to fall into bed.

It had been four days since I'd seen Joe. Not that I was counting. I rolled my eyes at myself and pulled my coat collar tighter around my neck. My apartment was close to work, only a ten-minute walk, but the rain made it feel like an hour. Still, it allowed me time to think, to worry, to answer a text from Anna. We'd spoken every day, as usual, but the conversations had been strained and short since we'd seen each other at the café.

Once I hauled myself out of the elevator and into my apartment, I dropped my bag, toed off my shoes, and hung my wet jacket on the rack by the door. Stretching my back, I raised my arms over my head and walked over to greet Batman and Robin. "I bet you guys are hungry, aren't you?" I asked my Molly and Barb fish. The Molly was solid black with a single gold scale on his back, thus earning him the moniker of Batman. Robin featured a prominent red face and mimicked every move that Batman made, hence his name. I ground a few multicolored flakes between my fingers and watched as the fish swam to the surface, bobbing their heads and opening and closing their mouths around the tiny flakes. "Sweet dreams, boys," I said, heading down the hallway to my bedroom. I stripped out of my clothes, quickly balling them up and throwing them into the basket in the corner. I groaned as I hit the bed and landed face-first into my pillows. Thoughts of Joe filled my head as I closed my eyes and let myself go.

$\sim$

IT WAS STILL RAINING a few hours later when I woke up feeling less ragged than when I'd gotten home. After a quick stop in the bathroom to freshen up, I threw on some old, worn jeans, a gray Henley, and grabbed my car keys and boots. I was a man with a mission. I wanted to spend as much time with Joe as I could. If we ended up friends, that would be enough for me. For now.

When I found parking a few feet away from the café entrance, I took it as sign. Or, that's what I told myself as I breathed in the sweet aroma of coffee beans and sugar. I placed my order and headed over to my table, my hand brushing at the seam of my jeans as I fiddled for something to do. Awkwardly, I sat and looked around. My breath caught as I saw Joe across the room, wiping a table down and throwing silverware into the bin. He looked...pale. Tired. Something was off in the way he carried himself and I felt a pit forming in my stomach. He turned away and pushed through the kitchen door, leaving me watching, anticipating his return. A few minutes ticked by before he barreled back out, one arm lifted as he coughed into his shoulder. He sniffed a few times as he languidly made his way over to my table, stumbling a bit before setting down my order.

"Holy shit, Joe. You look like proper hell." I reached out to touch his face, but he backed away quickly, wincing.

"Yeah. Just warm in here."

"Is that why you are shivering?" This time he didn't pull

back when I reached my hand to his cheek and lightly brushed it with the back of my fingers. Anger tore through me as heat burned my skin. "You're burning up! How long has this been going on? All weekend?" Grabbing the tray, I set it down, pulling him by the sleeve to the chair opposite mine.

"I'm fine, really. Just, you know… s-s-sorting out the weather. Really," he said, trying to stand up. "I should get back to work." He wouldn't look at me, instead kept his gaze centered on the waxed wood floors.

"I don't think so. You need to see a doctor." I told him, exerting a bit of force on his shoulder, effectively keeping him seated. "I'll ask Lulu to grab your coat and bag. I'm taking you home. You can't work when you are this sick, Joe." I pulled my hand from Joe's bony shoulder, just as he grabbed it and squeezed. "T-t-t-thanks anyway, but I can't go to the h-h-h-hospital." His face was flushed red, and his eyes were starting to gloss over.

"Why the hell not?" I hissed. "You have a fever and chills. You can't be here." Shaking my head, I sat back down in the chair across from him. "Explain to me why," I huffed.

"I…I, um." Joe uncomfortably turned to look at the counter, then back at me. "Look, I don't have ins-s-surance or anything. There's just…. I can't g-g-o to the doctor. Please." His voice quivered and he looked panicked.

I needed to think. Why didn't he have insurance? And what's more, why was he here when he was obviously sick? Did he need the money so badly that he couldn't call in? Lulu would understand. She'd have taken one look at him and sent him home with a to-go carton of soup and tea if she were here.

"Okay, look." I set my hand on the table, letting out a deep breath. "I'm a nurse. I can see you are sick and should not be working. Hell, you shouldn't be upright."

He looked like he could cry, his teeth worrying his bottom lip.

"Let me ask Sloan to get your stuff from the back and I'll take you home. Get you some soup and some Gatorade."

"No! No, I mean—" He fisted his hair with both hands and looked up. "Thanks for being so kind to me, but it's okay. I can get myself," he swallowed hard, "I can get myself home." Trying to stand, his unstable legs gave out, and he gripped the table's edge to keep from falling. I stood, helped him back to his seat, then gently gripped the nape of his neck with my palm. Lips close to his ear, I whispered, "I'll get your stuff. Just stay here a minute. *Please.*" My voice was pleading. With a tenuous nod from Joe, I stalked over to the counter and asked Sloan for his things. Then, I was on my way back to the table, his bag and jacket in hand.

10

Joe

I swallowed hard, setting off a string of coughs, fire raging in my throat. I was officially dying. I crossed my arms on the table and set my forehead down. How could I explain that I had nowhere to go? *Guess what, Madden? I'm homeless.* Another slew of coughing hit me until a warm hand was on my neck, gently squeezing.

"You okay?" Madden asked.

I nodded. I could tell he was worried about me the way his voice was lilting. But it didn't make much sense. He may have been trying to get to know me better, but I couldn't understand anything past 'are you okay'. He had no reason to care beyond that. I felt like I was missing something, but my head was too foggy to think.

With as much strength as I could muster, I stood and shuffled to the door, pushed it open against the cold air and stalked out onto the pavement. I pleaded with my body to just evaporate. I faced his way, but couldn't look him in the eye. "So, I'll just go home. T-t-thanks for watching out for me." Hooking a thumb over my shoulder, I turned to go.

"Joe, please let me drive you. My car is literally right here," Madden implored, his voice soft, soothing my ringing ears. Honestly, I couldn't think of anything better than getting into his warm car. "You don't have to let me into your place. I just want to make sure you get there safe and dry." I looked at my boots. This was why I didn't trust people. No attachments. I tried to walk away. Left. Right. Left. Then I heard him. He didn't take a step, which I was so grateful for. Instead he whispered, "Come on, Joe. Please."

"Please don't ask me that. I can't tell you. I don't want to tell you," I begged.

Madden stepped closer to me. My head pounded, my throat dry and scratchy. He was right. I needed to rest, and I was tired. So tired. Not expecting the contact, I winced when his hand came to rest on my shoulder. The look in his eyes just about did me in. The look of hurt. And I had put it there. "I know you don't trust me, Joe, and that's okay. For now," he said bending to look me in the eye. "But you will trust me. And you'll let me in."

After a few awkward moments he sighed. "Look. Come back to my place. I'm off work and I have a spare bedroom. Just until you feel better. It would make me—happy. It would make me happy to take care of you."

Nodding slowly, I leaned towards him, allowing him to put his arm around my shoulders. We walked slowly together as Madden directed me to his car. It looked shiny and black, fast and smooth. Riding in a car wasn't a frequent luxury of mine, but even I knew this was quality.

Always the nice guy, he opened the passenger side door for me, ensuring I didn't lose my balance as I lowered myself into the plush seat, and huddled up against the door as he stepped around to the driver's side. It smelled of what I assumed was new car smell.

We didn't talk on the drive and I was thankful. After a few minutes, he parked the car behind a tall, red-bricked building. Neither of us moved as the silence grew. I could hear my heartbeat in my ears and wondered if he could, too. My sinuses were tender and ached as I slid closer to death with every second.

Madden was gripping the leather steering wheel, his knuckles turning white. After what felt like an eternity, he turned his body towards me and let go of a breath.

"Look, I feel like I may have steamrolled you into coming back to my place, which was not my intention. It's possible I didn't think this through. It was obvious to me that you were sick and I had this overwhelming desire to take care of you. Still, I didn't take your feelings into consideration, and now that we are here—" He was silent for a moment. "Joe, I'll take you home right now if you feel uncomfortable being alone with me. No hard feelings. I may show up on your doorstep tomorrow with soup, though. I won't hold you hostage, but I can promise I'll take care of you, whether here or at your place. I want to."

"Madden, I feel like shit and my h-h-head feels like it's on a b-b-balloon about three feet to my left." I looked over at him dramatically. "Oh, I suppose that means you have it," I said, laughing. I really must be dying. "Look. I don't know you that well, but I am sixty-three p-p-p-percent sure I'm dying right now anyway, so if you take me upstairs and do anything with me, I'm better off."

He swallowed audibly and his face lit up in red for some unknown reason.

"D-d-did I do something wrong?" I asked, impatiently.

"God, no. Let's get going."

The interior light clicked on and blinded me as I climbed

out of the car, stepping onto the wet pavement. Madden met me at the front and his expression looked like he'd just won something. I was so confused by his reactions. His look of utter bliss when I agreed to something he offered me. He lit up like a plugged-in Christmas tree.

We walked into the building, me trailing behind a step, looking around for possible predators as I'd taught myself. I could see a few people milling around by the mailboxes on the wall. It was only early evening, but the busyness of the entrance worried me. I noticed the smell of leather when the elevator dinged its arrival and the doors swooshed open. Madden stepped aside and ushered me in, hand on my back, following me and pushing the '4' button. Now that we were alone in a lit-up, enclosed space, I broke into a sneeze attack. Because, of course, I did. Note to self—If you're going to sneeze, don't do it in an enclosed space surrounded by glossy mirrored walls. There's no escape. It was the sneeze heard AND seen around the world.

The doors swooshed open and I was standing inside the entry hall of his apartment, taking in my surroundings. My first impression: bubbles.

"What is that sound?" I asked as he toed off his shoes. Nodding at my shoes, I took my own boots off, setting them next to his on a small, short shelf. Looking around, I found his place to be nicer than anything I'd ever seen. The fact that I had zero comparison was not the point. It had high ceilings and white marble countertops with gray streaks running through them. They reminded me of the soap that I got at the shelter in Chicago.

The floors were thick wood planks, nicer than those at the café. Dark and long. The far wall had two massive windows with a fireplace centered between them, a wooden ledge on top covered in framed snapshots of people I'd never know. My heart lurched at the thought.

"What sound do you mean?" he asked, interrupting me from my fall down the rabbit hole.

"Bubbling?" I looked around, more focused on the refrigerator. Red, blue, orange and green papers were stuck to the doors with colorful alphabet magnets. Juvenile drawings of stick figures and trees without leaves lined the pages. I was confused. "Who drew those?" I blurted, my gaze boring into Madden.

"David did." He walked over to stand next to me. "He drew those years ago, actually. We were all so impressed because he was only a couple of years old. He's always loved art. He comes over every week or so to hang out and I always display his artwork. He's so proud of it." His reverent voice warmed me when he spoke of David. "Ah, the sound you are referring to is probably Batman and Robin. They're my fish. Do you want to meet them?"

"Superheroes? Yes. That's so cool."

The fish were brilliantly colored, their scales flashed with light, darting across the tank, swaying this way and that. I leant down on the countertop, my chin resting on my hands, just watching them glide effortlessly through the water.

Madden stepped up to the counter next to me and asked if I'd like to take a shower. "I-I-I don't have anything with me," I answered honestly. It was so obvious that I was not in the same world as Madden. We existed in two separate planes.

"I do. You can use my shower and I'll grab some clothes for you to change into. It might help make you feel better."

Before I could answer, he fled down a darkened hallway. Not knowing what to do, I continued to watch the fish. Yawning, my jaw popped from the strain and I let out a groan. I was just so tired, my body so sore, as if I were run over by a garbage truck.

"Joe, I've got everything set up, come back here and I'll

show you around," Madden called from the other end of the hallway.

I followed his voice and found the bedroom, lit up by the bedside lamps. Madden stood inside, an arm ushering me through another doorway. The bathroom was larger than I'd ever seen. It had a shower and a bathtub. Separated. There was a door on the opposite wall, but I couldn't see what was inside because the light was off. As if he'd read my mind, Madden explained, "The toilet is in there. It's just a door for privacy, is all." I must have looked like I'd never seen a bathroom before, because he draped his hand on my shoulder, urging me forward.

Pointing to a stack of clothes that looked like a pair of sweats and a t-shirt, he grabbed a towel and hung it on the shower door. "That's for you," he instructed. I just nodded in understanding, more dumbfounded than anything else. Opening the shower door, steam billowed into my face and I couldn't wait to get inside and breathe in that moisture. After he explained what the bottles inside contained, he left the room, turning the lock on the door handle, then softly closed it behind him.

I wanted to spend my life in this space. The water felt glorious, cascading down my sore muscles. I couldn't remember the last time I'd taken a shower without wearing flip flops, but this was heaven. I felt spoiled and special and wished my head felt better so I could enjoy the luxury. I'd love the chance to be here again when I didn't feel like I had an entire pillow full of cotton in my brain.

Dressing quickly in the clothing Madden left behind, I cinched the waist band of the sweats as tightly as possible, ensuring that they wouldn't slide right off. I was drowning in the t-shirt left folded by the bathroom sink, but it was so soft. It wrapped around my entire upper body, ending somewhere above my knees. Standing there, in Madden's bathroom, the mirrors fogged up and his smell surrounding me, I felt something close to comfort for the first time. In clothes that weren't even new, they felt like the most expensive fabrics I'd ever touched. They felt like security.

I made my way back to the kitchen, feeling tired and warm, my head as foggy as the bathroom mirrors. Madden fiddled with the television, so I took my place with the superheroes.

I jumped when Madden's hand landed on my shoulder.

"Didn't mean to scare you. I asked if you wanted something to eat but you were lost to the fishes." His voice held a tone of humor.

"Oh. I hyper-focus on things sometimes. S-s-s-sorry if I was rude to you."

Madden squeezed my nape and headed into the kitchen, his socked feet silent on the hardwood. I felt hollow and full at the same time. As scary as this was, starting a friendship with someone, it felt right. It felt filling.

Madden picked up a small orange jar with a brown lid and motioned between me and the tank. "They haven't had dinner yet. You can feed them."

"Really?" I squeaked.

He laughed. "Well, now that you ask, maybe I need to rethink this offer. I mean, these guys rely on me to ensure their survival. I can't just let anyone feed them."

"Oh. Right. I've never fed fish before." I immediately deflated, but a warm hand on my nape soothed the sting.

"Joe, I'm joking. They are just fish. The only way you can do it wrong is to not feed them, or basically dump the entire jar of food in." He handed me the jar, sans lid and pointed to the fish tank with a slight jerk of his head. "Go ahead."

"I-I don't know what I'm doing," I said, embarrassed.

He leaned over my shoulder, close enough to feel his body heat, and smell his spicy, fresh scent.

"Just take a pinch of the flakes between your fingers," he

directed, enveloping my hand in his. "That's right. Now, hold it above the tank where it's open and rub your fingers together to break them up as they fall into the water." His hand lingered an extra beat and I melted inside.

As soon as they noticed something breach the surface, both Batman and Robin zoomed up to inhale the fishy-smelling flakes of food, mouths gaping wide and round like little perfect 'O's. I was transfixed, stunned. I'd never seen anything like this before and couldn't help but let my mind relax as I curled up in the chair and just watched them. They were so vibrant and full of life. Not directionless at all.

After awhile, I tore my eyes away from the fish. Madden was no longer in the room. The squeaking and moving of furniture echoed from down the dark hall. Unsure of my place, I froze. Like a snowball, slowly melting into nothingness. Which, honestly, sounded a lot like me. Melting away into a puddle, causing more of a mess, leaving wetness behind. Gazing back at the fish, my eyes blurred, and I couldn't hold on. Curled into a chair by the tank, I started drifting.

Venom is here. I hear him walk into the kitchen, his steel-toed boots heavy as he makes his way around the house. Retreating as fast as I can to my room, I force myself into the closet and behind the wall of clothes, shrinking down into the smallest ball I can form. Suddenly, there's a hand at my back, drawing circles and a whisper in my ear. Venom? Oh, God. Wrenching away, I'm on the ground, Venom's hands clench tightly around me, pulling me up and into his warm chest. "H-hh-help!" I stutter a scream, fighting to get away, but his hands grip me and pull me tighter against his body.

"Joe, Joe, wake up, Joe. Shhhhhhhh, you're okay. It's Madden." Madden's deep, soothing voice tempered the panic and forced air back into my lungs. The gentle rocks and relaxing hushed sounds calmed me until I fully understood where I was. In his space. I must have fallen onto the floor by the fish. I quickly tore myself away from Madden's lap, mortified.

"Hey, hey, hey. Slow down." Gracious as ever, his hand slowly slipped around my wrist. "I was making up the bed in the spare room for you and you fell asleep," he continued, wiping a random curl from my forehead.

Allowing myself to fall back into his lap, his hand made soothing circles around my back. Through the fog of my cold and the darkness of my vision, I knew I'd remember this moment for a long time. For the first time in over a decade, I felt safe.

The warmth of his sweater warmed me from the outside in, like a marshmallow in a campfire. After a few slow blinks and calm breaths, I realized I'd been trembling. My face was hot and wet. Evidently, I'd lost the ability to control my bodily functions as my eyes, nose, and mouth were all leaking at the same time. In one blurred move, I was hefted up in his arms, flying in the air, like a bride on her wedding day. Moments later I landed on a cloud. Its softness conformed to my body like wet sand. Like it was made just for me. I let myself relax into it, and it swept me away, back into the pitch.

I woke to warm, unfamiliar darkness. My sinuses felt like lava packed volcanoes throbbing beneath my skin. Standing, I winced, stepping around the oriental rug, to the window adjacent to the double bed. Outside was wet and dark, the cars parked in rows like headstones in a cemetery. As my hand slid from the slats of the blinds, they clacked back into place in neat little lines. Madden. I could taste his name, like it was a tangible thing.

Not wanting to turn any lights on, brushing my hands along the wall, I found my way to the open kitchen and living area, following the neon light and the bubbling sound. I could almost hear the fish calling me. My name bubbling from their lips. They were fascinating and so free, as they darted about their small prison. Did they know? Did they have any idea how safe they were? How incredibly lucky? My breath hitched; they had what I was missing.

11

———

Madden

"I am so fucked," I said aloud, looking at my reflection in the bathroom mirror. After leaving a sleeping Joe in the spare bedroom, I'd gotten ready for bed, my mind playing a reel of our interactions. I wondered if I'd missed something. A sign or a piece of a puzzle that I should have understood or seen. After brushing my teeth, I searched the drawers for a new toothbrush for Joe, placing it in the spare bathroom with a travel-sized toothpaste I had from the dentist.

The fact that Joe didn't want me to take him home bothered me more than anything else. My mind was having no trouble forming scenarios of both deviant and ridiculous themes. And where were his friends and family? He'd never mentioned anyone in all the times we'd spoken. But I had never asked. The need inside me rose to find out all I could while he was here.

I lay awake for hours in the dark, my head spinning through scenarios. Why had I felt this strong need to take care of Joe? My feelings towards him had obviously moved from friendship to something more, but I didn't have the words to voice what that 'more' was yet. Making a mental checklist, I tried to sort through my thoughts.

Did I find Joe attractive? Check.

Did I want to be his friend? Check.

Did I want to kiss him? My entire body thrummed at the thought. Check mate.

Groaning, I flipped my pillow over to the cold side, desperately wishing for sleep.

SQUEEZING my eyes shut against the early morning light, I listened for sounds of life from the bedroom next to mine. "Joe," I whispered, just to taste his name. My body practically vibrated at the thought of seeing him in my apartment. A litany of thoughts plagued my mind. *What's happened to you, Joe? What do you need?* I threw on a pair of flannel pajama pants and an old t-shirt, well-worn and comfortable. After stopping by the bathroom, I lightly walked down the hall and paused, pressing my ear to Joe's door. I shook my head, scolding myself. No, not Joe's door, the spare room.

Hearing nothing at all, I cracked it open, careful to keep quiet. No Joe. Panic gripped me as I hurried down to check the front door. I released a gust of air when I caught sight of his boots, still at the door next to mine. *Where is he?* I made my way into the kitchen and almost fell over him. His body was curled up on the floor beneath the fish tank, tucked between the cabinets and island. Looking him over, I noticed the sparse expanse of freckles across his face and his perfect lips, pale in the dull light. He looked small and cold. I tentatively reached my hand to his face, cupping his cheek gently. Sitting back on my haunches, I gazed at his lean form. He looked so angelic, I thought, caressing his jaw with my thumb. His skin felt hot, a reminder that he was sick and needed to be cared for.

Stirring, Joe smacked his lips a few times causing his nose to crinkle up in the cutest way.

"Good morning," I said slowly, my hand trailing down his cheek. "Why don't we get you back into bed so you can rest properly?" I offered him my hand to help him up and his lips turned down at the ends.

"That's not—" He said, his words strained. The way he winced when he swallowed told me it pained him to speak, his throat obviously scratchy and raw. "I can't sleep in a bed. Have to have my back against something." He murmured out something else, but his raspy cough covered up the sound.

"Here, drink some water," I said and handed him a cold bottle from the fridge. "Maybe it will soothe your throat. I have some over the counter cold medicines and some Aspirin for the fever." I rooted through my cabinet until I found a couple of pills, then handed them to him. He eyed each one in his palm as if they were unclassified gemstones. Or he didn't trust me... And didn't that just hurt my heart.

"It's all fine to take, unless you have allergies to anything?" I prompted, my head tilting to the side. I should have asked beforehand. After quickly shaking his head, I said, "I'm a nurse, remember? I know what I'm doing." After giving him a wink, he dropped them into his mouth, taking a gulp of water. When a rogue drop found its way down his chin, I had to look away. "Now, let's get you back in bed."

I held on to him as he hobbled down the short hallway, dazed and fatigued. The urge to carry him to bed was strong, but I resisted the pull. He allowed me to grip his waist without flinching, but at the spare bed he hesitated.

"You can't sleep in a bed at all?" I asked, wondering what that was about. The mattress was too soft? Too hard? It was new, so I knew it didn't smell. All I wanted to do was to take care of him, but I kept coming up short.

"It's not safe," he responded through a yawn, his eyes half lidded. A bed was not safe? Damn if that didn't just cut me to the quick.

"Joe, you are safe here. No one else is here, and the door is locked. I promise you can just sleep." I tried to lift the comforter for him, but he brushed my hand away and turned towards the corner.

"It's fine. I'm used to the f-f-floor," he said, kneeling on the thin carpet, his body curled into a tight ball in the corner next to the bedside table. I stood for a moment, stunned at the sight. I opened my mouth to finally object, but he was breathing heavily, mouth slightly agape. Like an angel. The sight of his pale, slight frame scored on my heart. Grabbing a pillow for his head, I covered him with the duvet. "Sweet dreams, Joe," I whispered, lightly brushing my fingers through the fine tufts of hair at his temple, then I left the room.

UNWILLING TO LEAVE the apartment with Joe sleeping, I ordered groceries online and had them delivered. Online ordering wasn't something that I did regularly, but this wasn't a typical day. I'd spent the last few hours in the living room, splayed out on my couch with my laptop, reading various news articles, and catching up with some friends online. I'd never admit to getting up and sneaking a peek at Joe every thirty minutes or so. Because I didn't. Not once. And I certainly would not have stared at the strip of his abs that was revealed, showing his pale, warm skin pulled tight against his protruding hip bone. I didn't want to trace a path with my tongue. Nope, not at all.

His temperature had fallen, part in thanks to the medication I'd given him. Just that fact alone had made me infinitely more relaxed. As soon as the groceries arrived, I started a simple chicken soup for Joe. It was my mother's recipe and it was special to me. She'd made it for me anytime I was sick, and it always made me feel better. If I could impart a fraction of that on Joe, it would be worth it. Having no idea when he'd last eaten, concern knitted my eyebrows, bringing back an uneasy feeling. And with it, a shiver up my spine.

I'd sliced the celery, carrots, and was about to cut some onion when a series of sneezes, followed by a round of coughing came from the spare room. Wiping my hands on a tea towel, I grabbed a bottle of water and made my way down the hallway. Joe was sitting on the floor, hands covering his mouth, his hair sticking up all over like he'd barely survived a tornado. Smiling, I handed him the water.

"Here, drink this," I told him. Stroking the backs of my fingers against his forehead, I asked, "How are you feeling?" I was pleased when he didn't move away from the touch. Obviously, he had issues with people touching him, but I couldn't help myself. Apparently, I was a tactile person, because I'd caught myself mid-reach many times around him. I needed the physical connection. I needed to ensure that he was there, rather than an apparition I'd conjured from loneliness. It scared me to think he could one day disappear, or vanish, as if he was only ethereal, something I'd made up.

"I've been better," he croaked between sips of water. He finished the bottle, handed it to me, and wiped his mouth with the back of his hand.

"Are you hungry?" I asked, my hand now on his back, moving in small, light circles.

His eyes blinked slowly closed before he said, "I love it when you touch me, Madden." Through his shaky voice, I could feel how much it took out of him to say those words, and not just because he wasn't feeling well.

My heart stopped for a couple of beats before starting up a

wild pace that thumped in my ears. He'd sounded dazed, like his head was full of cotton, so I wasn't sure if he'd heard himself say it, but I let those words imprint on my stuttering heart. Stunned, we both sat there, him in a deep trance and me slowly writing the letters to spell 'Madden + Joe' on his back with my finger. I was getting in deep and it was too fast. Yet, there was a connection that I couldn't deny from my side. And I didn't want to deny it.

"I should probably get going," Joe declared, bursting into my thoughts.

Shaking my head, I said, "What? What do you mean 'get going'?" I heard the panic in my voice and felt the blood rush to my ears as the words left my mouth.

"It was really nice of you to b-b-bring me to your home and help me out, but I should, l-l-l-let you get back to your life. And work. And your fish. And whatever else it is you—"

Another bout of coughing ended his rant. I was more than pleased about that.

"Don't even think about walking out of here, Joe," I demanded, my voice harsher than I'd intended. Shit. "Sorry, I just mean... Well, I'm more than happy to have the company and you need taking care of right now. I'm off until Monday, so you should stay." I decided I needed to get this out there. Joe didn't seem like the type to assume the best out of a situation. He was like a stray cat, distrusting and hesitant. I didn't need to give him more reason to feel wary. "I'd really like you to stay. I like having you here, and I'm actually making you soup, so it would be highly offensive of you to leave now." I smirked, hoping for a bit of levity and he searched my face, looking for something. What, I didn't know. Eventually, he nodded and let me lead him into the kitchen.

～

"You know, I've never really seen fish before. Like, alive." Joe had positioned himself in front of the fish tank again, balancing on a kitchen chair. He looked so sweet perched there, a single leg folded underneath him, the other knee up by his chin.

"Alive? You mean you've only seen dead fish?" I asked, laughing.

"Well, yeah. Like, to eat. Not swimming. Not like this."

"Hey, Joe?" I had so many thoughts racing around in my head, so many questions and worries. I needed an answer to at least one of them. It seemed his illness was loosening his tongue, and I had to take advantage of it. After his earlier comment about my touching him, I figured some of his force-field was down. "Will you tell me about your childhood? What it was like? Or where you lived?" I didn't look at him, giving him space while I stirred the simmering soup in the pot. Minutes passed in silence and I sighed, realizing I had pushed too far.

"My m-m-m-mother was sick. She died when I was seven. My—," his voice broke, his hand covering his mouth. "Venom. He—He wasn't what everyone else's father was. I spent a lot of time b-b-by myself," he explained. "I was safe when I was alone. I am safer alone."

After wiping at his eyes, he cleared his throat and I immediately regretted asking about his family, but then he turned the tables on me. "What about yours?"

"Ah, well, let's see. I grew up with a sister who wouldn't leave me alone, so having a bit of privacy would have been nice. We got along well, though. Still do, in fact. She's great. And so is her little family, as you know." I smiled then, thinking back to the day in the café when Joe and David seemed to somehow connect.

For some inexplicable reason, I felt that Joe fit into my life, somehow. Like, our family puzzle had been put together, but a piece wasn't quite right. It fit, but it wasn't smooth. Maybe it was a stand-in piece. A place holder for when the lost piece was found and could replace it. Somewhere deep in my heart, hidden behind a veil as thin as cheesecloth, Joe belonged. I just needed to find where and how he fit. Turn his piece until it clicked.

I FED Joe hot soup and toasted bread until he couldn't keep his eyes open, then I offered him another handful of pills and a bottle of water. He started getting spacey about twenty minutes later, but he said he didn't want to sleep. He'd slept all day and wanted to 'just be'. I wasn't about to argue with that.

We fell on the brown, oversized couch, each occupying an end, our feet meeting on the same cushion in the center. It felt intimate and warm inside, like an evenly roasted marshmallow. Light, fluffy, and gooey.

Joe asked me to talk to him about everything. He said he wanted to know more about me. So, for the next couple of hours, I told him stories of my life. Both young and recent. About being lost in the woods when Anna and I were young. We happened upon a house at the end of the tree line, and the older woman recognized us and called our mom. We had been in so much trouble we didn't get dessert for weeks.

I listed off the names of the bands that I listened to growing up. I sang him a terribly off-key version of my sister's song that we danced to at her wedding. He never once made me feel as though I was giving too much away. In fact, he pulled stories from me that I hadn't thought of in years. He asked me questions that no one had ever asked before.

"What were you thinking about when you danced with your sister?"

"What are your favorite song lyrics, and how do they make you feel?"

"How did you know that nursing was your calling?"

I had been so enraptured by him and his thought process, trying to let him see my memories and share my stories, that I didn't notice when Joe had moved. His head rested on my thigh, and I was twining my fingers through the softness of his hair. His feather-soft downy hair. So light and smooth, like nothing I'd touched before. Like dandelion seed. My body shuddered as realization hit me. I could have stayed on my couch with him, just like this, for the rest of my life.

When the sun created shadows on the floors and high-lighted the walls, Joe looked up at me. My breath hitched. His face was full of wonder and awe and he looked so reverent. Like an angel. I didn't want to blink for fear it would wash the image away from me. And then he spoke, oh so softly.

"Madden, you make me feel," he whispered, still staring at me, unblinking. "You make me feel safe and free."

I watched his eyelids grow heavy, my hands in his hair, the sun spreading across his body like a blanket, his hair on fire from the light. He was perfection. I stared in wonderment at this beautiful man laid out across my lap. In just a few shared moments over the last few weeks, he'd become so special to me. I could have watched him all night. Just when I had thought he was asleep, he said something to break my heart into a thousand pieces.

"You are the only one I've ever let touch me, Madden."

SPENDING SATURDAY EVENING doing laundry and cleaning bathrooms wasn't typically my idea of a good time. Things changed, however, with Joe here. Most of his time was spent asleep on the couch, burrowed into the corner as far as he could get without becoming part of the piece itself. He was a nester, twisting and turning until he was perfectly comfortable, then not moving a muscle.

It was nice having him here in my space. I liked hearing his puffing breaths and his faint murmurs when he dreamed. It made me wonder where he went when he closed his eyes. From what he'd uttered the previous night, I knew that something bad had happened to him. There were so many possible explanations, knowing that he lacked the most basic human need, to be touched, held, comforted, and loved. I couldn't wrap my mind around that. I'd spent the last few hours thinking back to my life and sifting through images in my mind of being sad, scared, or worried and getting hugs from my parents. Back rubs. Holding hands with my sister whenever we walked to school and back or to the park together. I imagined what it would have felt to not have that. I couldn't even fathom the idea of it.

So, as I went on cleaning and wiping down things in the house, I thought about how I could do something for Joe. *If* I could do something for him. I knew he wasn't mine. Well, my head knew that. My common sense understood, but my heart. My heart was on a wholly different plane than the rest of me. Where practicality and sense didn't exist, and monsters couldn't reach.

Eventually, Joe sat up, rubbed his eyes and peered over the couch at me. "You hungry again, yet? It's getting kind of late, but you should probably eat something before it's time to actually go to bed tonight." I'd made a stew, but I wasn't sure something that heavy would be welcomed if he still didn't feel so great.

"Um, yeah, I think so. Actually..." he paused to weave his hand through his hair and winced. "Um, w-w-would it be too much trouble to use your shower again?" He was so hesitant, like he had asked for a $20,000 loan.

"Of course, you can use my shower. Follow me," I said, watching him unfold himself from the couch. He trailed me into my bathroom once again. "It will be easier if you use this shower, since it's got soap and shampoo and everything in it already. I'll just grab you a clean towel from the closet and some sweats. We can do your laundry later." Before he could say anything, I walked out, telling myself not to think of him getting into my shower. Wet. Using my soap. Fuuuuuck. When had things turned from me wanting to take care of him to me wanting to lick every inch on his body? Probably in the few hours that I'd spent earlier that day, with my hands weaving through his silky hair, his weight pressed against my body on the couch. It meant more than I'd have ever thought.

Returning with a towel, a pair of sweats with a drawstring, a t-shirt and a pair of boxers, I set them on the counter and turned around, biting my tongue. Holy fuck. He'd taken his shirt off and folded it onto the countertop. I held my breath as I stared at his chest. He was so beautifully pale and thin, with a smattering of light fur between his pecs that led to a trail pointing straight into his sweats. Before I could stop myself, my hand reached out and traced the line of ink running across his left pectoral muscle. It was a series of letters and numbers. Without thinking, I moved closer and realized it was coordinates. "A tattoo?" I asked, sounding like I'd never seen one before.

"Um, yeah." He sounded as breathless as I was. His cheeks reddened, and I followed the color with my eyes as it spread down to his chest.

"What are the coordinates for?" I asked, intrigued.

"Oh, it's close to Chicago. Where I lived as a kid." His face gave nothing away.

"Is it your house?"

"Um, no. Not exactly. It's—" He trailed off. I was about to tell him he didn't have to answer when he said, "The only thing I've ever cared about is there." He turned and stepped towards the shower, excusing me.

JOE WALKED INTO THE KITCHEN, hair damp and clinging to his cheeks. I couldn't look away. He was hesitant and I looked down and noticed his clothes and towel in his arms.

"Oh, hey, hand those to me and I'll throw them in the washer."

Taking a few steps towards me he said, "Thanks for the shower. I feel so much better now." I waved off his gratitude and headed towards the laundry room. At some point I needed to find out what his plans were. The last thing I wanted was for him to go. I wanted more time with him like this. With no distractions. But mostly, I realized that I just wanted *him.*

He was back at the fish tank when I returned. It brought a smile to my face. "You really like them, don't you?" I asked, tipping my head towards the tank.

"I do. I've never seen a fish up close like this. I find it sooth-ing. They just glide through the water without resistance. It looks like Batman and Robin do everything together. It must be nice for them to have each other, right?" It was a rhetorical question, but I knew there was some deeper meaning behind his words.

"No one is supposed to be alone, Joe."

12

———

Joe

"Apparently, I am," I whispered, more to myself than anything. When I turned to say something else to Madden, his face looked pained, as though he were trying to reign in some emotion. Once again, something I didn't understand. My head was still thick with being sick and I knew I'd been more open with him than I'd ever been before, but I didn't have enough brain power to decide if it was from feeling so awful, or from the strange familiarity I felt around him. Glancing over at him, I had to know. "Did I say something or do something wrong? Do you want me to leave? You are o-o-obviously upset, but I can't u-u-u-understand why unless you explain." It was the truth. My only thought was that I was playing house and he was tired of the game.

"No. Sorry, no," he said, stepping cautiously over to my side. His reassuring hand on my nape heated my body from my head to my toes. His touch ignited something in me. It grounded me. Made me feel secure, like I was enveloped in softness.

"Joe, I really, really like you. I want to be your friend, and I've enjoyed you staying here with me. It's been nice having you around, even if you've been sleeping most of the time," he explained, letting out a huff of a laugh.

"Okay, but you were upset, and I can't figure out why. It's k-k-kind of overwhelming for me," I responded, needing to understand. If I'd caused him pain or upset him, I needed to ensure I didn't do it again. He had become someone to me, even if I was loathe to admit it. Madden laughed, and it sounded like wind chimes in a gusty storm. It was radiant.

"Joe. You are funny, sweet, and so easy to talk to. But more than that, you have a way about you. You view the world differently. You see things that other people miss, ask questions that other people wouldn't even think to ask. And it makes me want to be around you more, to get to know you better. Maybe find out what I've been missing. To find out what it is about you that lights me up inside."

My brain was wired differently than everyone else. I'd heard that somewhere along the way when I'd researched about autism, while getting my GED. Ever since, the sometimes not so subtle differences astounded me. I was a very literal thinker; my brain just processed that way. Sometimes, if I picked up humor in tone, I could tell sarcasm and could appreciate it for what it was. Other times, I had no idea. My tendency to take things personally came mostly from misunderstanding. But the words that Madden had just thrown into the air with abandon? I didn't understand them all. There were too many emotionally charged words, and I was overwhelmed. My head pounding, I responded, blurting the first thought I could manage to speak. "Are you gay?" I groaned, my face in my hands. Maybe I could be the first person to die of embarrassment. My red cheeks had returned with a vengeance.

"I am," he said, tentatively, like he was trying to coax a stray dog into coming closer. "Are you?"

I sucked my lip into my mouth and thought for a moment. "I don't know. It's not so s-s-s-simple for me." When he looked down, I noticed my hands were clenched into fists.

"Can you explain that to me?" His head was tilted, his face so genuine, and something about that made my heart throb painfully in my chest. Oh, God. Was I going to tell him?

"Can we sit down first?" This wasn't something I could talk about casually, maybe not at all.

Madden slid his hand down my arm and took my hand, leading me to the couch. But the way he sat us—with him in the corner, me between his legs, my back against his chest—caused another painful stab to my heart. I felt secure in his grasp. Surrounded, literally, by his warmth and understanding.

With my body thrumming, I started my story.

"There once was a boy named Bird. He lived in a haunted house made of tar and brick and fire." I replayed my story, reliving moments, glossing over others. I told him about my mother and her counting. About Venom and his friends. About him waiting until I was fourteen before allowing them to do things to me that he turned his back on. About finding myself alone, more often than not, in my own house for weeks at a time, with no food, money, or electricity. I had no way of knowing if Venom would return, or if I had been officially abandoned. So, I walked away. In the night, I left because I couldn't live one more day in that house. I had nothing, either way. At least if I was on my own, my body would be safe and free from Venom's friends.

The last few years on the streets had been rough. I'd searched for jobs in every city. I couldn't stay in one place for long after what happened in Omaha. That reminder is still my nightmare to this day, but I couldn't tell Madden. Not yet. I didn't even think I could talk about what happened that weekend.

I lay against Madden, his breath on my neck, and his hands in my hair. I fed him my stories, the words seeping from my mouth. Some things were difficult to get out, honestly, but he never pressed me. And when my voice faltered, his hand massaged my back, giving me reassurance and the strength to continue.

When all was said and done, he pressed his lips gently to my temple and left them there. It wasn't a kiss. It was something both more and less. But, I felt it deep inside me and had a feeling it was important.

"Thank you for trusting me with all of that, Joe. It means a lot that you told me." His words were whispered into my hair, but I didn't answer.

"I, um. I never directly answered your question, and I will. You needed to understand what I went through to understand my answer. So, because of the multiple men who had been given permission to touch me as they pleased, I hate the feeling of anyone else's hands on me. The feel, sound, and scrape of their skin against mine, makes me feel like I've been buried alive and can't breathe." I heard Madden's sharp intake of breath but continued. "I've never been touched by someone who didn't hurt me."

"Joe, I—"

"P-p-please, just let me finish. I need to say this to you like this. Me close to you, but you not looking at me. It's easier. You make it easy for me. No one else has ever done that." I took a deep breath. "When you grabbed my wrist the first day, I was in shock. Not because you'd reached out, but because it didn't hurt. And I wasn't sure why. So, I let you touch me again. And again. And do you know what happened, Madden?"

"Tell me." His voice was a soft plea against my neck.

"It felt—soft. Soft and sweet and warm. And every time

after, it was better. And more than just tolerating a tactile response from you, I crave it now. It feels good and I want more."

"Oh, baby," he said in barely a whisper, his forehead pressed to my shoulder.

"I've n-n-never liked it before. And it scares me because I can't quantify the reason. But I trust that you won't hurt me. And you need to know that I've never trusted a-a-anyone before. So, don't hurt me. Please. While I think asking that is wrong, I need to."

"The last thing on Earth I want to do is hurt you, Joe."

I nodded. "Okay. Then you should know that I have had sex, but it has never felt good and it's never been with my permission. I know it would be different with you, but I don't know when or if I'd ever be ready. It seems like something that you would probably want with me at some point, so I will try."

I felt Madden stiffen behind me. Again, his reaction confused me. "Joe," he said, turning me sideways to look at my face. "No way. We are not just going to have sex. That's not what this is. That's not—" His face scrunched up and he looked pained. "Joe," he said again, this time his voice was agony. "Just, don't do that. Don't just assume that I want something, and your job is to give it to me. That's not... It's not what I want. At all."

"So, you don't want to have sex with me?" I asked in clarification.

When Madden's eyes went alarmingly wide, I laughed. After the initial shock of my reaction, he laughed too. And it felt a little bit like what I'd imagined a *moment* felt like.

"*This* is something, though, isn't it? You and me, I mean. *This*. It's something?"

He nodded, swallowing hard. "Yeah, Joe. This is something."

"Okay. Okay, good. What comes next?" I asked.

"Next? What do you mean?" His voice was unsure, making me blush.

"I don't know what comes next. We just said that we have something. I've never had something before, and I don't want to get it wrong."

Madden turned me in his lap so that my shoulder rested against his chest. I pulled the hem of his shirt into my fingers and gently caressed the material, feeling calmer with each stroke.

"There isn't a rule book on having a friendship or a relationship, Joe. We just continue talking and taking another step forward, making sure our feet land together."

I looked at him and said, "I'm going to need help. Sometimes my balance is off."

I woke up sweaty, scared, and with no way of knowing the time. I'd dreamt that I was running, unable to get anywhere. I couldn't shake the feeling that there was someone else, waiting for me to fall asleep. I hated being alone after waking like this. It wasn't until I thought about where I was that I remembered Madden's huge bed. Maybe, just maybe, he could chase away my nightmare long enough so that I could fall asleep again.

I crept to his door, pushing it open, carefully stepping inside. It was dark, but the light of the moon poured in through the bathroom window, reflecting in the mirrors. I could just make out his form and he shot up like I'd called his name. "Joe? What is it?" Without answering, I walked over to him. He stared up at me, eyes questioning. My only answer was the harsh reverberation of my heart. After a few seconds, he lifted the blankets and the sheet in invitation, then scooted back, giving me room. Room that I shouldn't want, but accepted without further thought. I needed the safety that only he offered.

"I had a dream and got scared and thought maybe I could fall asleep again if you were with me. God, that sounds so dumb. I'm sorry. I shouldn't have woken you up." His warm, soft hand gripped my wrists as I turned to leave.

"Hey. C'mere and get in." I hesitated, then slowly crawled into his bed, into the warm spot he'd just vacated. He was inches away, not touching me, which I appreciated, but wasn't sure I wanted. Soon enough, his hand found mine between us and he tangled our fingers together. "This okay?" He whispered into the dark room.

"Yeah." Before I could fully process the touch, I was asleep.

As the sun pierced the blinds, a sense of place took root in me. I felt rested and happy. A hand tightened in mine and a warm breath grazed my neck. "Good morning, Joe. Did you sleep okay in here?" The voice was deep with sleep and sounded like home. The kind of home I'd always imagined, with people who cared, who made you feel safe and warm. Here, in Madden's apartment, in the space of two days, he'd somehow given me that.

"Mmmm," was all I could manage. A few minutes later, feeling a bit more human, I turned onto my side and looked at him. His eyes were closed, his face relaxed. He looked younger this way. "Was it okay that I came in here? I probably shouldn't have and I'm sorry for waking you."

Without cracking an eyelid, he responded, a small smile tugging at his lips. "It was very okay. I slept so well knowing you were right here with me."

A few minutes passed in a contented silence. I got up and went to the hall bath, deciding on a long, hot shower. Realizing too late that I didn't have anything to wear, I wrapped the towel around my waist and opened the door, hoping to find my clothing in the laundry. But it was nicely folded on the floor in front of the door, clean and perfect. I was embarrassed at how big the grin was, that appeared on my face. Madden was so good at anticipating and taking care of my needs. And we'd barely begun to scratch the surface of friendship. Was it always this easy, or was it just Madden?

"I hope you like pancakes," Madden said, smiling over his shoulder from the stove. He was whisking away, dark hair damp from his shower.

"Actually, I love them. T-t-thank you," I said, grabbing a chair from the table and heading over to the fish tank. "Have you fed the boys yet?" I asked, watching Batman and Robin float past.

"Nope. They were waiting for you." He threw me a sly smile and winked.

I knew that he was joking, but I couldn't help but wish it were true. Thinking that someone or something cared about me was something new, and felt like butterflies locked in a cage.

Taking the briny flakes between my fingers, I crushed and sprinkled them along the top of the water, watching for their mouths to break the surface. They didn't disappoint.

"If you want to get out forks and knives from the drawer by the sink, I'll bring the plates to the table and we can eat."

Giving my friends a little tap first, I went in search of utensils, then pulled my chair back to the table. When Madden set two plates down, filled with hot, steamy pancakes, I grinned at him. I felt like my face would burst into flames when he said, "I love your face right now. I'm going to have to try to see it this happy more often."

"Thank you," I replied, meekly.

"Man, you must really like syrup," Madden said, laughing.

I looked down at my plate and replied with a grin, "Yeah. Pancake soup is totally a thing. A normal thing." He laughed while I turned a bright shade of pink.

"So, I called Lulu yesterday and told her you were sick, and she said to let her know about today. I guess you are scheduled on a shift from 2-6 today, but if you don't feel well enough—"

I cut him off. "No, I need to go in. She's counting on me and I won't let her down."

He set down his fork and let out a long breath. "Joe, it isn't about letting her down. If you aren't feeling well, it's okay to take some time."

"I'm fine now. Thanks to you. I really appreciate you taking c-c-care of me." I didn't voice how safe I felt in his home. In his arms.

"I'll take care of you as much as you'll let me. I hope you know that. And I'll walk you to work later, okay?"

All I could do was nod. The fluttery feeling in my stomach heated my cheeks when he smiled at me.

THE KITCHEN WAS one of my favorite places in the café. It was sweet and full of spices, but the colors were beautiful too. Squinting my eyes, I could easily pretend I was in a flower garden. All the various spices held tones of browns and oranges. There were lettuce and vegetables, breads, coffee beans, dishes in varying, unmatched colors. It was a kaleidoscope of hues and I loved taking a minute here and there to enjoy its strange wonder. After losing myself for a minute, Lulu hip checked me with a smile.

"I'm glad you're feeling better, my dear. I was worried about you. It sounds like Madden is taking good care of you." Her voice was low and even, and I knew it was for my own privacy, but I still blushed.

"He made the best pancakes I've ever had for breakfast."

Turning to face me, her eyes taking me in, she mused, "I've known Madden for a couple of years now. He's been in and out of this café and we've had plenty of chats. He's a good man, Joe. And trust me, I'm not saying this to get into your business, but if you need a friend or anything else, he's definitely the first person I'd go to." She started to walk away, then turned and added, "And he's very pretty to look at." Then she winked. I blended in with the red velvet cupcake batter.

WHEN I WALKED out of the kitchen at six, with my bag in my hand, Madden was there. He was talking to Lulu at the counter and it startled me to see him. He said something to her, she nodded and started wiping down the counter. When he looked my way, and walked over to me, a wide smile took over his face. "Hey, Joe. How was your shift?"

"W-w-what are you doing here?" His smile dimmed, and I wanted to push his lips back up again.

After shoving his hands in his jean pockets, he answered, "I wanted to walk you back to my apartment, but I should have asked you first. I'm sorry."

It was then that I realized I'd offended him by asking. "Madden. I asked why you were here because I didn't expect it. That's all. There was nothing to read into it but surprise. We never talked about me going back to your place. I mean, I figured I'm feeling better and you'd want your space back."

The look on his face confused me, yet again. "Right, well I shouldn't have assumed." He ran his hand over his bottom lip, stirring up a strange sensation inside me. "I had the day off and made dinner, so will you come over and eat and we can talk?"

"Um. Sure. But, I think I said something to upset you again." I sighed. "Look, I say things that are very literal. It's just me. I feel like I'm always saying the wrong things around you. Things that make you feel bad."

"I don't want you to worry about—"

"Well, I am. The last thing I want is for you to t-t-think that I'm a jerk. I'm not." I smiled, unable to hold it in. "Well, I'm not trying to be one anyway. But it is easier for me if you tell me how you feel in words because I have a hard time understanding anything else."

Madden nodded, putting his hand on my back to start us walking. I tried to process what was going on between us while we walked. He told me about the phone call he'd just made to his sister as I walked in silent contemplation. He thought I'd just end up going back to his apartment after my shift. Why? He'd told me that he wanted to take care of me. That he *wanted* to. He'd been nothing but nice and understanding, and provided food and a warm, safe place. And he'd touched me. Not just physically, but emotionally as well. I *felt* when he was near. And I realized today, standing in the kitchen of the café, I felt, saw, and heard more now. As if he'd done something to me. Opened me up wide. I wanted to do something to make his face light up. We were walking side by side, careful not to touch each other. Thinking about last night, how it made me feel when I needed comfort, and he'd reached out his hand to mine. It felt so good, so warm and perfect. So, with trembling fingers, I reached for his hand and slid mine inside. His breath hitched as we walked, but he continued his story, squeezing my fingers in his. I felt as though my heart burst in anticipation and opportunity. To possibly be able to make Madden a little bit happy too. And that smile I'd hoped for? Yeah. I'd gotten that too.

13

Madden

I've always considered myself a cautious person. I look both ways before crossing the street. I read the instructions on medicine bottles. I never rip the tag from my pillows. I never wear my heart on my sleeve. Until now, apparently. Because the simple act of Joe threading his fingers with mine, did something to me. Yes, I'd had boyfriends and been on dates and held hands. I'd fucked quite a few guys as well, especially during college. Being with a man is nothing new to me. But this, this felt like more. Like the first time. At least, the first meaningful time. Denying the fact that I had strong feelings for Joe would be an insult. I knew it and felt it. It should have scared the shit out of me. Not having known him long, it shouldn't have been this fast or easy. But it felt right. To me, anyway. Promising myself I wouldn't push him, I bit my lip and opened the door to my apartment, my hand on his back as he led the way.

"I think I'm going to take a shower, if that's okay," he asked as he opened the jar of fish food, giving the boys their dinner. "I hate to ask for more from you, but can I borrow some pajamas or something? I don't have anything other than this." He said, gesturing to his body.

"Sure thing. I'll grab you something and put it by the door for you."

I didn't have much with a drawstring, but I found a pair of track pants and a t-shirt that was too small after being dried a few times. Placing them gently by the door, I moved to the kitchen to heat up the dinner I'd made us.

As I put the ravioli in the simmering sauce, I listened to the hall shower, thinking of Joe. It was easy with him. It didn't make any sense, but he just fit with me somehow.

And now, with him here in my place again, I needed to figure out what I wanted. The reality of the situation was, I'd missed him today. I'd been sitting on the couch, checking my watch for the fifth time in a half hour and it struck me. I felt as though I'd forgotten something that was vital to me. Knowing he was back here with me, well, it felt right. Part of me just couldn't see myself coming home after a long shift to my empty apartment again. Not after having Joe here, filling in the empty spaces with his love for Batman and Robin, and his ridiculous unicorn socks.

Just as I finished plating dinner, he walked up behind me, and tapped me on the shoulder with his index finger. I jumped, startled, then laughed at his wide-eyed expression.

"I didn't mean to scare you!" He said, laughing.

"It's fine, Joe. I was just lost in my head, but I'm glad you're here. Dinner's ready." Handing him his plate, I grabbed mine and the silverware and followed him to the table. I never ate at the table alone, preferring to sit in front of the television, or even in bed. It had been nice to have a companion.

Joe picked at his ravioli with his fork, dissecting a square, watching as cheese oozed out under the red tomato sauce. "Is it okay?" I asked, worried that he didn't like tomatoes.

"Yes, it's great." He looked at me and bit his bottom lip adorably before asking, "What is it?"

Hell. He'd never had ravioli. "It's ravioli. It's just a pocket of pasta that can be filled with different things. This one is filled with a few different types of cheeses. And I just put it with tomato sauce."

"Okay. Thanks for the ravioli." The grin he bestowed upon me made me feel like I'd conquered some epic battle in his name. Like a hero. God, it hurt. It was fucking ravioli and he was looking at me with wonder. He turned me into the ravioli hero.

I watched as he took his first bite and swallowed, my eyes focused on his throat, his Adam's apple bobbing as he worked the bite down. As my gaze lingered, he turned the color of the sauce.

Changing the subject, I said, "So, can we talk about you going back, er, home?"

"Yes. But you invited me. I can leave now, if that's what you're asking."

It seemed he was as confused by my question just as much as I was by his response. I hadn't meant to sound like I wanted him to leave, but he'd put his fork down, and the scowl on his face made me wonder if he was ready to bolt.

"That's not what I meant. I don't want you to leave. And I don't mind feeding you either. In fact, I like this." I gestured to the space over the table between us wildly, in a sudden panic. "I like having someone here to eat with, talk with." Joe nodded his head and relaxed a bit, still obviously unsure. Thrilled that I hadn't totally fucked this up, I took another breath. "What I meant to say is, what are you planning on doing now?"

He finished chewing and swallowed, taking a sip of water

from one of the bottles I had lined up in the center of the table. "We are friends, right? Or more?"

Unsure of where this was going, I nodded. "Of course, we are."

"So, I can tell you anything? And you won't get mad?" He looked up at me with a twinge of fear when he asked, and it hurt my heart.

"Joe, I—I can't promise not to get mad, but I promise to listen to you and help you if I can."

He took a minute to think and then nodded distractedly. "Okay. So, I don't actually have a place to live. I've set up a tent behind the gym, but I have a membership there so it's fine. I can do my laundry and shower and keep my stuff there."

He didn't look up at me as he bit his bottom lip, shoving a pasta shell around his plate. "Okay," I said slowly, processing.

"So, that's where I am going after this. I didn't want you to know before. It's embarrassing. And now you'll never think I'm a good person."

"What? Why would you think that?"

"Because you can't be friends with someone who has nothing, Madden." Before I could react, he continued, "Someone like me has no business being friends or anything else with someone like you. I have nothing and you have a life. You matter to people."

"You matter to me," I responded, anger building inside.

"No. I don't. Because nothing lasts and no one stays, and I have dark shadows following me. Waiting. And I don't deserve—"

I cut him off by swiftly pushing my chair back, scraping wood against wood. Hurrying over to him, I bent over, hugging him tightly, holding his head to my chest.

"I care about you, Joe. I don't care about the other stuff." I wasn't even sure what I was saying anymore, he just needed to understand that he was wrong. "What I mean is, I want you around because you make me feel good. I like who I am when you are around. And I want you around. Here. To stay."

"You don't even know me. Not really. Why would you want me to stay again? I've already spent too much time here, w-w-with you."

My mouth opened and closed a la Batman and Robin at the thought that he had no idea how intrigued I was by him. My lips turned up a bit at that and fuck me if he didn't blush.

"I want to know you. I think we've gotten to know each other a lot more in the last couple of days and I don't want the bubble of the weekend to end yet. I like you, Joe. I like you a lot and I'm not ready to say goodbye."

Joe stood, quickly walking down the hallway towards the bathroom. I heard the door shut and the lock snick as I sat, confused, at the table. *What happened?* Giving him a moment, I waited at the table with my head in my hands, my heart banging against my ribs. Water ran in the bathroom. A couple of minutes later, Joe padded down the hallway in his socks, his face blotchy and red.

As much as I needed to understand him and his reaction, the hardness of the kitchen table wasn't the place for this conversation. "Let's go sit down. I want you to tell me what happened if you can. I don't want to make you unhappy, Joe. That's the opposite of what I want. But I need you to talk to me." I led him to the sofa, planting myself a few feet away to give him space. He nestled his body into the corner, making himself small. It made me want to pull him onto my lap. But, of course I didn't.

"I'm sorry."

Leaning forward, I gently spoke. "You have to stop apologizing because you don't owe me an apology. If I said something wrong, or made you feel like you had to leave the room, then surely I'm the one who owes you an apology? But you should never be sorry for having feelings. Never. And never let anyone tell you otherwise."

As he pulled his legs up under his body he nodded, licking his lips. All I could do was wait. "It's just—," he broke off, searching for the words, so I gave him a moment. I'd wished I had the means to comfort him, but I didn't quite understand what he needed. I could only hope that I'd get the chance to understand him that well. Blowing a breath that teased at his hair, he started again. "You said something that freaked me out. Y-y-you... You said you aren't ready.... You aren't ready to say goodbye to me."

I nodded. "I did, and I meant that, but I still don't understand." I was missing something critical here. I searched his mottled face, thinking of what would make those words cause such distress.

His eyes were wide, lips parted. "Madden. Who are you? How can you be real?"

"I don't—"

"I know. It's just... I've never known anyone who wanted me around before. I've never had anyone ask me to stay. Well, except for Lulu, but that's not really the same, is it?" His eyes looked worried now, like maybe he'd misunderstood what I'd meant. He didn't.

"No. No, it isn't. It's not the same at all. I don't lie, Joe. I meant what I said. I think you are funny and smart, and you make me feel good. You make me want to show you everything that you don't know about. I want to watch movies with you and eat new foods with you and see how you react to everything. I want to give you pleasure and see how you respond. And mostly, I want to share all kinds of experiences with you."

He tilted his head to the side, like a puppy, and I laughed. He smiled. "Why?"

I moved closer to him, sliding my body next to his. His eyes widened. "'Cause you make me feel awake. You make me take notice of things. See the world a bit differently. I look at things and wonder if it's something you've seen before. Or if you've ever experienced the particular situation I find myself in. And I don't just stop there. It's not a fleeting thought. I find myself wanting to find out. To ask you. To show you or tell you about it." I dropped my hand from the back of the couch onto his shoulder and finished with, "Joe, please stay. Don't leave tonight."

With upturned lips he nodded. I felt relief and joy for the first time since I could remember.

WE'D DECIDED on a movie night with popcorn. I liked M&M's in mine and Joe told me he'd never had popcorn with a movie, let alone with candy, so it was perfect. For awhile we sat in silence, me contemplating the potential experiences he'd never had. I could almost see the world open up for him. The thought of experiencing all of that with him had me grinning like a fool. And he noticed.

"What's got you smiling like that?" He asked, sitting up to look at me.

"Nothing. Nothing at all. Just watch the movie." I was still grinning, though.

He pushed against my chest, his hands firm. "Tell me," he pleaded, his lips turning up at the ends.

"Uh-uh. Nope," I answered, shaking my head.

"Okay, fine." He slumped in the corner, his bottom lip sticking out like a petulant child and I couldn't help myself. I tentatively reached my hand towards him, testing the waters. He didn't look at me or try to move away, so I continued until I'd turned his face to me, my thumb and forefinger gripping his chin.

"Hey, I'm sorry. I just enjoy being here like this with you." I let go of his face and got up to refill our sodas. When I turned from the fridge Joe was standing there in his socked feet, looking like someone stole his favorite...well, anything. "Baby, what's wrong?" I couldn't help the endearment. It just came out and honestly, I'd meant it, so I wasn't going to apologize for it.

"I don't like being a joke. When you laugh at me, it hurts. And I'm not used to feeling hurt. Not anymore. It just hit me, like a tornado blast out of nowhere. And you told me to be open and honest with you. So, I am. I don't like you laughing at me. I don't know what I did, but it hurt my feelings."

It was as though the air was sucked out of the room. I'd never wanted to hurt his feelings, never in a million years. As I stood in the kitchen, Joe's upset face peering up at me, I wondered how much of this was just Joe and how much had to do with his past. I was getting closer to solving the puzzle, though. I now had a corner piece. Something concrete to guide the rest.

It was so fucking obvious. He was upset because I hurt his feelings. I had the power to hurt him. Oh, God. He cared about me, too. And just like that, my heart cracked open. My arms spread wide, I slowly embraced him and said, "Oh, baby. I didn't mean to hurt you."

My phone vibrated with an incoming text just as I was finishing up the last of my charts before my lunch break. I was hoping to pick up something quick, then see Joe. *Joe.* Just thinking his name made me feel like I was hovering above the ground. I'd turned into such a cliché, but it was worth it. Knowing that he was in my apartment right now, trusting me after last night. Well, maybe not full-on trust, but a spark of something. And it felt precious to me. Like a thinly woven thread that he'd handed to me to keep, it attached him to me. A barely there nothing, but to me it was everything. And I would do whatever I had to, to keep it.

Last night I had lain awake for hours wondering—hoping—that he would slip into my room in the dark. The previous night worried me, seeing him standing at the door, so fragile and afraid. I could never imagine the endless possibilities that tormented his dreams. The circumstances that had led him here, hard his life had been. How brave he was to fight for what he had. He was someone to look up to.

I thought of all the experiences that I wanted to share with him, and the places I wanted to show him. I just wanted to have him there. It lit a fire within me. *He* lit a fire within me.

As I ran to the burger shop on the corner my phone rang. Hoping it was Joe, I pulled it from my back pocket and frowned when I saw it was my sister. "Anna?" I asked, confused as to why she'd call when she knew I was working. The text notification I'd received earlier had been from Anna as well.

"Madden," she huffed, quickly and without her typical cheeriness. "Madden, everyone is fine. Well, fine health-wise. I think. I hope. Shit, I'm sorry!"

"Anna." I took a breath. "Try speaking in sentences. Proper sentences. Where are you?" I tried not to get myself run over as I ran back out into the street to make my way home.

"I'm at your place. I came over because I had to pick up new soccer cleats for David, and the store is just down the street from your place, and I baked pies earlier, so I brought you one. Blueberry."

I smiled. "Okay, so you saw Joe at home?"

"Yeah, I used my key, and he was sitting on your couch, in your pajamas, staring out the window. The TV was on, but he wasn't watching it. I tried to get his attention but calling his name didn't work, so I walked over and put my hand on his shoulder."

"Oh, shit. What happened, Anna?" I asked, more than

worried, picking up my pace now I was only a few minutes from home.

"He jumped about three feet off the couch and turned white. Like, white, Madden. And then he raced to the bedroom and slammed the door shut. David started rocking, Joe started yelling 'I'm sorry' and it turned into quite a fiasco."

I could hear urgency and worry in her voice as it quivered, but she wasn't the one I was worried about.

"Anna. Anna, do me a favor. Please." I was out of breath, trying to calm myself down so I wasn't frantic. "I'm at the corner, almost there." I took a deep breath. "Can you please go to the bedroom door and tell Joe that I'm coming home and that he can just wait there for me? Please, just tell him... Just tell him that everything is fine, you are leaving, and he can stay where he is." My stomach clenched as I made my way up the stairs in my building. As I reached my door, Anna pulled it open and slid her phone from her ear. I was in her arms before I could even register her there, but I needed to see Joe. "Anna, thank you, but can you please wait outside?" Her eyes widened as I pulled out of her embrace. "I'm sorry, but I need to talk to Joe. I need to... fuck. Please, Anna?" I was practically pushing her out the door.

She must have seen the panic on my face because she called to David, who was sitting at the table. I ruffled his hair as he rushed by and shot Anna a quiet 'thank you'. As I walked down the hallway, I listened as the front door clicked shut, the sound louder than I remembered it being. Oh, Joe. What did he need? Was he just overwhelmed?

I raised my hand to knock, pressing my palm against the door instead. I had so many emotions rolling through my body, and I didn't want to sound panicked or stressed. Earning Joe's trust wouldn't happen if he was scared of me.

After a few deep breaths, I whispered, "Joe. Hey, it's Madden. I'm alone." Nothing. I didn't hear anything at all. After scratching the door with the edge of my thumbnail, I tried again. "Joe, it's Madden. I'm alone and I'm going to open the door. If you don't want me to come in, please tell me now," I said, waiting a few beats before slowly lowering my hand to grip the handle. That's when I realized my hand was shaking.

I slowly crept into the room, my gaze darting in every direction for Joe's slender body, but he wasn't there. There was no sign of him at all. Walking to the bathroom, I peered inside seeing only myself in the reflection of the wall-length mirror. "Joe?" I whispered, heading back towards the bed. No answer, not even a breath. I ran a hand through my hair, took my phone out of my scrubs, and sat on the bed. That's when I noticed the closed closet door. While I may be a clean freak and somewhat of a germaphobe, I'd always left the closet open. It was a habit from when I was a kid and the cat used to get trapped in my closet, and pee on my shoes. I sat for a minute to figure out how best to proceed.

Joe had met both Anna and David. What had scared him so terribly? What could have caused this reaction? Unsure what to do, I knew I couldn't leave him stuck in the closet. I walked over and sat down against the wall adjacent to the door. "Joe? You okay?" I asked. I waited for a minute or so, and then held my breath while the door handle turned, the door opening a crack. I was once again met with silence.

Taking the open door as an invitation, I crawled over and nudged it wider with my shoulder, enough for me to fit through. Joe sat with his back against the wall, directly behind where I had sat just moments ago. His legs were tucked up tight against his chest, his arms wrapped around them. My hand hovered just above his shoulder for a long moment before I softly set it down. Joe's head jerked up, his expression broken through his tears.

Oh, hell no. He wasn't allowed to feel like this. I crawled over to him, wrapped my arm around his shoulders and pulled him into my lap. He came easily. I kissed the top of his head. "Oh, baby. I'm so sorry. I'm here now, just relax." I rocked him slowly for a while, smelling his soapy neck, the sweet smell of my strawberry shampoo in his hair. I doubted I could ever forget his scent as long as I lived. Marveling at the man in my arms, I realized something. It wasn't earth-shattering, but it rocked my world. *This was a man that I could fall in love with.* I took a shuddering breath and let it out.

A few minutes passed in silence before Joe looked up at me, eyes glassy and red, his lashes wet. The look was cemented into my brain, never to be forgotten. He looked torn. Shredded from guilt. As though he'd done something wrong and needed forgiveness. I'd have given my soul to never have to see that kind of wounded look on him again.

His lip quivered as he started to speak. "I didn't expect anyone to come in," he said, sniffing. "And then she grabbed my shoulder, and I couldn't think." I nodded in confirmation and he buried his face in my neck and breathed. It was all I could do not to moan.

"Joe, it's okay. She told me she tried to get your attention, but you were lost." I shifted so I could see his face. "Where did you go?"

At once his body slumped against me as if the weight of the world was on his back. His right hand found the hem of my scrub shirt, gently rubbing at the raised edge. It was something I'd seen him do before, now realizing it as a self-soothing mechanism. My hand found his nape, applying gentle pressure.

"Joe, you don't—"

"You left for work and I sat down and looked around at everything. You have no idea what it's like to have nothing." His head shook a bit. "I see your place and it made me think of where I grew up. It was 2,300 miles from here, but so much further. I never felt like I belonged there. Like—like I was wanted. Or that I was safe from danger or fear. I real-r-r-realized today that I feel that here. Safe, I mean." His shiny, huge blue eyes looked up at me, his fingers pausing their ministrations on my shirt. "I never really knew what safe felt like until now. Until you. And I was sitting on your couch, in your space, feeling like I could belong somewhere for once." Joe's head dropped against my shoulder when he said, "And then someone grabbed me... and I panicked. I'm so sorry." I could feel his pain radiate through his labored breathing as I rubbed at his back once more.

"Joe, baby. I'm sorry Anna showed up like that. I should have told her you were staying here. I just didn't think about it because she hardly stops by. But I'm sorry she scared you."

His forehead, nestled in the space between my jaw and collarbone, was a feeling unlike any I'd ever known.

14

———

Joe

We stayed on the floor in the closet for a long time, me nestled into Madden, him gently stroking my back. His apartment felt like safety. This was epically better—in his arms. On every inhale, my brain reacted to his scent, creating havoc in my body. My breaths were more like pants. I could hear my heart beating an irregular rhythm. How I had blood flowing there I didn't understand, because my pants were tight against my erection, trying to break free. I shifted, trying to alleviate the strain, at the same time trying to hide the bulge.

Would Madden be upset if he knew? I hadn't felt this before —not like this. Never like this. Just thinking about it had me achy, my face reddening. I prayed he wouldn't notice.

There were more moments of silence where I basked in his scent, warmth, and touch. Happiness radiated through me and, surely, he had to feel it, too. If I could, I would live here in his arms like this, protected from the world.

Not telling Madden the real reason I freaked out wasn't a lie. An omission didn't technically count as a lie, because the other person wasn't aware of it, right? I just couldn't bring myself to go there yet. What would he think? Would he still want me around if he knew? I shivered at the thought.

Before I was ready, Madden shifted and pulled me to the side, effectively removing me from his lap. My lip jutted out in a pout before I could even register the action, and he chuckled.

"My back is aching from sitting against the wall like this," he said, checking his watch as he stood. I heard several cracks as he arched this way and that, his back protesting the move. He leaned down, stretching his hand out to mine, giving me a boost up, which I accepted, letting go as soon as I was up.

I had no experience in attraction. I had experience in one-sided lust. In assault. Staying away from anyone who could hold me down or gave me *that* look. So, this was uncharted territory and I was starting to feel lost inside. Like I needed time to work this all out in my head. What it all meant. What I was feeling. Really, I just wanted not to think about anything right then.

"I'm going to call in sick for the rest of my shift. Why don't we pick a movie and I'll make pancakes for dinner?" He was already typing into his phone when I registered what he'd said.

"We can't have pancakes for dinner," I said quickly, my voice panicky. "Pancakes are breakfast food. Not dinner."

Madden's eyes widened as he threw his phone onto his bed. Gently resting his hands on my biceps, he said, "Okay, it's okay. We don't have to have pancakes. I just thought you liked them so much it, might be nice to have for dinner."

My head started shaking back and forth on its own accord. "No. Pancakes aren't a dinner food. You can't just eat them whenever you want. They are breakfast."

"Okay, we won't have pancakes tonight. It's okay." My head was against his chest again, my heart racing. He didn't understand, but it would be fine. Everything would be fine.

After I'd calmed down enough, Madden asked, "How about pizza?" I nodded. I hadn't eaten pizza in months. I loved it, too. Pizza was a very respectable dinner option.

"Yeah," I whispered, clearing my throat. "Yes, pizza is good."

Madden grabbed his phone and ordered pizza, then sat next to me on the couch, leaving a foot or so of space between us. I didn't understand why. Starting to get used to him touching me, I wondered what I had done, then remembered the pancakes. I stared straight ahead and said, "Sorry about the pancakes."

"Joe, look at me." I couldn't. Shame silenced my voice. He shifted closer to me on the couch and my skin prickled in reaction to his proximity. "Please don't be upset, Joe."

I sighed and turned to look at him. His eyes were pleading. "Madden. I don't understand. I'm not upset, you are."

"No, I'm not. At all. Why do you think that?" He moved his left knee onto the couch, so his leg was against mine and he was facing me. His body heat felt amazing against mine.

"Well, I kind of got loud about the pancakes and then you didn't sit next to me, so I thought you were mad at me. I d-d-d-don't want you to be m-m-mad."

As soon as I said the words, I closed my eyes and felt his palm cupping my left cheek. When his forehead rested against mine, I felt butterflies take flight in my stomach. His breath against my skin was just a whisper. "I couldn't be mad at you, Joe," he said. When his thumb grazed the skin beneath my eye, I let out a sound somewhere between a whimper and a moan. Putting his lips against my forehead, he whispered, "God, Joe. What you do to me."

WE DID END up watching movies on the couch, pizza resting on the coffee table in front of us. I'd never seen much of anything, so he was thrilled to fill in the blank spaces of my vast empty cheesy movie hole. Simply being close to Madden had me more relaxed, and in the moment, than I could ever remember being. This must be what having a family feels like. The sense of belonging was overwhelming.

I was slouched down in one corner of the couch, Madden in the other corner, massaging my feet on his chest. Never had anyone taken such good care of me. I was starting to think that I wanted more than just being friends. Was I ready for that? I truly didn't know.

"Why don't we call it a night? You can go shower, and I'll clean up out here. I need to call Anna back, too."

I nodded and sat up, grabbing his arm when he did the same. "Madden, thank you."

"What for? I didn't do anything, Joe." His smile was so tender it made my heart light up.

When I thought of his words, I started to laugh. "Right. You've only done everything." I started down the hall, but turned and said, "Thank you."

I'D BARELY STEPPED out of the bathroom when Madden walked through his bedroom door and stopped, eyes wide. I recognized that look. It was the same look I'd gotten from men since I was a kid. Well, the men Venom brought around anyway. I felt my face heat, red blooming from my ears and down my chest. I was wearing sweats, but I hadn't put my shirt on. I wasn't sure how I felt about the way Madden's eyes wandered down my body, stopping in certain places. Maybe he was cataloguing me, though he'd seen me before.

I stepped around him. "Goodnight," I said, as I squeezed

past, not sticking around to hear if he responded. As soon as the door to my room was closed, I leaned against it and slid down to the floor.

I had so much going on in my head that I needed to process. Reading people was not something I was good at. I tried to read into body language, but that was difficult as well. During my years living rough, I'd spent so much time at libraries and bookstores. Once I had some practice with reading, I tried to read as much as possible. Especially about science and facts, about living with autism, trying to understand where the differences lay between my brain and everyone else's. The issue was that everyone under the umbrella of autism was different. Some were stronger in some areas, weaker in others. I still wasn't sure where I fit. It was hard to fully diagnose myself. After all, how would I know if my reactions were atypical. Or if my mind perseverated on specific tasks. It was just me.

After a while, I decided to let everything marinate, and got into bed. I figured it was worth a try, but after lying down I immediately sat up and climbed off. It felt wrong, so I grabbed the bedding and made my way over to the corner. I didn't mind sleeping on the floor. It was cleaner than anywhere else I'd slept.

Just as I had gotten comfortable, Madden tapped at the door, then called my name. *Did he change his mind and want me to leave?* "C-c-come in," I called, voice catching.

Poking his head in, he looked directly at the bed, a frown marring his features. When his gaze found me, his shoulders slumped. Before he could say anything, I sat up. "Should I go?" Again, I wished I could read people. I was so lost.

Madden's frown deepened, making me wince. "Go? Why would you go?" he asked.

"Um, you don't seem very happy to have me here right now. You're looking at me like—" before I could finish, he was across the room, standing in front of me. I had to crane my neck to see him.

"No, I don't want you to go. I'm sorry, Joe. I'm sorry if I scared you earlier. I have no excuse for making you feel uncomfortable." He stepped back a few steps as I tried to stand, my arm on the wall for balance.

"It's probably obvious by now, but I don't understand things like you do. I don't see everything in body language, and I don't hear everything you say in the way you mean. Also, I've never done this, Madden. I've never spent this much time with a single person in my life. Honestly, not even my parents. No one has ever wanted to be around me this much, and now I'm scared." The words just poured out of me, then my eyes started burning, and before I knew it, I was in his arms, creating a giant pool of wetness on his t-shirt.

Madden cradled me and rubbed my back, like I'd gotten so used to him doing. I calmed quickly, hiccupping like a child. I was always a mess these days. I had never wanted so badly to understand other people.

After a few minutes, I realized we were slowly swaying, my mind spacey. He guided me towards the door, and I stopped, his grip pulling at my arm. "What are you—" I was cut off by Madden shushing me gently, fingers weaving through mine, leading me down the hallway to his room. "I'm not—" I tried again to protest, but Madden wasn't having it.

At his bed, he pulled up the coverlet and sheet, ushering me in. He scooted in beside me, sitting up against the pillows, mirroring my position.

"Look, Joe," he said, his tone serious. "I can see that this is difficult for you to understand and navigate, but I don't want to make anything harder. You seem to take my reactions and gestures to be somehow against you."

"No, I—" again, he waved me off, trying to finish his train of thought.

"From what you've told me so far, your childhood wasn't great. I get that. I also know that you have—" he shook his head. "You're on the autism spectrum, and from what I've seen with Anna and David, there are quite a few barriers between communication, both verbally and physically. I don't want to make this hard on you, Joe. I really like you. I like spending time with you. I want to spend more time with you. And I want you to trust me." He waived his hand in the air again, which I figured to mean he wasn't done talking. I nodded at him to continue.

"Trust is hard and takes time. I know that. I just mean, I don't want you to keep assuming I'm trying to get rid of you or push you away every time I ask you a question."

He paused, taking in a gulp of air. I watched his hand fiddle with the edge of the sheet, my mind focusing in on the movement.

"Joe?" Madden lifted his hand from the bed and waived it in front of my face. "You okay?"

"Oh, y-y-yeah. Sorry," I said, sheepishly.

"It's okay. You just haven't said anything for about ten minutes, and I couldn't get your attention. You okay?"

I nodded again, my mind hazy. I didn't want to talk anymore. I was tired and I wanted to sleep. "I need to sleep, Madden."

"Okay," he nodded. "I went to your room tonight because I wanted to talk to you, but also because I wanted to be close to you again. I was hoping you'd sleep in here with me. Would that be okay?"

"Yes. Thank you." I rolled onto my side, facing the opposite direction and felt Madden scoot down into the bed behind me, but not touching.

After a minute of waiting, it was making me nervous. "Madden, if you want to get closer or touch me, can you please just do it so I can sleep?"

I heard him chuckle, then slid his body loosely against mine, one arm over my hip. "This okay?" he asked.

"It's fine. Good night." I could feel his smile against my hair.

"Good night, Joe."

"Hey, sleepyhead!" Madden was in the kitchen wearing navy scrubs, his dark hair wet, socked feet sliding across the wooden floor as he reached for ingredients for what looked like...

"Are you making pancakes?" I could have been embarrassed at my joy, but I didn't care. I was practically vibrating with it.

"Well, I figured it is breakfast, after all. And you seemed to have a bit of a thing for pancakes, right?" He turned and winked at me. I suddenly had a hard time breathing. I nodded, unable to keep the smile from reaching my eyes. "They're almost done, so if you want to have a seat at the table, go for it."

Moving quickly, I grabbed two waters from the refrigerator and sat them at what I now considered 'our places' at the table. I also brought two sets of silverware from the drawer and placed them on napkins on the table before sitting down in my seat.

As I watched Madden move effortlessly around his kitchen, I realized I wanted this to be *my seat* more than anything. I wanted to wake up after sleeping tucked up against Madden's warm embrace. Feel the coarse hairs on his legs brushing against mine as he moved in the dark. Just the thought of going back to my tent after a couple of days with Madden was too hard to contemplate this early in the day. I set my forehead on the table.

A warm hand gently squeezed my nape and pulled me out of the fog. I felt his forehead rest against my shoulder as he said, "I get that you don't always understand me and my gestures and expressions. But I don't always understand yours either. Did something happen just now?" Another gentle squeeze and I shook my head. "Can you tell me why you aren't looking at me?" Again, I shook my head. I heard him sigh against my bicep. I didn't want him to be angry. I just didn't know what to say. When his warm hand fell away, I craved the security of it immediately.

"I'm not going to force you to talk to me, but can you just tell me if you're okay? I just want to make sure there isn't anything you need."

I closed my eyes against the table and sighed, before shaking my head.

"Okay, that's something. I'm going to sit right here next to you and eat my pancakes. I hope you'll join me at some point, but you don't have to. I'll still be here."

I could hear his knife scraping across the surface of the pancakes, as he buttered each of them on his plate. Then came the snick of the syrup bottle lid. A few seconds later, I heard chewing, and a delicate swallow, before he uncapped his water and took a drink. My eyes squeezed shut as I tried to pull my thoughts together.

"Joe?" Madden's voice was weary. I hmmmm'd in response. "If you don't want to answer my question, it's fine, but I'm going to ask anyway." He paused, and I could hear his intake of breath, before he asked, "Is this—what's happening with you right now—is this something that you do frequently?" Before I could respond, he continued. "I mean, do you need some alone time, or time to think? Because we've spent a lot of time together in the last couple of days and...well, as much as I've loved it, maybe it's been too much for you?"

I owed him an explanation. After an eternity, I lifted my head and looked over at Madden, expecting anger. Instead, his face held a tender smile, and his hand reached out to cover mine across the table. Warmth, like an electric blanket, surrounded me.

"I just sometimes get too many thoughts in my head and need a break. Like my brain pushes everything new out to sort through what's currently there. It's hard to explain. It wasn't about you, though." He nodded, forking another piece of pancake as if none of this ever happened. Then he pointed his fork at me.

"Can you eat now?" he asked. I nodded. "Good. Because I made these for you. I'd hate for you to miss out."

A smile crept up my cheeks as I picked up my fork and tucked in.

He'd made me pancakes. For breakfast.

15

Madden

Having spent the night with Joe pressed against me was bittersweet. His scent filled my bed, his warm body filled my arms. It was a type of heaven I didn't know I qualified for. I was aching by the time I woke up, not wanting to let go of Joe, but afraid of what I'd do if I didn't. I quietly rolled away from his long, lean form and took a longer shower than typically necessary. I needed relief and found it, moaning Joe's name as it made its way down the drain.

I was feeling happier than I could remember when Joe appeared from the hallway as I was making his favorite meal. His hair was sticking straight up in the back and his mouth looked adorably pouty. I turned back to my preparations as my face flamed thinking of his mouth and what I'd done in the shower just twenty minutes before.

He seemed his usual self until I'd brought the plates to the table. His demeanor worried me, but I was finding more and more that I didn't really know Joe that well. Not like I'd thought, anyway. He had so many facets of his personality. I sat next to him, watching his body twitch with each breath, his sticky-up hair so endearing, I knew I wanted to find out everything I could about this Rubik's cube of a man. And I wanted to know that I had the time to make it happen.

After breakfast, Joe got cleaned up while I finished in the kitchen, getting myself ready to go back to the hospital. I had a long shift scheduled and needed to talk to Joe about coming back here again tonight, when he was done with work. Something inside me just wanted to hold him dear. It was a new-to-me urge, and it had a tight hold on me somewhere deep, burning in my chest.

When Joe walked into the room and his gaze settled on the fish, I took my chance.

"Hey, so after work, you should just come back here. You can do your laundry, and we can hang out. Neither of us works until later tomorrow, so we can just chill here."

His eyes never strayed from the fish, but I saw the curve of a smile on his lips. A whispered, "yeah, okay" was the only response I received, but it was still a yes. A hummingbird took flight in my chest.

I turned away. Even though he wasn't looking at me, my stupid-ass grin took over my face, and I tried to cool it off by grabbing a water from the fridge. I didn't want it, but I'd just take it with me to work. Hell, when had I turned into THAT guy?

~

THE THING about Adam was that he loved to talk about himself. He could go on and on, tell story after story, and never come to a lull in the conversation. He had been in charge of the break-room for the last thirty minutes, holding three other nurses hostage, with his tales of late night debauchery. All I could do was roll my eyes hard enough, crossing my fingers that it caused an earthquake, so everyone could run away in the commotion. It didn't work.

When the laughter from his last joke died down, I pulled him into the hallway, thus releasing his prisoners. Letting go of his arm, I huffed out a laugh, walking down the hallway, pulling a patient chart when I reached the desk.

"You are antsy today, Mads. What's gotten into you?" He asked cheekily, his hip leaning on the desk. Arms crossed, his smile turned naughty. "Oh, holy balls! You got some last night. Joe from the café?"

I gently pushed him away from the desk, his arms windmilling to keep his balance. Okay, so maybe not as gently as I'd thought. I had to laugh, though, which lightened the mood. The last thing I wanted to do was talk about Joe with Adam right now. It was so new and different, and I wasn't ready to bare my feelings to anyone yet. Not until I knew how Joe felt, what he wanted.

Things with Joe were complicated, for sure. He was hard to read, slow to trust, and jumpy as a frog on fire. Even after all of that, though, there was still something special drawing me to him. A spark of wonder, I guess. I liked not knowing exactly what to expect with him. I loved the way he needed me. It fed into my ego and lit me up inside.

"Look, Adam. I really don't want to discuss Joe with you yet. Nothing has happened between us, so don't give me that face." He looked slightly irritated, but I knew him well enough to know it wouldn't last. "I'm just not sure about anything, yet."

The teasing smile vanished, and he looked concerned, as if I told him I was dying.

"You really like him. This is different." I nodded, because, yes, those were both true statements. I just didn't know what else to say. He nodded back. "Fair enough," he said, patting my shoulder as he walked away. I took a deep breath and knocked on a patient's door.

MY SHIFT ENDED at ten that night, which coincided with Joe's shift. I pulled open the door to the café as Lulu yelled, "Sorry, we just closed," from somewhere in the back. I flipped the sign on the door to assist with the closing process.

"It's just Madden. I'm here to pick up Joe whenever he's ready." My voice carried in the empty room, making me cringe. Before I could figure out what to do next, Joe came rushing through the kitchen door, surprise lighting up his gorgeous face. I was stunned. His face was flushed, contrasting with his almost white hair, creating a halo over his head. *Wow*. This guy was letting me take him home. And possibly sleep in my bed, against me again.

"What's wrong?" Joe asked, and I realized I hadn't said anything.

Shaking my head, I said, "Nothing at all. In fact, just the opposite. Are you ready to go?" When he smiled up at me, I took his hand in mine and led him out the door, yelling a quick "goodbye" to Lulu.

Out on the sidewalk, Joe still had a smile on his face. "What's going on?" he asked me. I shook my head and turned to him.

"I'm just happy, Joe. I'm happy and you're here, and we are headed to my place to spend time together." As we crossed the street, the corner of his lips turned up again.

"I don't think anyone has been this happy to see me." Oh yeah, way to ruin a good mood. A shiver ran down my spine, and I stopped walking abruptly. Our linked hands brought him to a stop, about two feet ahead of me, and he whirled around. "What happened?" he asked me.

I stared at him, under the streetlight. "You don't even know, do you?"

Stepping forward, his hand still in mine, he asked, "Know what?"

I reached my hand up, tentatively. When he didn't object to the movement, I touched the hair that had grown out, covering his ear. Twisting it in my fingers, I answered him. "That I care about you. A lot, Joe. More than I thought I would."

His eyes widened before looking down at my shoes. After a few seconds, he nodded, pulling me forward. We walked in silence back to my apartment.

It was late, but neither of us had eaten. Kicking off our shoes at the door, I told Joe to take the first shower. I could get his laundry started, and order pizza while he cleaned up, then I could take one myself. I watched as he wandered down the hallway, his retreating form warming my blood. Just simply having Joe here to take care of, to worry about, was a special treat. I felt like I'd stolen something and didn't want to give it back. Leaning back against the kitchen counter, I listened to the sounds of water running from down the hall, thinking of what my life had become these last few weeks. It was as if I had purpose now. It was a type of epiphany, as though my mind had finally caught up with my heart. I knew I cared about Joe. That was obvious in the way I wanted him around. I worried about him, for him. Keeping him safe and happy had somehow become my number one concern.

Knocking on the bathroom door, I yelled out, "What kind of pizza do you want tonight?" I hadn't asked him last time, and I noticed that he didn't eat much of it. He seemed to have eaten around the pepperoni, which I didn't comment on at the time. I had figured I'd ask him about it later, but had forgotten.

The water turned off and I heard a muffled, "One minute," called out from behind the door. I smiled to myself. This was a scene I could get used to. Joe, naked in my bathroom. Wet from the shower.

The door cracked open and there he was. Pink, wet, and wearing the blue towel I'd left him. "Sorry, j-j-just whatever you like is fine." He tried to close the door, but I put my hand out to stop him. His eyes widened.

"Why don't you just tell me what you like on your pizza, so that I can make sure you have what you want?"

"Oh. Um," he said, his tongue sliding out to wet his lower lip. Was he trying to kill me? "Well, have you ever h-h-had pineapple on yours? I mean, we don't have to, it's just that Sloan is always talking about how he loves pineapple on his, and no one else at the café likes it, and he said that it's because people get it with ham, but bacon is better, but no one ever tries it. They always just walk away with their hands in the air." He finally looked up at me, and confusion ran over his features. "W-why are y-you smiling?"

"You've never had pineapple on pizza before, Joe?" His cheeks turned a delicious shade of pink, and he looked at his feet.

"No, I—I've never ordered my own pizza before. I k-k-know that sounds stupid to you. You probably have pizza all the time, b-b-but I don't, and I just thought maybe I'd try it, but we don't have to. It's fine." This time when he finished talking, he didn't look up.

"Hey, Joe?" I heard him grunt in response. "Will you look at me?" I asked the top of his head.

"It just makes talking to you harder." I took a step back. He still hadn't looked up.

"Why? Why is talking to me hard?"

"It makes me very uncomfortable to know that you are looking at me when I'm speaking. I can't explain it, I just don't like it. So, I don't do it." He turned away, but I reached for him.

"Thank you for letting me know. I'm going to get you a

bacon and pineapple pizza, and I'll get myself a pepperoni and black olive pizza, and we'll just hang out, okay?" I just wanted a nod. Nothing more, nothing less. What I got was a megawatt smile. And damn, if that sight didn't make my pants that much tighter. I wasn't sure how long I could keep this up.

16

Joe

Watching Batman and Robin, I had decided, was my new favorite calming device. There was just something about the colors and the bubbling sounds, and how active they were. I could probably get lost in watching them for hours at a time. I had been doing just that, when a harsh buzz rang through the apartment.

Covering my ears with my hands, I dropped to the floor, curling myself into the smallest ball I could. Blood rushed through my ears, but I felt the beat of Madden's feet on the wood as he made his way down the hall.

His hand on my back, he squatted close. "It's just the pizza delivery. I just need to pay him and get the pizza. You okay?" His hand was rubbing circles again, giving me something to concentrate on. I nodded. After a long pause, he stood up, and I heard voices, the door opening and closing, and then he was back.

This time, he was sitting on the floor in front of me, his forehead to mine. He didn't say anything, but just sat there, breathing next to me, with me.

After a few minutes, our breaths matched, and a thrill swept through my body. I blinked my eyes open, and he was right there. Not rushing me. Not yelling at me. Not asking questions. Just... there.

I didn't say anything. I didn't need to. He seemed to know what I needed. I stared at his mouth, visualizing his breaths, in and out, in and out. We stayed there, on the floor together, for quite a while, and then my stomach let out a fierce growl, and we both started giggling.

When we quieted, Madden's hand rested on my shoulder, head tilted to the side, as if a dog, waiting for instructions. I don't know why I did it, but before I could think, I turned my head, and placed my cheek on his hand. It was so warm and soft, and I could feel his goodness running beneath his skin. Something clicked in me—something important, vital—because I knew right then. I knew with everything in me, that I could trust Madden.

MADDEN PLATED UP THE PIZZA, and I grabbed some bottled water. Since I hadn't seen so many movies, we decided to eat on the couch. I set the waters on the coffee table, just as he brought our plates over, and handed me one. I smiled at the plate. I was going to try something new. Pineapple on pizza. I felt my stomach clench and my face heat up again. If I didn't like it, would he be upset?

Eyeing me, he cleared his throat. "If you don't want pizza, we can make something else." He started to stand, but I grabbed his hand.

When I finally looked at his face, he was looking at my

hand, where I was rubbing the hem of my shirt absently. Catching my gaze, he looked up and smiled. "You do that all the time, you know? Rub your shirt between your fingers."

"It's called stimming," I explained, quietly. "It makes me relaxed and kind of zoned out. I do it when I get upset, mostly, and need to calm down, or when I'm worried or tired." He nodded slowly, thinking about what I said. "Does it bother you?"

"Not at all. I just wondered about it. Do you only use your shirt?" He dropped his head and waived his hand between us. "Forget I asked you. I'm sorry."

I stole his hand, and held onto it. "No. I used to have something as a kid. That's what started it, I think. It was a stuffed animal with the softest fur. And then it was gone." I looked from his hand in mine, back to his face. "Most of the time it depends on the fabric. The softer the better. I like your shirts, though. They are very soft."

The smile that formed on his face was too much to bear, and I had to look away before I was burned by it.

Madden grabbed my plate and handed it to me again. "Will you try it? The pizza. I promise I will never get mad at you, Joe. We'll just throw it away and have something else."

Nodding, I picked up the piece of pizza and smelled it. It smelled like pizza with pineapple and bacon. Closing my eyes, I took a bite and slowly chewed. And chewed. When I swallowed, I opened my eyes to find Madden looking at me like I had the key to some untold fortune. I laughed.

"Well," he said, smirking. "What's the final answer? Does pineapple belong on pizza?"

Setting my slice down, I stood up and cleared my throat. Then, I raised my hand to my mouth, like a microphone, and made a royal announcement. "It is decided. I officially rule that pineapple belongs on pizza," I said, holding up a finger to indicate I wasn't finished. After chewing and swallowing, I added,

"But only sparingly and/or in small pieces, because it's good, but it takes over the whole thing."

As soon as he burst out laughing, I dropped the air-mic and took a bow, falling back onto the couch, half-landing in his lap. When my shoulder bumped his arm, my slice of pizza went flying over the back of the couch. It landed on the floor with a decently loud splat, which caused another round of laughter from Madden, and a shocked expression from me. With an evil smirk, he started tickling me. First under my arms, then over my ribs until I was squirming and thrashing on the couch. I tried to get to him, but he twisted around, and I grabbed both of his wrists, pinning them to my chest. I moved to straddle him, then forced his hands up next to his shoulders, against the back of the couch. After a second, we both realized it was an awkward position, though I wanted nothing else in that moment. Hell, all weekend. His eyes widened, and I knew what I wanted.

His gaze bored into mine as he let out a long, stuttering breath. Slowly, I leaned forward and pressed my lips to his. In seconds I was on fire.

He let me lead, though I had no idea what I was doing. I wanted him to know I wanted this. I gasped when he finally took over, reciprocating what he offered. Gentle, light touches of skin against skin. My hands let go of his, and he immediately put one on my nape, brushing the other through my hair.

Kissing Madden was better than I could have ever dreamed. It was warm, wet, and he tasted decadent, like something I wanted more of. After a few minutes, I leaned back, catching my breath. I felt like someone had lit a match inside me. Unsure how to proceed, I bit my lip and looked down. He was still looking at me, breathing heavily, a small smile formed on his shiny, swollen lips. Lips that were against mine just seconds ago.

"Did you—" he started, then blinked hard. "I mean, was

that okay?" he asked, almost shyly. If there was one thing I knew, it was that Madden was not shy. It made me feel momentarily powerful. I reached for his biceps, pulling him against me again. This time I took charge and kissed him. Tentatively at first, like he had with me, but then I introduced my tongue to his lips. I licked a path under his bottom lip, teasing, then to the seam between. His lips parted on a gasp, and I took advantage of his intake of breath, sliding my tongue inside. Completely new at kissing, I brushed my tongue lightly against his, waiting for him to take over. He didn't disappoint when he sucked on my tongue and moaned. Reaching his hands up into my hair, he licked at my tongue, coaxing my own to join in. Angling my head, he explored every inch of my mouth.

I felt his strong body against mine, then felt him, hard as a rock beneath me, and tried to figure out how I felt about it.

Too much was going on at once, and I decided that the kissing was too good to miss. After a few minutes of the oral assault, I pulled back again, this time taking deep breaths, and searched his face. I had no idea what I was looking for, sure he could see how much I loved every second. I envisioned a neon light on my forehead screaming Yes, yes, yes! Like a limp doll, he rested his head against my chest, breath calming, warming my very soul.

"Hey, Joe?" His whisper was breathy, making my insides flip.

"Yeah?" I panted.

"Are you okay with that?"

I nodded. "I want to do that again."

"Oh, God. Yes, please." His tone mischievous.

AFTER WE'D CLEANED up the dishes, and put away the leftover pizza, I fed the fish. Madden hadn't even asked me. Told me it was my chore, that everyone here had to help. He picked the fish as my responsibility. Staring at them, my heart raced.

"Joe?" His hand on my shoulder caused me to jump.

"Sorry, I was thinking. I didn't mean to do that," I explained.

He nodded and asked, "Can I ask you why you did?"

I bit my lip, trying to find the words to make him understand.

"Was it what I said? About staying here?" he asked, head tilted in question.

"Yes."

"Okay, do you want to think about it for a while, or do you want to talk about it with me? I'm fine with either."

My jaw dropped open in surprise. It was as though a turbine engine powered-on in my chest. Was Madden trying to understand me? Was he giving me what I needed? Clear boundaries? Two simple choices. In a world of endless possibilities and unfounded results, he was helping make my little corner of the world easier to navigate.

No one had ever done anything like that for me before. Ever. I didn't know what to say. He was waiting for an answer, so I said, "Okay, we can talk about it. I d-d-don't even know what to say, because I'm not sure what you mean about staying here." I flushed red in embarrassment.

He pulled out a kitchen chair and motioned for me to sit, then took a seat next to me. He told me that he enjoyed spending time with me, and that he wanted to get to know me better. That I make him think differently. That I make him happy. I stopped listening at that point, because it was too much to process. I saw his mouth moving, and I had to put my head down on the table.

Madden immediately stopped mid-sentence, and I felt his hand on mine. I wanted his touch. I wanted his hands on me, and his mouth on me, but wasn't sure how to ask for it. Maybe it would only last that night, and then this little vacation from my life would vanish, like everything else did.

His thumb rubbed against my wrist, and I turned my head against the table to look at him. He was smiling at me. Smiling. I felt exposed, undone, and confused all at once.

"Joe," he whispered, still smiling. "Baby." I blinked hard. "Do you like staying here?"

"I...yes." I thought it was loud enough for him to hear.

"Do you want to go back to where you're staying?"

"No." His smile returned with a vengeance.

"Did you like what we did on the couch earlier?"

I opened my eyes and looked right at his. "Yes."

Color erupted on his cheeks, and I realized he was embarrassed. So, I said, "The pizza on the couch earlier was so good. What's not to like?"

When surprise and shock lit up his face, I laughed. That just caused his nostrils to flare, and I knew what was coming. I jumped out of my seat, and ran towards the hallway, grabbing onto the wall as I rounded the corner. As soon as I heard the loud banging of his footsteps behind me, I let out a squeal and a giggle. I made it to Madden's room, and threw myself face down on the bed, my face buried in my hands in the darkness. My entire body thrummed knowing he was after me. I heard his footsteps. I felt my heart racing. What should have triggered a mountain of sensory and traumatic reactions only made me squeal. I was safe here. I knew it. Madden wouldn't hurt me. I gulped in a deep, profound breath before I was pounced on by the man who had saved me.

17

———

Madden

Caught completely off-guard, I pulled my jaw off the floor, and followed Joe quickly down the hallway, not knowing what would be waiting for me. This was a new side to Joe. Would he be scared that I was on the chase? Because he instigated the shenanigans, I was hopeful that he would react well, but I didn't want to push him. When I made it through my bedroom doorway, I halted, taking in the sight. Joe was curled into a ball in the middle of the bed, hair sticking every which way, face smashed into the blanket. I saw his body convulsing, but I wasn't sure if he was laughing or crying. Honestly, it could have gone either way.

Slowly making my way towards him, I quietly called to him. "Joe, baby. Are you doing okay?" The bed creaked as I leaned my weight on it, but he didn't move a muscle. I was frozen, completely unsure of how to proceed. Oh, I knew exactly what I wanted to do. I wanted to wrap myself around him and never let go. I wanted him to ask me to take advantage of him in a dozen different ways. But he would have to ask. I would never risk his safety, or comfort, by making the first move. Ever. My hand itched to reach out. I curled it into a fist at my side, trying to keep from moving too much, when I heard a giggle. My face broke out into a smile.

"Oh, Joe. You are in so much trouble, now!" I pounced, molding my body over his, grabbing at his sides, my fingers tickling down his ribs. His laughter heated my soul. It reverberated through my body, until I didn't know if it was him laughing or me. My cheeks ached as he started wiggling and flailing around under me. I released him, getting onto my knees, and straddled his body. He deftly flipped over, and I felt him hard underneath me.

I bolted off the bed and stood in the bathroom doorway, catching my breath. Fuck, fuck, fuck. Wiping my hand over my face, I took a few deep breaths, then glanced his way. His face was red and flushed, as he looked back at me, confusion written all over it. I took a step back, not sure what to do or say. I just needed a minute to figure out what Joe needed. Before I could get my head together, he sat up, his lips turned down.

"I'm so sorry, Madden. I didn't mean to—" and in a flash, he was out the door, down the hall. In shock, I stood there, staring at the empty void on the bed. When I finally shook myself out of it enough to realize what had happened, I heard heavy boots on the wood, and I sprang into action.

"Joe, stop!" I yelled down the hallway as I sprinted into the kitchen. His hand was on the door, as if he were leaving. "Where are you going? Are you—are you leaving?" The distain in my voice was a shock, even to me. It caused Joe to flinch.

"Well, yeah, I was. I mean, you were upset. I could see that. And now I've messed this up. I am leaving. You don't need to worry, though. I won't say anything to anyone or do anything to you when you come into the café. I'm not crazy."

I felt as though my head was going to explode, trying to unpack that suitcase of garbage he'd just laid at my feet. My hands at my temples, I shook off his words. "What?" I yelled. "You're just leaving? Just like that? No, Joe. No, I don't think so. I understand you probably don't have a lot of experience with... well, with friends, or relationships. But you don't just walk away. I don't want you to go. I..."

"What? You—but why?" Joe's face was unreadable.

"Can you just take your boots off and sit down for a minute? Can we discuss this without me having to worry you will run out the door at any second?"

He stilled, then looked at his feet. The laces on his boots were loose and hanging on the floor. He could have tripped down the stairs like that. Jesus. My arm reached out to grasp his shoulder. I wanted to direct him to the couch, but he flinched and took a few steps back, his feet unstable beneath him, as he fumbled to the floor.

My heart lurched in my chest as I watched Joe scramble back on his hands, until he reached the cabinets. He started to curl into himself, and I knew I couldn't let that happen. There was no way I would allow him to hide from me. Not now. Not ever.

"Joe, baby. Listen to me, okay? I'm not going to get any closer than this." He nodded, but I noticed his shaky hands. "I would never hurt you. Ever. I know you have no reason to believe me, but I would do anything for you to understand that. There is nothing you could do or say that would make me hit you or yell at you in anger, okay?" I gave him a minute, then continued. "You are safe here, Joe. If you want me to leave, I'll leave. But this is a safe place for you. I wouldn't let anything ever happen to you here."

After a couple of minutes of heavy breathing, emanating from both of us, I turned away, and started down the hall. I knew he was overwhelmed. Too much had happened at once, and he needed to process. I got that. I needed him to understand that this, my apartment, was a safe place for him to do that. Just before I made it into my bedroom, I heard his timid voice call my name, so softly. Reversing my direction, I made my way back to the kitchen, fear lacing through me. He was still in the same position, curled against the lower cabinet, his hair covering his face.

"Madden?" Voice smaller now, I worried what would come next.

"I'm right here, Joe. Tell me what you need."

He didn't answer, so I stood still...waiting. When his hand reached out for me, I didn't even hesitate. I took it, reveling in the warm feel of his skin touching mine. He pulled me close, directing me to sit next to him. I complied, worried I was sitting too close. He let go of my hand, and I heard his quiet voice between us.

"Why did you run away from me?" he asked.

"I wanted to give you space. I want you to feel safe, Joe. I don't know—" he shook his head, cutting off my words.

"In your room. You—I was. I don't understand. You jumped away, but now you don't want me to leave. You didn't—" he paused, shaking his head. "I don't understand, Madden."

It made perfect sense to me. I didn't even understand *my* reaction to him on my bed, so I should have known he wouldn't know what to do with it. "Joe, I'm so sorry. I didn't mean to make you feel bad about anything. I was surprised, because we were having fun earlier. And I enjoyed it. A lot. Kissing you was... well, it was amazing. I didn't want to push you too far, and then, I realized that I was putting you in a precarious situation. I freaked out for a minute. I don't want you to leave. I never wanted you to leave."

Joe didn't say anything, but after a few seconds he nodded, looking straight ahead, then his head fell to the side, resting against my shoulder. It felt better than an innocent gesture should have. It shouldn't have lit me up from the inside out, but it did. When I thought about it, I realized that every move, word, phrase or gesture he made meant something. He was very purposeful in everything that he did, which just made this moment, this night, one to remember.

When I rested my head against his, he spoke. "Madden, I feel really good around you. It's scary to me, because I haven't felt good around anyone for a long time. Maybe ever. I don't want you to get hurt, though."

"Why would I get hurt, Joe?" I asked, my lips against his hair.

He didn't respond for a while, and then, after blowing out a deep breath, he told me that trouble always followed him. I sat there, with his head against mine, thinking. Wondering what the future held for Joe. If I was in it anywhere.

JOE HEADED to the hall bathroom and shut the door, smiling over his shoulder at me. I made my way to my room, turning off lights as I went. Brushing my teeth, I couldn't help but replay the loop of tonight over in my head. From Joe's comedy act over the pizza, to his heated looks and swollen lips. We eventually did watch a movie, but with his body tucked up against mine on the couch, my hand in his hair. This time, he had one hand resting on my thigh, and I thought I was going to combust. I'd never had such a visceral reaction to another man in my life. I bet I could come in my pants like a teenager, just from watching him abuse his bottom lip.

Turning off the bathroom light, I pulled my shirt over my head and threw it in the laundry basket by the door. After taking the rest of my clothes off, I walked the several feet across the room to my bed, and jumped in surprise.

"Hey, is this...is this okay?" Joe lay on the far side of my bed, one of my t-shirts hanging loosely over his narrow shoulders. He looked like an angel. I felt like a demon.

"God, Joe. Yes, it's okay. I can't think of anything that you could do that wouldn't be okay. That wouldn't make me over-joyed, if I'm honest." I stood there, at the side of the bed, my legs touching the mattress, not really knowing what to do next.

"Okay, cool. I just—," he paused, eyeing me suspiciously. "Can you please get into this bed, so I can talk to you without worrying that you'll run? You're freaking me out here." He smiled, and I huffed out a strangled laugh. I was seeing a lighter, more relaxed side of Joe, and I fucking loved it. It made my guts clench in a fantastic way.

"You know that I'd never try to make you uncomfortable, right? I'd hate it if you couldn't trust me, and I'd never want to break that trust, Joe." I sat up against the headboard, pillows smashed behind me. As soon as I said it, Joe sat up, too, mimicking my pose.

"I trust you. That's why I'm here, Madden. And you are special. To me, I mean. And in general. Maybe more than special. You make me want things, Madden. Things that I shouldn't, or never thought I could ever want. And I've never wanted like this before. Not something I couldn't take, or get money for. This is new territory for me. And I understand if you don't want that. Don't want me. Because I'm so—,"

I cut him off, my hand on his cheek. "Don't you dare finish that thought. Don't you dare, for one minute, think that I don't want this. Want you." My fingers stroked along his jaw. "God, I want so many things with you, baby. We don't have to figure everything out right now. Not yet. Not when you aren't ready to know for yourself. I won't ask you for more than what you can give me, Joe. I just want to be here, watching you, being with you, while you figure it all out. Just let me stay, baby. In here," I finished, pointing at his head. He nodded, and before he could say anything, I added, "And then maybe... Maybe one day, you'll let me in here." My hand went to his chest, right over his heart. I knew I'd overstepped, but I couldn't help myself. I'd never wanted anything as much as I wanted him.

I slid down into bed, threw the extra pillow on the floor, watching as he did the same. I wasn't sure what to do, what the protocol was, after we'd made out a couple of hours ago. What happened now, in my bed, me in my boxer briefs, and Joe in his underwear and t-shirt. Before I could panic, I felt the mattress dip, and Joe was there, his left side pressed against my right, his head cradled against my shoulder. I heard, then felt, his intake of breath. His hand entwined with mine, he whispered, "Goodnight, Madden."

Oh God, this man. Turning my head, I kissed his hair. "Goodnight, Joe." Sweet dreams, baby.

18

Joe

I awoke to the smell of coffee, and the sounds of dishes clinking together from the other side of Madden's apartment. The smile that covered my face was impossible to hide. I wasn't ready to get out of bed, to let this dream life end. *Nothing good could last.* This wasn't my life, but it was everything I never knew I wanted. Scratch that—needed. And fuck if Madden wasn't becoming necessary, which was why I had to leave. I couldn't risk getting any more involved in his life. I couldn't risk what might happen if I were to be found again.

A shudder tore through my body at the thought, but the smile broke through again. Madden. He'd managed to plant a seed that took root in some dark and empty corner of my insides. And he kept feeding it, watering it with his words. Nurturing it with his touches. I felt the change yesterday. He was so warm and happy. His eyes were open and soft. I couldn't stop myself from needing to know what he tasted like. Needing to feel him against my tongue. It changed me. I felt it as it happened. I felt it grow inside of me, sprouting leaves and petals from its stems. It grew and grew and grew, until it reached up and pushed its way inside, somewhere vital. A little nudge here. A tiny fissure. Now I'd never be the same, because whatever seed he'd planted had burrowed up into my heart. I knew it wouldn't last—couldn't last. It was enough to force my hands to ball into fists, and my eyes to scrunch tight.

I laid there for a while, planning and plotting my half-hearted escape in my head. Thinking of how I should just get up right now and walk out the door. I didn't have to worry about packing anything. I had nothing. I could literally walk out the front door right now, go pack up my tent, and keep walking. To the next town. Then the next. Until they all blurred into a sea of lights and tall squares of brick and metal. Same as before. Like I'd done so many times.

Everything was different now. Me, Lulu, Madden, the café. Even Sloan, in some weird, vague way. And Adam. I had things to lose. *How did that happen?* I'd promised myself that I'd never care about anything ever again, but I forgot to promise not to care about people. Because that one was new. I'd never had people to care about. Not really, until now.

I burrowed down into the bed, pulling both the sheet and the comforter over my head. I'd never seen a bed this big, let alone touched one. And now I'd slept in one. Twice. The Cheshire cat smile was back. Full force. Before I could stop myself, I was making snow angels in the sheets, giggling.

"Just when I think I couldn't like you any more than I do, you do something so cute it makes my teeth hurt." I gulped at Madden's voice and immediately froze, arms and legs splayed like a bug on a windshield. "You're going to have to take me to the dentist soon, Joe," he teased. I knew it was a joke because of the way his voice pitched up when he smiled.

"Hey, I want to take you somewhere today, so you have to

get up now. I made French toast. With lots of syrup for you, sweet boy. So, get up!"

The covers were ripped off me. In a flash he was on the bed, legs straddling my body, tickling me. I was doubled over, yelling for him to stop. It hurt. It was like sensory overload. I couldn't deal with the intense feelings. "Madden, stop. Oh, God, please stop. Stop!" He must have understood then, that I wasn't playing around. He was instantly off me, kneeling a foot away, worry creasing his brow. I couldn't catch my breath. Sitting up, my lungs heaved, and I felt like my skin was too tight, and pulling at me.

"Shit, Joe, I'm so sorry. I didn't think. Tell me what to do."

I tried to regain a bit of composure, but Madden wasn't having it. He fingered my unruly hair, placing the long strands behind my ears. Then, he put his forehead against my forehead, ever so gently. And nothing happened. Maybe he was trying to siphon my thoughts into his head. I had no clue, but it helped. I found my breaths quickly matching his. Then he smiled at me.

"How about we go and see about reheating breakfast, hmm?"

"I don't—," I let out a long, shaky breath, pulling back from him. "How can you want that? Want me? Don't you see I'm not like you, Madden?" My hands went out to my sides, in frustration.

"It was too much for you, and I should have realized it. I'm sorry for that, but if you can forgive me, I'd like to eat with you, then get cleaned up, and take you somewhere. We both have work later, so we should hurry." I sat there, stunned, as he patted my leg and got up. As if nothing had happened. I heard him whistling in the kitchen as he opened and closed the door to the microwave. The telltale beeps of buttons. Okay, then.

"I'll feed the fish!" I yelled, skipping my way down the hallway.

"I know you will," he laughed.

~

"I DON'T GET why you won't tell me where we're going." I was pouting and acting like a five-year-old but I couldn't have cared less. Madden had gotten ready while I'd washed the breakfast dishes. Well, put them in the dishwasher. But that was still helpful. I had put on my jeans, which he'd washed for me once again, and then he let me borrow a t-shirt that he claimed was too small for him. It was still a couple of sizes too big for me, but I wasn't about to complain about smelling like Madden all day. Especially since I'd sprayed some of his cologne on that I'd seen on his dresser. He'd tentatively taken my hand and walked me to his car.

I was nervous. Being driven around the city in a car was not something I ever thought I'd get used to. Rubbing the soft cotton of my borrowed shirt between my finger and thumb, I turned my body towards him. "Please, tell me?" Surprises were never something I looked forward to, not with my history.

"No. I told you before, it's a surprise. But I really think you'll like it." He looked over at me, a huge smile on his face.

"You really think I'll like being taken to the woods and murdered?" I was never good at small talk, and by the horrified look on Madden's face, he didn't find my comment funny either. "I'm sorry. It was a joke, but I'm nervous. I'm not really w-w-worried you're going to k-k-kill me." I attempted a smile, but I came off looking like a crazed clown. So, I went with what I would have wanted from him. I leaned over and put my hand on his on the armrest between us. It seemed like the right thing because it got a better response.

"You know, Joe, I don't think I'll ever get enough of you touching me." Madden pinned his eyes on the flush that took over my body and smiled gently. "You are so different now.

More comfortable around me, I think." Squeezing my hand between us, he continued. "The fact that you're starting to trust me enough to let me see the real you—," he stopped abruptly. His eyes fixed back on the road, but he swallowed hard. Like he'd gotten choked up.

"Hey, are you okay? Are you sick?" I tried to let go of his hand, but his grip just tightened around mine.

"God, Joe. I just really like you so fucking much. And I'm probably going to fuck this up like I did this morning."

I shook my head fiercely. "No, you didn't. I'm the one—."

"Jesus, Joe. You're the one who's fighting every day to create a life for yourself. You are so brave, and worthy of having everything you'd ever want. I look at you and how far you've come, and I'm so proud of you."

"What are you talking about? Brave? I'm not brave, Madden. I fall apart if a stranger brushes against me. That's not brave. I have nothing." I fisted my hands and faced the window, looking out. "I see the world. I know it's full of people who could hurt me. People who can harm others, for no reason. They steal things, lives even. There's so much pain and bad out there. Even people who are supposed to be good, they aren't. You can't trust good."

We sat in silence for a few minutes, both of us brooding. I didn't want this. This feeling between us. Like I'd thrown a rock at a perfect window. A small pit had formed. If it wasn't fixed soon, it would become a crack. And I couldn't have a crack between us. So, with a shaky breath I whispered, "You're different to me. I haven't figured it out yet. I'm trying. And it's like—," I held up a hand, silently pleading for a minute to find the words. He nodded, giving me what I needed. I searched and searched. Sometimes I felt like I was seeing words but couldn't read them. Like, they were too far away. "It's like when you see someone, and you just have that feeling that they are evil. Like, just the way they swing their arms when they walk, or the way their mouth moves when they talk. Sometimes it's just like, like, this color surrounds them. Like a darkness that you can just see. It's like that with you, but the opposite. I don't know why yet, but I'm starting to see it more clearly." My voice waivered and I swallowed a couple of times.

"What color do I have around me?" Madden didn't take his gaze off the road, but he pulled his bottom lip into his mouth. It sent a wave of lust through my body. That was new, too. The feeling I got when he touched me, when he put his hands in my hair. It was a different touch now than it was before. Now it heated my skin and made my nerves light up like fireworks. I closed my eyes, wanting to keep it with me, for when this ended.

"Joe?" Madden asked as he looked over at me, a crease between his brows.

"What?" I responded, blinking.

"Color?" He was smiling as if he'd known what I was thinking.

"Oh, um. Right. Yours changes. Mostly it's yellows, greens, and purples. When you touch me or look at me when you think I've done something unexpected, you have this sort of rainbow tinge. Like so many colors want to come through and they are fighting to get out."

After that it was quiet in the car again, but every time I sneaked a look at him, his lips were turned up at the edges.

"ARE YOU KIDDING ME? This isn't real. How can this be real?" My eyes bugged out. I couldn't keep my ass in the seat. I was doing my best impression of a prairie dog, bouncing up and down, the seat belt strap digging into my collarbone.

"Not a joke. I was hoping that you'd be excited, but I may have underestimated." Madden was downright giddy when he looked me over. "To be honest, I'm so relieved. I worried you'd be upset or that it wasn't the right thing."

"Madden. This is the perfect thing. I've never been before. Ever! And I've always, always wanted to go to a zoo. Can we see all the animals? Can we touch any? Can we feed them? Are they sad? What if I fall in? What if they hate me? Oh, God, Madden, what if the animals see me and run off?" At that point my lungs were heaving for real. I heard a chuckle beside me and then a gasp when he realized I was having difficulty taking in air.

"Joe, just breathe. Lean forward. Here," he said pushing my head between my legs. His hand lightly rubbed at my back, like I'd become so used to in the last few days. It was grounding and I realized it almost gave me instant relief. After a couple of minutes, Madden moved his hand up to my nape and squeezed. "You okay now?"

"Yeah," I gulped. "Yeah." I shook my head and smiled at him. "Dude. I'm afraid the animals won't like me." That's when Madden's face broke open, and wind chimes danced in his laugh.

He squeezed my neck again, then let go. I instantly missed the contact. So, I did what any other man would have done in my position. I whined. A really embarrassing girly sounding high-pitched whine from the back of my throat. In trying to redeem myself, and cover up my embarrassment, I reached to put my hand to his face. To cup his face. To show how much this surprise meant to me. Instead, I caught him as he was turning and ended up sticking a finger up his nose.

"Oh, my God. Just go without me. I'm better off here in an enclosed cage of my own." I was horrified, my hands pressed to my face, listening to Madden laugh so hard he snorted. Full-on pig snort. I broke out in a laughing fit, and a minute later we were clutching our stomachs and crying. But it felt good. "I don't think I've ever laughed that hard before," I said, smiling. His eyes were twinkling from the moisture pooled there.

"C'mere, Joe," he whispered, pulling me close over the center console. When our faces were a breath apart, he said, "I so badly want to share everything with you."

MY FIRST THOUGHT was that I should have brought an oxygen tank. I was overwhelmed, in love, and disgusted. Overwhelmed by the crush of people, children with grabby jam hands, babies in strollers throwing mashed up pieces of masticated yuck, and parents who'd already lost their tempers. It was barely nine in the morning. Just the thought of Madden surprising me with a trip to the zoo had me soaring. I loved that he had thought of this. That he'd thought of me. It made my chest squeeze and ache, but there was so much going on that I folded those thoughts up like a paper map then shoved them away for when I was lonely and alone again. Having never been around animals before, I'd never realized what the smell would entail. I was living in a cartoon fantasy where animals cleaned themselves and proudly showed their beautiful sides to the world. Despite the pungent scents, my face ached from smiling so widely for so long at one time. It was undoubtedly the best day of my life.

After we made our way through the ticket counters and followed the fray past the admission lines, the park opened up into the Great Northwest, full of eagles, goats, and cougars. I was entranced. I could have spent days at each exhibit, just watching the beautiful creatures. They were all made so differently: Strong and capable for their specific needs, all sinuous muscles and fur. I wanted to memorize every detail. I burned to understand their motivations. Why, over the course of time, did their fur, teeth, or ear-shape change? I felt as though I was sitting in a library full of books that I'd never have time to read, yet they all contained information that felt so very vital to me.

I'd registered Madden standing next to me, silently watching each animal, but his eyes kept landing on me. At first, it made me feel exposed. In our time together I'd showed him my wounds and let him pick open the scabs. Allowed him to open me up. A little bit here, a bit more there. But this was different. His face told me it was. He wasn't judging me. He wasn't making fun of me for being so childlike, so enthusiastic about the animals. He watched me with a fondness I'd never seen before. Never directed at me, obviously, but this slow, steady, relaxed Madden was looking at me like I was looking at the animals. With a desire to learn more. To understand. To take me apart and examine my pieces and then put me back together again. I shivered at the thought. That maybe he truly wanted to know me. What motivated me. What I liked and what changed me over time.

"Hey, there's something up here a bit that I really want you to see. Something I think you'll enjoy." His voice sounded hoarse and tight, like he'd been singing all day. His eyes were wide and hopeful, though, so I didn't ask, just smiled up at him and, with his hand at my back, he led me down the path to the next set of exhibits.

"I know you love Batman and Robin so much and I figured maybe this would be something else that you'd find fascinating, too?" He'd ended in a question, his voice gaining lilt. He was nervous. I looked at the gigantic glass enclosure in front of me. The thick glass stretched impossibly from floor to ceiling, water taking over two-thirds of its height. Above the water line was a giant cluster of rocks, covered in small pebbles, some green vegetation sprinkled throughout. Gliding through the water and waddling along the rocks were about five dozen penguins. Each of them dressed to the nines in their tuxedos, buoyantly tearing through the water, faster than I'd ever expected. Like bullets being shot from a gun. Over and over they streaked past the glass, thick bodies rocking in movement, webbed feet moving the water around them.

My body took over, and before I knew it, I was pressed against the glass, hands splayed out, eyes wide. I wanted to reach inside and touch them. I wanted to live in the tank and learn everything about them. They were so magical. They moved like they couldn't even be real. Time seemed irrelevant; I was lost in the rhythm of the movement, their crisp, black bodies dancing through the blue water. My eyes were unfocused, my mind trying to memorize each second of the scene in front of me. Madden's hand in mine brought me back to reality and I turned and smiled at him. "I can't ever pay you back for all that you've given me," I said, shaking my head. I looked down at the wet puddle on the concrete floor and dipped the toe of my shoe in the center. I needed to feel something tangible in that moment.

"I don't care about repayment. Just seeing how much you love this is worth way more than a few bucks." He placed a kiss on my hair, and I didn't panic or tighten. And knowing that... Knowing that my body accepted Madden's touch without thought... That was a gift that I'd keep to myself, but one that I'd cherish. We stood there quietly, just breathing. Soon, a group of students rushed in, loud and laughing. They were jumping around each other, arms flailing, and I could feel my muscles tighten. Before I could think, Madden stepped behind me, wrapped his arms around my waist and bent to rest his chin on my shoulder. It wasn't a grand gesture, but it meant everything to me. That he knew what I needed in the moment, didn't even pause to think, just reacted. I'd never felt so safe. I knew right then that if anything happened, he'd protect me. He wouldn't allow anything to happen to me. I swallowed and relaxed into his embrace, feeling tingly and a bit numb.

19

Madden

The car ride back into town was quiet. Both Joe and I had a lot on our minds and by silent agreement we took the thirty-minute drive to process the day individually. I felt heat in my belly thinking about the last few days with Joe. I had allowed myself to get tangled up with emotion when it came to him. It was a whirlwind that I wasn't prepared for or expecting. Hurricane Joe tore through my life and after spending some concentrated, meaningful time with him, he'd left my life upside down. But that didn't seem right. Maybe just shaken up. I lived a routine existence before. I had Anna and her family. I had Adam and work. Days and nights blended together with traumatic experiences at work the only things that cut up the ticker of time running across the bottom of my screen of life. But with Joe, I was embracing and crafting moments with him. I wanted more and more time. For it to stop altogether, or maybe just pass us by, like hitchhikers on the side of the highway. I wished for more time with him without the real world intervening. I'd known I used his sickness last week as a reason to take him home. I'd seen the opportunity and seized it, now so unbelievably grateful that I did.

Being with Joe now was like he'd unzipped the bubble that he was living in and let me inside. I feared for when we both went back to work, back to our regular lives. Would he push me out, rezipping the opening one tooth at a time? Next time, would I have to start over? Could I reach out and hold his hand? Would he allow it again, or would he hesitate? Make me work my way back in to where he could trust me again? And that thought terrified me. Because I didn't want to lose any part of him. I didn't want to fight my way back into the bubble just to realize it was unrecognizable the next time. But I would. I would do anything.

I looked over at Joe who was sitting peacefully next to me. His hands were splayed on his thighs, head back against the head rest. He looked like he could fall asleep at any moment. And the way the sun played across his face made him look so warm and bright. I didn't want to let him go.

I pulled over at our exit then parked in a shopping center lot. Joe looked over at me, confusion marring his perfect face. I gestured with my hands. "C'mere." He came willingly, pushing his face into my neck, his arm around my waist. It was cramped and awkward in the car, but I had to hold him. I felt him relax into me and then his lips were at my throat. Feeling the soft flutter of them against my skin made little bumps rise to the surface. He smiled against me then kissed my pulse, leaving a wet spot. As I swallowed, he chased my Adam's apple with his mouth. Before I knew what was happening, he was on his knees on his seat, arms around my neck, planting kisses like warm rain on my neck and jaw. "What—what are you doing?"

He didn't answer, just started rubbing his nose on my jaw, my neck, up my ear. "Fuck, Joe. I-I. You have to stop." Breathless, I barely uttered the words when Joe let go and slumped against his seat. I winced and adjusted my erection. "I'm sorry, I don't want you to stop, but we're in a parking lot and we both have to get to work."

Joe didn't respond to me, just stared out the window. "Hey, tell me what you're thinking." His posture was straight and firm. "I wasn't rejecting you." He blinked once. The next blink brought a tear with it down his cheek. Oh fuck. I reached over but he leaned away towards the door, his face towards the window. "Joe, don't hide from me. I swear I want you more than anything in this world. I just can't... I can't right here, right now. If we were anywhere else—," I leaned forward, hoping he'd look at me. No dice. "Please, look at me, Joe. Let me see your beautiful face."

A laugh escaped his mouth and he tried to take it back just as quickly. He looked over at me, his hand covering his betraying lips. "Joe, if we were in my apartment right now, I wouldn't have stopped you. You know that, right?" I watched as he closed his eyes, wondering what was going on in his beautiful brain.

"I got carried away. It's so new and I just had the greatest day with you. It was like, *the* greatest day ever. And you gave it to me. I'm just—I'm so happy and I don't want it to end yet. And I look at you and every time I touch you now my body reacts. I've never had that happen before. I like it. I like the way I feel when I touch you. When I taste your skin. And your mouth. The way your body feels against mine. And I just want to forget everything else. I want to let it all go. My reactions, my crazy. I just wanted to feel you."

"Fuck. I'm pretty sure you are going to kill me."

"YOU LOOK DIFFERENT. Did you cut your hair or something?"

Adam perched on the side of the counter in the nurse's lounge, a spoon hanging out of his mouth. I had assumed it was for the yogurt cup in his hand, but he just kept gnawing on it like it was a chew toy.

"No, I didn't cut my hair," I replied lamely, running my hand over my hair like a dumbass. "Nothing's different. You suck." I was in a pissy mood. I'd dropped Joe off at work, taking the time to park the car and kiss him soundly on that sexy pouty mouth of his before I walked him into the café and ordered a coffee to go. It was harder to leave him than I would have ever thought. I felt like I'd torn half of my heart out and left it there when I climbed back into my car. Everything felt quiet. Like someone had turned down the volume on my life. It was now just a gentle hum around me, easily blocked out, and I hated it.

I glanced up at the cheap digital clock on the wall where seven-fourteen PM blazed in red lines. I'd left Joe for his four o'clock shift, so we'd only been apart for just over three hours and I felt the loss like a wound to my soul. How did he become so essential in such a short amount of time? And now, what was the plan? Go back to only seeing him on breaks for coffee? He had no phone so I couldn't even call him. I had no idea what he did or where he was when he wasn't on shift. And I had no right to ask, but I wanted the right to know everything. Still, I had no recourse but to sit back. It wasn't as if I could just ask the guy to move in with me. Right? No, that was insane. Wasn't it? I bit my lip.

"Dude. For real. What is up with you? You've been broody since you got here. You had an entire weekend off and I didn't hear from you once. You okay?" Finally, the spoon was back in his yogurt cup lying on its side on the counter. I had no idea what to say. I felt like that stupid bubble that I was in with Joe would burst if I spoke of it. It was such a fragile thing and I and I didn't want it to pop.

"I'm fine. Just been thinking a lot, that's all." I tried to stand up from my place on the couch but Adam's hand pushed me down, then he landed next to me.

"Thinking about what? You seem contemplative and it's freaking me the fuck out. Now what the hell is going on?" He eyes did this whole puppy dog thing that always made me give in. He smirked because he knew it.

I let out a long sigh then told him about the last few days with Joe, leaving out the details of our night of making out on the couch and my bed. That was something I was keeping for myself. My heart fluttered when I explained how sick Joe had been and how much he'd slept. I told him about Anna calling me and what he'd been like when I got home. He just listened, not reacting other than the typical head bobbing and frequent smiles. I felt my face flame when I told him about my reaction on the way home from the zoo today. It was difficult for me to wrap my mind around, being so seemingly attached to someone this quickly. But I just kept going back to the same thought. *It just feels right.* And it had.

"Well, I gotta tell you, man. You are different around him. And I've only seen you with him a few times at the café, but it was obvious back then that you had feelings for him." Adam sat back and crossed his right ankle over his left knee. "Caring about someone looks good on you," he added with a smug smile.

"What? Earlier you basically said I was being an asshole and now you say this looks good on me?" I wanted to change the subject.

"You didn't stop smiling once while you told me about your weekend," he mocked and glared at me.

"I—," shaking my head, I started smiling again like a fool. "Fuck. I know!" We both started laughing at how ridiculous this all seemed. After a long silence, Adam huffed a long breath.

"I'm happy for you. You've always been one of those guys who does complicated. Like, full-on relationships. You want connection, love, and romance, and that's great. 'Cause it sounds like he's definitely not the kind of guy who could do anything else. But I'm worried for you, too. I don't want to see you hurt."

"No, I know. But I'm too far in this. I don't see a way out that I won't be hurt by. Christ, it's been a few hours and look at me." I ran a hand down my face. "What am I gonna do, Adam?"

"Well, I don't know. He's had no one, right? So, it might take a long time to build up any kind of trust. If ever, I guess. I wish I had the answer, my friend, but I feel like you know what you're doing. He's not running scared. From what you've said, he's letting you in, so enjoy it."

I let that sink in for a minute. Adam patted me on the shoulder and stood. "I've gotta hit the bathroom and then check on my patients. You good?"

"Yeah," I said, waving him away. "Thank you. For listening."

"Always, brother."

I had to get back to work as well, but I needed another minute to get my brain back in check. I had this burning in my chest like I'd inhaled a swarm of yellow jackets. I was a planner. I was not an edge of your seat kind of guy, but with Joe, I had to rethink everything. He needed my full attention and I wanted to give it to him. I wanted to give him everything. I'd never felt this out of control before. But it wasn't as though I'd reached a crossroads. It was more like my path was shifting. Instead of having to choose left or right, my path diverted, changed course. As I sat on the tan leather couch, in the loud, dark nurse's station, staring at the ugly spotted ceiling tiles, I contemplated that. I had changed course. Like my entire life's plan shifted itself to make way for something. And it wasn't a conscious decision. I didn't pick which way. It just...*veered*. And it hit me.

Like a comet blazing a fire through the sky, set on its course towards me, it hit me. And I knew. I was in love. My life found its own path because of him. I loved Joe. As if in a daze I shook my head. "I love Joe," I whispered to myself. The rush of euphoria ran through me like a bolt of electrical current, zapping each of my nerves with heat. Oh, God. I felt like all my questions had been answered. As if I'd climbed a mountain and finally reached the top and found treasure there. And maybe I did. But now, now I had to figure out how to secure the treasure and keep it.

20

———

Joe

I'd had some sort of out of body experience. Or body snatchers took over. Maybe I was suffering from some unknown disease and was in a coma and none of this was real. That seemed the most likely explanation of how my life had changed in the last few days. I had no idea how to process any of this. It made me feel so many emotions and not all of them were welcomed.

After Madden brought me to work, grabbed a coffee and said goodbye, he told me he'd be back during a break if he could, but wanted me to head over to his place after my shift. He had a full twelve-hour shift and wouldn't be there until the morning. When he placed a key in my hand, I'd almost dropped it. I had to ask him what it was for. I couldn't understand how he could just give me the thing that unlocked his entire life.

Staring at the oversized freezer doors in the kitchen, I was no closer to figuring anything out for myself, but Lulu was there, staring with me.

"Are you waiting for something to happen, kiddo?" She asked me. It shook me out of my trance, and I realized I was stimming. Letting go of the hem of my shirt, I huffed out a long breath.

"Look what he gave me," I told her, holding my hand out and open for inspection.

Glancing at my hand, her lips formed a giant smile, taking over her face. She looked at me, then back at my outstretched hand. I waited a beat before she finally spoke. "Madden is a lovely person, Joe. He's driven, exciting, loyal. He's always happy. Always. He likes making people happy. It's what he does." I nodded. "I think it's wonderful that he wants to make you happy, Joe. I think you deserve some happiness in your life."

That was hard to hear. I felt my skin shrink against my body, but Lulu didn't notice. She continued, "He really likes you, I see it in him." She sighed audibly. "I don't want either of you getting hurt, but you need to talk to him about how you feel. Is that the problem? You don't know how to talk about how you feel?"

She never pressured me, so I felt like I could really think about my response. After a while, I said, "Lulu, I don't know how to do any of this. I don't understand what he wants, what this means, what the restrictions are. I mean, what if he's home with someone when I walk in? Or, what if I am there and he wants to be alone? What if he doesn't mean anything—," Lulu made to wrap her arm around me, but thought better of it. Instead she looked into my eyes with a fierce scowl and said, "Joe. You deserve love and respect and friendship. You deserve every single good experience that life has to offer. Maybe it takes you a second longer to decide on things, but it doesn't make you less anything. Do you hear me?" What else could I do but nod as a tear slipped from my eye. "Good. Now, that's settled, I think you need to talk to Madden. I know it's hard for you, but you need to think about your feelings and questions, and when you see him again, you need to ask them. If you don't, you'll be staring at this freezer until next month and I need your help with the wild customers out there. You good?"

I nodded again and she turned to leave, stopping at the door. "Joe, don't let anyone make you feel like you can't take the time to make a decision for yourself. If they do, they aren't worth giving more thought to anyhow."

MADDEN STOPPED in about an hour before my shift ended. He had purple marks under his eyes, and I wanted to press my fingertips to them. His face held so much wonder to me. It was so perfectly aligned and laid out. Tonight, though, he had a line in between his eyebrows that hadn't been there earlier. Before I could process a question in my head, he spoke.

"I missed you." His body eased as the words hung in the air between us, and I was reeling. It cut me to the quick. In three words, he said everything that I'd been agonizing over for hours.

"Joe? Is that... Are you okay?" I watched his hand come towards me then felt his firm grip on my shoulder as my eyes closed. "Did I overstep? Make you uncomfortable?"

I shook my head, then rested it on his hand. "You just said exactly what I was trying to put words to all afternoon."

With my eyes closed, he pulled me into his warm embrace, arms pinning me tightly to him and the firm hold settled me. It centered me. I could breathe. I was tempted to hug him back, but I couldn't move, and I didn't want to. Ever.

When his lips pressed a gentle kiss to my hair, I pulled back and looked up at him. After gazing at each other for a heated moment, he leaned down and kissed my forehead and I almost exploded on contact. That was the single most intimate moment of my life.

"Use the key and stay with me. I'll be home late, but I want you to be there, yeah?" I nodded. I wasn't about to say no after this.

When my shift finally ended, I left Lulu and Sloan in the kitchen, all the clean dishes dried and returned to their assigned shelves, and started walking. I wandered down familiar streets, the lights of the storefronts blazing neon colors on the path ahead. When I reached the door to the familiar brick building, I smiled. I knew exactly what I was going to do. I had a plan.

FROZEN IN PLACE, my heart hammered as I listened to the front door close, and the sound of footsteps plodding across the tile. I couldn't help the smile that spread across my face, even as I tried to bury it into the pillow. Footsteps made their way down the hall and then I heard the isolated silence of nothing. Where did Madden go? I waited... For some sort of movement throughout the house. Some sign that he was here. That it was really him that walked through the door. When I didn't hear anything at all, I sat up.

"Hey, baby. I didn't mean to wake you. I'm sorry."

"You didn't. I just didn't know if it was you and then I didn't hear anything."

He sat next to me on the bed, leaning over me with his weight on his right arm. It felt incredibly safe.

"Honestly, I was hoping you'd be here, but I wasn't sure. I've been thinking about you all day. I couldn't wait to come home and find you all warm and soft in my bed. Thank you. Thank you for being here, Joe."

I sat up slowly, then wrapped my hand around his neck like he'd done to me so many times, but this time was different. Because I pulled him down and kissed him. It was a soft kiss. Our lips gently pressing against each other, moving together as one. Heat licked up my body from my toes to my ears and back down again. It was agony and ecstasy all at once, but not in an overpowering way. It made me want to get closer to him, not run. I wanted to climb into his lap and feel his body against mine like I had the night before. When I heard a moan, Madden pulled away just far enough that only our foreheads were touching.

"Are you okay?" I asked him tentatively.

He laughed and I watched as his eyes fell closed again. "Yeah, I'm great. You made that sound and I need a minute to breathe is all."

I felt my face light up like a space heater. The moan had come from me?

"Hey, I need a shower and I need to grab something to eat. Did you have dinner before you got in bed?" His fingers were busy brushing my hair back behind my ears, causing me to shiver.

"Um, yeah. I had some corn bread and chili at work before I left. Well, I tried to. The chili had these red beans that I just don't think I can eat." I made a gagging sound and he laughed. I wanted to bottle up his laugh and hide it in a safe place where I could hold onto it forever.

"Well, that doesn't sound like a proper meal. How about I put some leftover stew into a pot to heat while I shower and then we can eat in front of the television. You can put on another episode of Friends if you want. Then we can get back in bed."

I didn't miss the heated look he gave me when he mentioned getting in bed. I nodded and he leaned forward and gently rubbed his lips against my forehead again. I felt myself hold in a breath as he stood and went to his dresser for clothes.

"Did you get some pajamas to wear or do you need some?" he asked as he rooted through the drawers.

"No, I just have a t-shirt on that I found in the drawer." I thought I heard a squeak come from him, but it must have been the dresser drawer when he closed it. He threw a clean pair of flannel pajama pants at me without looking over, then made his way into the bathroom and shut the door. I laughed to myself. He forgot the stew.

WITH OUR BELLIES full and our eyes tired, we headed to Madden's bedroom, both of us sleepy and slow in our steps. I'd wanted to stay awake, if only to watch him. To watch his reactions to what was on the television. I loved watching his face, cataloguing his features and expressions. I knew so many now and could finally start interpreting what they meant in some instances.

By the time we made it to the bedroom, the air felt thick with something I couldn't name. A shiver ran through me, anticipation of what was to come. As if Madden sensed it, he grabbed my hand and told me, again, how happy he was that I was here when he'd arrived home. How much he'd missed me, and what a surprise it was to see me in his bed. He also assured me that if I wasn't comfortable sleeping in his bed, I could use the spare bedroom.

I let that thought run through my mind. Madden stayed silent, and I understood that he was giving me time, to process my feelings and thoughts. He was trying to be there for me. To understand me, give me what I needed so I wasn't overwhelmed. Through that space, I trusted him even more. He wanted to know who I was. Me, Joe Calloway. It meant everything.

"Madden. I want to be here, in your room, in your bed, with you. Thank you for giving me the option of the other bed. It means more to me than you know."

Squeezing my hand, he let it go and we both got ourselves into the bed, under the covers, then instantly found each other again. I felt free, and alive. And *seen*.

Turning to face him, I moved as close as I could to his body, wrapping my leg around his, our bodies touching from chest to toe. I savored the feeling. Raw emotion cut through me and suddenly I wanted more. I wanted to feel him all around me. To be covered in his scent, his heat and his weight. I just didn't know how to ask for it.

"What's going on in your head right now, Joe?" His breath against my hair was delightful. "Hmmm?" he added when I didn't answer him. "Whatever it is, I won't say no without good reason. I won't be mad at you. I won't get angry. I won't hurt you, Joe."

Damn him. I felt a tear well up in my eye, then roll down my face, leaving its wet impression on his shoulder.

"Baby, talk to me. Whatever it is, you can talk to me. I want you to always be able to tell me what you need, what you feel. And I'll wait. I'll give you time. But don't cry. I can't handle you being sad."

I shook my head, burying my face in his chest. I wasn't sad. His words made me feel like flying. Like I could mean something to somebody. And, yeah, maybe that did hurt just a bit. I started to tell Madden what I wanted. What I needed. But with my face pressed against his chest, my words failed. Leaning back, I whispered, "I want to feel you all around me. I want your weight and your arms and legs wrapped around me, Madden. I need it."

"Anything, Joe. Anything."

He let go of me, then maneuvered himself so that he was lying above me, his weight balanced on his forearms. Already I felt grounded. "Please," I whispered, and he dropped down on top of me, slowly feeding me his weight and his heat. It was glorious.

With his arms around my shoulders, his head in my neck, I breathed. In and out. And then there was nothing.

21

____

Madden

I could have lain wrapped around Joe all night. It felt perfect. The easy way my body molded around his. The feel of his tightly wound muscles letting go and giving in to sleep. It was deeply intimate, yes, but it was so much more than that. It was trust. Acceptance. I was giving him something he needed without expecting anything in return. I loved every second of the submission.

As soon as his breaths turned deep and slow, I delicately pulled myself off Joe and missed the contact immediately. Giving in to temptation, I lay on my side and spooned him, leaving no room between us, hoping it would be enough contact for him to sleep well, and enough to satisfy my need to be close to him.

Falling asleep that night was easy. With his fresh smell all around me, his body heat scorching me from the outside in, I was out within seconds.

∼

A LOW, dull vibrating sound woke me from a deep sleep. I reached to turn off my alarm then realized it was a text message. Glancing at the screen, I saw two words from {Anna}: **We're here.** Oh, shit. Then came the knock at the door. I groaned then turned to hear an answering groan from Joe. I had to smile as his sweet pouty lips pursed against the air. He was still asleep, but shifting from the noise, and I wished I could stay curled around him all day.

I reached the door in a t-shirt and sweats, my hair styled closely to a Muppet, but what could I do? Anna stepped in with David in tow. He made his way straight to the couch, just like he always did, then said hello as he began systematically untying his shoes.

Anna walked in, threw her purse onto the table, her keys clanging loudly as they tumbled out. "Hey, brother. Did you work late last night? Did we wake you up?" Her features were pinched in worry.

"Yeah, I worked my regular shift, but I didn't get to bed right away, so I'm tired. Did I know you guys were stopping by?" I asked, looking over at David. "I don't know if I have any—,"

"No, don't worry. We won't stay long. We stopped over because David has a makeup session for his therapy, and he wanted to see his uncle." She spoke loud enough for David to hear, but he wasn't paying attention.

I walked over to him, sat on the chair adjacent and asked him about his day and therapy. Anna was busy in the kitchen making coffee, which smelled amazing. Somehow, she always made better coffee than I ever could, even in my own house.

"Um, Madden..." Anna said warily from the kitchen.

"Yeah, what's up?" I answered, then turned her way, jumping into the kitchen, putting myself in between a sleep rumpled Joe and Anna.

"I smelled coffee," he said, his voice low and growly. The kind of low I felt deep in my groin. Grabbing his arm, I pulled him with me over to the table and sat him down on a chair. Thank the gods he was wearing a t-shirt and sleep pants. I could see Anna giving me a death stare, which I was successfully ignoring.

"So, as you can see, Anna and David stopped by to say hello." I waved at Anna and pointed at David with my chin. I could see the second that it registered that we weren't necessarily alone.

"Oh." His sweet face flamed red and his eyes grew wide. It brought an embarrassingly huge smile to my face.

I stood up and tried to help Anna with the coffee, pulling out the cream and sugar, and set them on the table. She side-eyed me until I was done, then grabbed my t-shirt and pulled me into the hallway. I was in trouble.

"You're sleeping with him?" she asked, her voice at least two octaves higher than usual.

"No," I replied, cautiously, looking behind me at where Joe sat, coffee mug between his hands. "I mean, yes I'm technically sleeping with him, but we aren't having sex. Jesus, Anna. Why am I telling you this? It's none of your business, is it?"

Her hand reached out and landed on my forearm lightly. "Madden, you just met this guy. Do you even know anything about him? Why is he sleeping here? What are you—,"

Reeling back from her touch, I harshly whispered, "No. This has nothing to do with you. I appreciate your worrying over me, but I really like him, Anna. Like, really like him." I ran a hand down my face. "And I sound like I'm in eighth grade, but it's true."

I turned to face Joe again, but he wasn't at the table. He was sitting close to David on the couch. Closer than David would normally find allowable. They looked like they were talking, their heads inclined towards each other, Joe gesturing with his hands. Was he explaining something? I looked back at Anna whose gaze was on her son.

We both stepped forward at the same time, intently listening to what was going on between them.

"I'm glad you came by. I was at my favorite bookstore last night and I got you something." Joe stood up excitedly and almost brushed right past us. I threw a look at Anna and then followed Joe into my bedroom, watching him pick up a bag from under my bed.

"What is that?" I asked him. He was holding the item in the bag, but it was flat and rectangularly shaped. I had no idea what it was.

"Um, I need your help. I walked by the bookstore last night and since I had some money, I bought this. For David." He handed me the gift and stood there, staring at it in my hands.

"Can I open it?"

He nodded, so I reached in and pulled out a book. *The Encyclopedia of Dinosaurs.* "Wow, baby. You bought this? For David?" He nodded again. I moved to sit on the bed, and he mimicked the move, sitting next to me, our pajama-clad thighs touching. I looked at the book, then at him. "This," I said and paused. "This was very nice of you, Joe. I really think he'll love it."

"I know he will. That's why I bought it."

I laughed. "Okay, I agree. So, what's the problem?"

"Well. I've never done s-s-something like this b-b-before. Given something. A gift I mean. I'm not sure." He looked up at me. "I don't know what to say."

Being around Joe, my cheeks were going to ache because of all the smiles. I stood up then held the book out to him. As he accepted it from me, I said, "I bought this for you. I hope you like it." When his gaze went from the book in his hand to my face, he looked confused. "That's how you give him his gift," I said. "Easy."

"Right. Easy," he repeated.

I cupped his cheek and drew my thumb across his lips. This sweet guy was making me fall for him and he didn't even know it. "Let's go back out there so you can give him his present, and then they can leave."

He smiled up at me, but it didn't reach his eyes. Grabbing my hand, he stood and pulled me down the hallway.

DAVID LOVED THE BOOK, of course. I don't know that I'd ever seen his eyes light up like that before. It was the look of pure bliss and my Joe had put it there. I was so proud of him. And it was so special to me to be around to witness so many first times for him. I felt something swell deep inside of me, at the thought of Joe quickly becoming the most important person in my life after a few weeks. Just watching him made me smile. I wanted to protect him, to love him.

AFTER ANNA AND DAVID LEFT, Joe and I sat on the couch, exhausted. It had been a long couple of days, and I needed a bit of normalcy. I looked over at Joe who was lying across the couch, his feet in my lap. His eyes were closed, but I knew he wasn't asleep. His thumb and forefinger were busy working the hem of his shirt, causing a smile to form on my face. He was so perfectly perfect.

"Hey, Joe," I whispered and watched his eyes slowly reveal themselves. I motioned for him to turn around and lay across me, his head on my lap. Once arranged, I rested my left hand on his chest and used my right hand to play with his hair. We sat there, the sun shining through the window for a long time, neither of us talking. It felt like a moment, though, to me. We were having a moment without words, but it was full of trust and respect, and maybe a little bit of love on my part. I was falling in love with Joe, I knew.

Lost in thought, I didn't notice when Joe turned to look up at me, but when I finally met his gaze, his eyes were liquid pools spilling over. I brushed the overflowing tears away with my thumbs and bent down to kiss his forehead. I watched as his eyes closed and more tears traced down his face, under his ears.

"Baby, don't cry. It hurts to see you like this. Talk to me." I looked down at him and noticed he was back to stimming, his hand on the hem of his shirt. "Are you worried about something? Is something wrong? Are you sick?"

Shaking his head after every question, I had no idea what it could be. We'd had such a lovely evening last night, then a perfect night's sleep. He was happy earlier. I tried to think of what could possibly have upset him, but came up empty.

His voice was shaky, but he managed to croak out, "I am afraid to hurt you. But I'm afraid to hurt me, too." The tears spilled furiously this time as he started sobbing in my lap. I pulled him into me, turning him and making shushing sounds until he was straddling my lap, his head between my chin and collarbone. Even though he was upset, this felt right.

Every time our bodies were pressed together like this, the pure *rightness* of it hit me, hard. When Joe was done, he sat up and looked at me. In a small voice he said, "Don't hate me because I'm beautiful." My eyes widened, and we both started laughing.

After we got ahold of ourselves, I grabbed his face in my hands and I kissed him. I couldn't stop myself. My body ached for him as I pressed my lips against his, loving the tender feeling of them. He was so warm, I needed more. Pulling him against me, his hands moved from my shoulders to my back, then up further against my neck. I could feel his hardness against mine. Biting back a moan, I pulled him even tighter against me, loving the way he came to me without reserve now.

I needed to taste him everywhere. I wanted every part of Joe. Gently lifting his chin, I moved down his neck, kissing and licking and sucking a path to his collarbone and shoulder. Moving his shirt this way and that to free up more skin, I grunted as he drew his arm up, silently offering his approval. With his shirt out of the way, I dove in. My fingers traced down his chest, thumbs brushing over his nipples, earning me a squeal of delight. It sent a spark right through to my cock, sending it leaping against my zipper. I couldn't remember ever being this turned on and needy before. The need to be inside Joe was overwhelming. I pulled away from him and heard a small huff of breath in reaction. It made me smile.

"Did I d-d-do something wrong?" Joe asked, his voice tinged in worry.

I shook my head. "Of course not. I just needed to catch my breath. You make me feel so good, Joe. I don't want to overwhelm you. Or me. I need a minute to calm down."

Joe stood and I handed him his shirt. He quickly tugged it back on, but not until I had taken in the marks on his chest. He had bite marks from me. "Oh, shit, Joe. I'm so sorry." I was horrified that I'd hurt him, but when he looked down, he shrugged, a smile on his face.

"I didn't even notice."

22

Joe

I was different. I didn't think it showed on the outside, but it must have. Lulu was looking at me all afternoon with big eyes. From the first time she saw me, as if she knew what I'd done with Madden. But that was impossible.

I kept an eye on her all day. I kept seeing pinks and yellows around her, which made me question what was going on. Why would she be staring at me all day for no reason? Had I done something wrong?

I spent the better part of an hour prevaricating over Lulu. She had a friendly, happy aura to her, yet every time I turned around, her gaze locked on me. Eventually, I headed for the kitchen, in desperate need of a break. When I saw Lulu duck through the door, I followed.

"Hey, Lulu?" I asked as she made her way into the massive freezer at the back of the room.

"What's up, babe?" She responded over her shoulder, lifting

her knee to balance the box in her arm as she unlatched the stainless-steel door with her other hand.

My skin heated at the endearment, a reminder of Madden calling me baby. Every time I'd thought of his velvety voice saying that word in my ear, I felt a bullet of desire shoot through me. That feeling was new for me, but I didn't really think too much about it. I hadn't ever been in a place to have any kind of relationship, living hard like I had been. I'd seen plenty of back-alley sex, slept next to rent boys in the past years, but I'd never allowed myself to go there. I couldn't even think about someone touching me like that. Putting their hands on me. Me putting my hands on them. Among other things. Lips, tongues, roving mouths. My stomach felt queasy just thinking about it. I needed air.

"Can I take a little break? Maybe walk around outside for a few minutes?"

"Sure thing. We've been slow in the last thirty minutes up front and we've got about thirty more until the next rush. You okay?" Lulu stopped in front of me, a giant carton of cream in her hand. Her gaze roamed my face. I let her look her fill then nodded.

"Fine, thanks. Just need a quick breather."

"Grab your jacket. It's cooling down out there."

"Thanks, Lulu," I answered. I watched her push through the door to the front and wiped my hands on a couple of paper towels before grabbing my jacket off the hook by the back door.

THE NIGHT SKY had always brought such wonderment to me. I used to dream up different names for the stars, make up stories of how they were formed, how old they were. I would have loved to study them. There was just something so peaceful and reassuring about their placement in the sky. They'd existed for centuries, longer than I could ever comprehend. Light years away, their existence was so sure and calculated, calming. For minutes I sat in the alley down the street from the café, my back against the brick wall, staring up in peace.

"You looking for a good time, kid?" His voice came out of nowhere, buzzing in my ear.

Scrambling to my feet, I pulled my jacket tight across my chest. "No. Just going back to work." Turning in the opposite direction, I tried to take a step, but was pulled back by a tight grip on my hood. My stomach heaved as I felt his hands on me, focusing on the voice. He'd found me again. Devin, the monster.

"Nah, I think you were looking for something back here in the dark." His voice was scratchy and deep, like he'd smoked gravel cigarettes.

Taking a deep breath, I squeezed me eyes shut. There was no way this was happening. I'd been careful. Not staying in one place too long. No friends. Until now.

"Please, just let me go back to work. Someone's going to be looking for me." I sounded pathetic but I didn't care. My throat was tightening, my heart fluttering.

"Is that right?" The deep voice hissed in my ear. "Well, then. We'd better be quick. I know you know what to do," he finished with a laugh. My gut clenched; I panicked when he pushed me down by my shoulders.

"No!" I screamed as he let go of my shoulder with one hand and grabbed my mouth, cutting off the sound. Tears prickled at my eyes and I closed them tight, shaking my head. I was shaking uncontrollably at the feel of his hands on my body, as if I could feel each tiny line and swirl of his fingerprints painting colors on my skin. Peppering my body with their marks. Changing my pigment, causing the blood to rise to the surface. Physically altering my appearance, even if just for a short length of time. Pain flared inside me. I was going to be violently ill soon as my body reacted to his closeness. I wanted Madden. More than anything in the world, right then, he was my safety.

A hand tightened around my mouth as tears poured down my face.

"What the fuck? Just get on your goddamn knees, kid, like you deserve. You know you want it. Just like you used to, yeah?"

I twisted around so that I was facing him now, his hand falling away from my mouth. I screamed again then sharp pain to my throat cut off my airway. The hand previously at my mouth now held my neck tightly. Too tightly. Shaking my head, I kicked out, hitting him in the shin, wishing I had steel-toed boots. His grip fell away, I ran.

Turning the corner, I found the back door to the café and flung it open, tripping over my feet and landing on my knees on the cold tile floor.

"What the hell?" Sloan stood by the sink, a coffee carafe in his hand, eyes wide. "Oh, my God, Joe, are you okay?" I heard the carafe bang against the sink and then his hands were on me.

"Nooooooooo!" I wailed, slapping his hands away. "Don't touch me! Don't touch me! Don't touch me!" I screamed. Crawling under the table beside the door, I wedged myself behind the back counter then curled my body into a ball, into my safe place. I let my body take over and numb my thoughts as I rocked back and forth in the dark corner. I had ruined everything.

23

Madden

"Adam, what time are you getting out of here tonight?" Our shift had seemed unusually long, though it was only around eleven PM. I still had hours to go, but Adam had started earlier than I had today. And yeah, I was jealous. I wanted to stop by and see Joe before I made it home, but after the café closed for the night, I knew he'd be curled up in the corner of my couch. I'd taken to calling it his nest. He would take all the pillows from my bed and make a small fort, surrounded by our combined scents. He told me that it made him feel safe when I wasn't there. My heart melted the first time I'd walked in and seen him, all bundled up, smashed in the corner. It was magical. He looked like an angel.

When I'd asked him why he didn't go to bed, he looked at me with wide, expectant eyes. I shrugged, not understanding. He told me then that he couldn't be in my bed without me. It was just something that felt wrong to him. It made his skin itch.

Understanding dawned on me. He was uncomfortable being exposed and prone without me. And fuck me, that touched me more than I'd thought anything could. Ever since, when I'd get home late and find him nestled on the couch, my heart shifted under its protection of bone and beat wildly.

I'd been missing him since my day shifts turned into overnights for the past few weeks. On the rare occasion that he was at the café when I showed up, my stomach would flip, and I had to hide behind my coffee cup before anyone could see the smile that automatically formed on my face. After the revelation I had about my feelings for him, every time he was near, they grew stronger. And all I ever wanted to do was see him. To feel him, hold him next to me.

"I'm off at one, why?" Adam was finishing up a lab order at the desk and I caught him smirking at me. Raising his eyebrows, he pushed, "You have somewhere to be?"

"Not really, no. Just—. Fuck, I don't know." I needed coffee. That's what it was. I hadn't slept much in the last few days and the lack of rest was getting to me. Yeah, I didn't believe it, but Adam knew better as well.

"You don't know? Come on, man. Just say it. You want to go see Joe." If I could have punched the know-it-all smirk off his face, I would have.

"Shut the hell up. I'm just tired is all," I said, flinging myself onto a stool.

"Hey, isn't that the guy from the café? The sad, black eyeliner guy?"

I turned quickly to see Sloan tearing down the hallway, looking wild. As he got closer to the nurse's station, his eyes went wide. I stepped up, raising my hands to show him I wasn't a threat. Bending over, his hands on his knees, he wheezed out, "You have to get to the café. It's Joe."

"What? What happened? Is he okay?" Before he could even answer me, I was halfway down the hall.

"Mads, I'll cover you. Call me!" I heard Adam yell as I turned the corner.

"Fuck! Fuck. Joe, baby, please be okay," I whispered, tearing through the corridors and into the street. Thank fuck the café was so close. I was there in a couple of minutes, not registering any of the steps I'd taken. I just needed to get to Joe.

Pulling open the door, everything looked normal. Deserted, but for two couples sitting at tables with phones in hand, coffee mugs and napkins decorating the tables. Then Lulu stepped out from the kitchen door. As soon as her gaze met mine, her posture visibly loosened. "Madden, he's in the kitchen. Something happened. I have no idea what, and he's not talking."

"What do you mean? What happened? Is he okay?" I was panicking and I needed to calm the fuck down. I needed answers.

"He went out back to get some air, he said. Then he came back about 25 minutes later screaming and curled up under the table chanting 'don't touch me' over and over." Her eyes were glassy with tears, and I pulled her into an embrace.

"Can I go in there, Lulu?" She wiped at her eyes and nodded.

I stepped into the kitchen and saw a dark figure curled up tight in the corner. My heart cracked open.

"Joe, baby." I made my way across the tile floor. When I was a few feet away, I dropped down onto my knees and looked at him. He was so small, curled up into a shell of himself. His fingers were pressed so tightly around himself that they were white with tension. Another part of my heart cracked.

I had no idea what to do. My first instinct was to grab him and pull him into my lap, but this was Joe. I knew that would escalate a bad moment into pure terror for him. Instead, I inched closer, whispering as softly as I could. "Hey, Joe. It's Madden. I'm here. You're safe. You're safe now." When I was close enough to feel the heat from his body, I pulled myself up and sat, my back against the wall, head tucked down under the table. "Baby, it's Madden. You are safe. I'm here. Can you hear me?" The need to touch him was overwhelming now. His hair was sticking up above his ear, and I wanted to put my fingers through it. I wanted to take him into my arms and never let go. I wanted his trust more than anything in the world. "Joe, please. I'm here. Please talk to me." Nothing. "Joe, I'm going to touch you unless you tell me not to. I'm going to rub your back with my hand if you don't stop me, and you are going to know that you're safe." I waited a few long seconds then slowly, gently, placed my hand on his back. I felt his entire body jump at the contact, but then relax. I started making shapes and letters, slowly and gently, like I had before, praying that he'd know it was me and calm down.

I was petrified sitting there under the table in the kitchen with Joe. What the hell could have happened to cause this? What could I do to make him feel safe? To keep him safe?

"M-M-M-Madden?" A tiny voice broke into my thoughts and I took a breath that I didn't realize I'd been holding.

"Baby, yeah, it's me," I said as soothingly as I could, still stroking his back. I could feel a bit of tension loosen under my fingers and I let out another deep breath.

"H-H-He t-t-t-touched me, M-Madden." What the actual fuck?

I went from broken to furious in three words. "Who, Joe? Who touched you?"

Joe didn't answer, just shook his head violently, then looked up at me. His eyes were red and wet, his face marked with tears. Before I could say anything, he was up and crawling into my lap, his wet face buried in my chest, arms around my neck. I felt like a God in that moment. I wrapped my arms around him, my lips in his hair, breathing in his scent. Under any other circumstances I'd have been hard as a rock. But my boy needed me, and I *needed* to find out what happened.

"Can you tell me what happened on your break, Joe?" I felt him blow out a sigh, then shake his head. "You said 'he touched me'. Who touched you, Joe?" Keeping up my ministrations on his back, I hoped he'd feel that safety and care that I was trying to exude. When I felt wetness at my neck, I realized he'd started crying again. I winced and felt my heart balloon. This tender boy had the ability to break me. He owned me. In that moment I knew it to be true. I'd do anything to keep him safe, to make him happy. I gave him a few more minutes, eyeing Lulu in the doorway. She'd just popped her head in and watched us curled around each other and put her hand over her heart. I knew exactly how she felt.

"Joe, how about we get out from under this table so I can see your beautiful face? Please?" I felt him nod into my shoulder, then start to pull away, just enough for me to get up. His hands were balled fists in death grips attached to my scrub's shirt. As soon as he let me stand him up, I saw it. Purple stains against his skin. Bruising. My blood boiled, I saw red. Fingerprints on his neck. "Who did this to you?" I whispered, trying for a calm tone that I wasn't feeling. "Baby, I have to know who it was. We have to report this."

"No! I just want to go home. Please, I don't know who it was. I just want to go home, Madden. Please take me home."

I had no choice. I wasn't going to stand here and argue with him, but I was going to find out the story and see about finding whoever attacked him.

"Okay, okay. But first, can I see your throat?" He pulled away quickly before I could even finish the question.

"No, just take me home, please?" His plea was like a vice around my heart.

"I will. But I need to check you out first. I need to ensure you don't have any lacerations or internal damage to your throat. Did you lose consciousness at all? You could have trauma to your vocal chords. Jesus, Joe, I just—," I couldn't finish my thought before tears stung at my eyes. I pulled him in close again and kissed the top of his head. "Let's get you home and then will you let me examine you?" I shook my head at the way that sounded, but I saw ease in his expression. Thank fuck. "Come on. I'll take you home."

"Thank you. I just want to go home and feed Batman and Robin and forget this ever happened."

The smile that lit up my face at him calling my place home almost pulled my cheek muscles. Almost.

I CALLED and thanked Adam for staying to finish up my shift as soon as we walked into my apartment. Joe gently tossed his shoes by the door, then made his way to the fish tank, settling himself on the kitchen chair directly in front of it. He hadn't said much since we'd left the café, but his shoulders were loose, and his face held more color. I didn't want to push, but I wanted to know who I needed to murder before I lost my mind. I prodded him again, asking if he'd tell me what happened. After a minute, he sighed and turned to look at me, a defeated mask on his face.

"I don't know who the guy was. Just a guy, okay? He grabbed me. I kicked him and ran. I'm okay now." I wanted to believe him, but the marks on his neck told me otherwise. And I knew Joe. This wasn't him.

"Joe, please. You can't just—"

His pleading eyes bored into me, "Yes, I can. I want to forget this ever happened. There's nothing anyone can do anyway. Let's just forget it, please?"

I shook my head. How? How was he able to just forget something like this? He was a mess on the floor an hour ago. I sat and watched his reactions. He glared at me for awhile, then returned his focus to the fish. I was tense and angry. Angry at how much he'd gone through. At how cruel the world could be, how cruel people could be. All I'd ever wanted to do was protect him from everything. It was a fierce feeling that I'd never encountered before. It made me warm all over as I sat at the kitchen table, watching him track the fish with his eyes. God, he was a beautiful creature. I could watch him all night, but I wanted more. I'd missed him, and having him in my space again just felt right, gave me a sense of purpose.

I stood, my hand on the back of my chair. Joe didn't move, his gaze on Batman and Robin. Slowly, I walked around the table to where he was sitting, slightly hunched over, sideways on the chair. He had his arm resting on the back of it, his chin on top. I patiently stood next to him, watching, waiting. When he finally looked up at me, he must have seen the longing in my eyes, because he sat up straight, then stood. We never broke eye contact and the feeling between us intensified as he moved towards me. I felt his hands graze my hips, then wrap around my waist as his head landed against my heart. The minute my arms were around him, he let out a long, contented sigh and it was all I could do not to pick him up and take him to my bed right then. He was all I'd ever wanted.

"Can we watch a movie or something?" I nodded, my chin brushing against his hair, not wanting to let go yet. His hands curled into fists in my shirt and he pulled in closer to me. It all felt so familiar.

We held the embrace for a few more minutes, then he let go of my shirt and took a step back, his chin shaky as he bit his wobbly lip. I immediately tensed as a tear spilled from his eye. I lifted my hand to wipe it away, and he turned into my palm. "Sorry, I'm a mess. I thought I was all cried out." His voice was small and unsure, and I stepped forward, reaching for him again. Backing away, he held up a finger, signaling for me to wait, then made his way down the hall to the bathroom. Thinking the reality of what happened tonight must have hit him, I grabbed a couple of bottled waters and set them on the coffee table, then threw myself down on the couch, giving him the space that he clearly needed.

When I heard the bathroom door open, I turned expecting him to be ready to watch a movie. Instead, he stood in the hallway, looking young and lost and almost broken. "Oh, baby, come over here and sit with me," I crooned, patting the cushion on the couch.

"Um. Can I—. Can we—." His hands were clenching into fists at his sides and I could tell he needed something. "Madden, I need you," he whispered, his eyes glistening again.

"You have me," I answered, making my way over to him. Standing in front of him, unsure, he looked up at me with those sad eyes and I asked him, "Do you want to get in my bed?"

"Oh, please. Can we?" I chuckled at his instant relief.

"Of course." I led him by the hand to my room and went straight to my closet, pulling out a t-shirt and a pair of sleeping pants with a drawstring. I left him to get comfortable while I went and turned the lights off around the apartment, then grabbed the bottled waters from the table before making my way back into the bedroom. My heart clenched at the thought of spending the night with him in my bed again. If only the circumstances had been different. But I would take Joe anyway I could have him, even if friendship was the only option up for offer.

Joe was already in my bed, the sheets and comforter pulled up around his neck. I didn't know if he was just cold or if he didn't want me looking at the markings that I knew were there. I sighed, getting my head on straight. I hoped Joe wouldn't have lied about knowing the guy from the alley. So, going to the police wouldn't have done any good, only caused even more unnecessary trauma for Joe. It just hurt me to know that someone had his hands on Joe. My Joe!

Two eyes peered up at me as I made my way to the bed,

setting the waters down on the side table. "Do you want the light off now?" I asked, fingers poised over the switch.

"No, not yet. I want to talk to you first." I didn't know what to think of that. I nodded, then excused myself to get ready for bed, taking a pair of sweatpants with me into the bathroom. As I brushed my teeth, I contemplated what I wanted, like I had a million times in the past month. All I could think about was that I wanted Joe, in whatever capacity I could get him. If it was just a friendship, it would kill me, and I'd probably end up old and alone, but I'd do that for him. What I wanted though, that was so hard for me to comprehend at this point. Because I'd never wanted anyone like I'd wanted him. I wanted him in my life, in my apartment, in my bed. I wanted to kiss him endlessly. To cook for him and come home to him and take him places he'd never been or seen. I wanted to know every single thing he liked, things that made him moan, things that turned him on, things that made him laugh. I wanted all of it with him, but I didn't know where or how to start. This had to be on his timeline. And I would wait.

I rinsed my mouth and washed my face, then turned out the lights and crawled into bed beside Joe. He was now lying in the center, leaning on a few pillows. His hair fanned out above his head. I wanted to touch him so badly my hands stung. I couldn't do it. With what he'd just gone through I was out of my element, completely unsure how to act, what he needed from me.

"Thanks for letting me stay here. It has changed my life, Madden." His voice was stronger than I was used to, like he'd gotten a shot of confidence since walking into my apartment.

"Don't thank me for that, Joe. I'm glad you feel comfortable here. It means a lot to me. You know that." It meant everything.

Joe squirmed a bit, raising up to rest his back against the gray textured headboard. I followed suit, rearranging the pillows behind my back, folding my hands in my lap over the bedding. Butterflies came to life in my stomach at the formal tone that had settled over the room. I opened my mouth to relieve some tension, but Joe started talking.

"All my life I've been alone, and it's been fine. I mean, I've been fine. I know I don't have much, but I haven't really needed anything either. But last month you brought me here. You opened your home, gave me something that I've never had. Actually, you gave me so many things I've never had." His eyes clenched shut and I reached my hand over to squeeze his forearm.

"Baby, I—" he interrupted me, shaking his head.

"No, I want to tell you. Because it's important. You're important." His eyes opened and bore into mine.

"Okay."

"I w-w-want you. I've never wanted another person before, but I want you. You make me feel things that I didn't know I was capable of. Like happiness and safety. And need. And I don't even know what it means, but I know I need you. But I'm scared, too. Because I have nothing to give you that you don't already have. Nothing worth wanting. All I can give you is me, which isn't worth anything, but I want you to have me."

Just like that, I was standing in the center of a tornado. My ears were ringing, my throat dry, my head a mess. This boy. This man. He wanted me and was brave enough to tell me, even though he didn't fully understand what it meant, what he was feeling. But I knew how I felt, had known for weeks. The words were bursting from my chest, trying to escape. But I couldn't. I couldn't throw something like that on him. Not yet. I would, but not when he wasn't sure of what he was feeling, what he needed. No, I'd hold on to the "L" word until I couldn't wait another second. Until I knew he was ready to hear it.

"Joe, you are so fucking brave. You make it hard for me to think about anything else because I can't stop thinking about you. I'm glad you're here and I want you to stay. Stay with me.

Please. Just…stay. I want to take care of you and feed you and show you things. To be here when you get home from work. I want you to be the last person I talk to at night and the first person I talk to in the mornings. I want you here as much as you want to be. Okay?"

"You do?" His eyes were wide and wet, and the question in his voice made me moan.

"Yes, I do. I want you here so badly. Please say you'll stay."

"I'll stay if you want me to stay, but I won't be a burden and I won't make a mess. I promise. If I'm here I'll clean and—," I cut him off with a kiss because he was being ridiculous. He was so innocent in so many ways that just broke my heart. No one should be so afraid of overstaying their welcome twenty seconds into the offer.

"I want you here with me. I can't imagine that will change, but I promise to tell you if it does. Does that sound okay?"

Joe nodded, then bit his lower lip, tongue comforting the sting after. I couldn't look away. My body was thrumming with desire in one move of his mouth. Before I could think, my hands were framing his face and my lips were parted against his. I carefully swiped my tongue across his lip as he had done seconds before, tasting his sweet mouth. I knew I couldn't push past his limits, but we'd made out before, so I had to hope that this was safe for now. But the instant I let my teeth scrape against his jaw he let out a sound somewhere between a whimper and a moan and I lost my mind.

My fingers threaded through his shaggy hair, pulling and twisting. I felt his body shift and suddenly he was on me, straddling my lap, plowing his tongue into my mouth with just as much force as I'd given him. His needy hands were on my neck, in my hair, squeezing my biceps. With every heartbeat he caressed another part of me, like he needed to feel me everywhere. It was surreal and sobering to think that I was affecting him just as much as he was me.

After a few minutes, I pulled back, needing a breath of air. He looked flushed and debauched, needy. All I could do was stare at his face, searing this moment into my memory forever. His flushed cheeks, neck, bruised and swollen lips. The burn of the graze of my stubble across his jaw. He looked utterly ravaged and it took my breath away.

He was breathing heavily as well, a small smile on his red mouth. He leaned forward, his hands braced on my shoulders and whispered, "I've been so afraid. But I want you to know me. Like no one ever has before."

I shivered at his words, resting my forehead on his neck. Nodding, my words stuck in my throat like sandpaper against tree bark.

"Madden, I want to know what you want. What you're thinking and feeling. It's hard for me to understand unless you tell me." He whispered in my ear, the words more intimate than anything I'd experienced before. Like we were the only two people on the planet right now.

"I just want you, Joe. However much of you I can have."

Joe sat up, shifting his body around so he was no longer on top of me, but next to me. He started getting under the covers, ready to go to sleep. I sat still, just watching him in the soft lighting of the lamp on the bedside table. His hair was so light it practically glowed. His face relaxed into the pillow, large eyes looking up at me like I held the key to something important.

"Are you going to come down here so you can be my spoon tonight?" Joe asked like he would ask for sugar in his coffee.

I almost swallowed my tongue. "Yeah. Yeah, of course." Reaching for the lamp, setting the room into darkness, I scrunched down into the bed and rolled onto my side towards Joe. We were facing each other now. After a few seconds his hand came up and then fell back to his side.

"C-c-can I t-touch you?" His hesitancy floored me. So innocent and unsure.

Leaning up on an elbow, I brushed a rebel strand of hair behind his ear and said, "You don't ever have to ask for permission to touch me. You can touch me whenever and wherever you want. And I'll like it," I added, winking at him. "But that doesn't mean that I'll think it's reciprocated as well. I don't. I want you to be comfortable and confident knowing that I wouldn't ever hurt you. I wouldn't. And I won't ever go further than you want me to. If you tell me to stop, I will stop. It doesn't matter what we are doing. I promise you, I'll stop. Do you trust me to stop?"

He answered me quickly and surely, "Yeah, I trust you. Thank you, Madden."

We stayed like that, lying in bed together, turned towards each other, just breathing. Watching each other. It felt good. Good to be seen by him, for him to let me see him as well. Like another layer of brick was breaking down from the walls built around him, and I loved it. I loved feeling like I was the only one who got to see him like this. Vulnerable, relaxed. Maybe a bit happy. I wanted so badly to tell him what was in my heart. But I knew I couldn't, not without ruining things. Instead, I reached over and traced his pale eyebrows with my index finger. Then a line over his short, pointed nose. Around his full, red lips. Across his jaw line and up his cheek. Then the backs of my fingers brushed lightly over his bicep and down his arm. The touch sent my pulse racing. It wasn't sexual at all, but it was intimate. It bridged the distance between us, connected us.

"Goodnight, Madden," he said as he grabbed my hand in his, exhaled, and then closed his eyes.

24

Joe

I was walking through a dense forest. It was daylight, but dark through the canopy above me. I was standing in the middle of nothing, a tiny speck in nature. Spinning in a three-hundred-sixty-degree circle, I realized each direction appeared to be the same view. There was no path, no obvious direction. No white rabbit leading the way. I was lost. When it hit me, I felt my lungs heave and my heart beat faster and faster. How did I get here? My head hurt and I realized I'd been clenching my hands into fists in my hair. Letting go, there was hardly any relief. I had no plan, no way out, no idea what I was doing there. The last thing I could remember was falling asleep with Madden, his hand clasping mine in the dark. This didn't make sense.

Feeling around in the pockets of my jeans I turned up nothing. I had no money, no phone. Obviously. What had I been expecting? Think, Joe. I took another look at my surroundings, everything still nondescript, just lush greens and browns. It looked like the sun was lowering in front of me, so that must be west. But what was west? I had no idea where I was. Should I go west? South? Fuck. I breathed in and out, thinking. It wasn't cold, so that was something. Wait. It's cold in Oregon, so I wasn't in Oregon. I had to be in Oregon. What the hell was going on?

I might as well move. Westward ho and all that. Follow the light. I trudged through the thick web of trees, crunching on smaller fallen branches as I went. It seemed strange that I hadn't heard any birds. I hadn't even seen any animals out here. Weren't there supposed to be animals in the woods?

Finally, after walking for what seemed like hours, I reached an open clearing full of tall, light green grass and wild-flowers. It smelled of wet earth and funerals. Or what my mind thought a funeral would smell like. I'd never been to one. Not even my mother's. A few paces into the field I saw a path and a wide opening between the trees. As I picked up my pace and made my way through the landscape, I could see that there were two paths. Because of course there were. My head hurt and I wanted to be home. My lungs pushed out an ironic chuckle. Home. Right. I didn't really have one of those, did I. Not even a question, just my snark coming out to play. And just like that, I broke down. I fell to my knees, my face in my hands. Sobs tore out of my chest, tears burning as they leaked from my eyes. I had spent hours trying to get out. Trying to find my way. Nothing was ever easy for me, dammit. Why couldn't I just have one thing? Was that too much to ask? One thing good in my life? One thing that wouldn't cost me everything? Immediately, I saw Madden in my mind. And yeah, if there really was anything I could want to have for my own, it would have been him.

It was as if my body knew before my mind did, that he was safety. It knew not to run when he touched me, every time he touched me. It took a couple of times until my brain caught up. I was dazed, to be sure, but it felt almost pleasing. And then, when we were laughing on the couch with pizza, I felt this intense heat flowing through my body, tingling in my extremities. It was as if something in me had awoken after 22 years and I wanted to chase after that feeling again. When we kissed it was like everything in my head flew out the window, like an entire flock of birds retreating from a single tree. All the pain, all the sadness, the loneliness, just gone. Evaporated from my mind. All that was left was the sweet taste of Madden's mouth, the smell of his soap mixed with the overwhelming scent of vanilla. The scratchy feel of his stubble on my face, on my neck, against my hands. My head was full of Madden. Like some sort of torture, giving me this slice of heaven, but the worry that it would all come slipping through my fingers was always there, right at the surface. I knew I couldn't count on this, but I wanted to so badly. More than anything, I wanted him.

A sudden jarring motion had me jumping up and I felt familiar arms clamp around my waist. Catching my breath, I looked over to find Madden, his arms around me, wide-eyed and confused.

"Just a bad dream," I whispered grabbing my chest.

"You okay now?" His hands pulled me back down on the bed, and he loomed over me, propped up on an elbow.

I took a minute to look at him, into his deep green eyes flared with truth and honesty. His ebony hair that stuck up in clumps in the back. A small, crooked smile playing on his lips. He was so solid, so sure of himself and his path. He had a dream and went for it, even after the horrifying death of his parents. He was alone, yet he made something of himself. Against the odds, he'd finished high school, moved halfway across the country, and put himself through college and nursing school. He'd made himself a home and a life. He must be so proud. I knew I was, and I'd barely met him a few months ago.

"Baby? What are you thinking?" His brows lifted and creased. I realized I had been staring. With his eyes roaming over my face, I decided it was time to take what I wanted. I was brave last night, trying to explain my feelings. Even if I was going to have to leave soon. I couldn't let Devin get anywhere near Madden. But I wasn't ready to leave him yet. Especially after him asking me to stay again last night. No, my time was running out and now I needed to be brave again, to show him. Take what I wanted. No, what I needed.

I reached up my hand, wrapped it around the nape of his neck and pulled him down so that his nose was lightly brushing mine. My skin immediately heated. "Madden, please," I croaked.

"Please what, Joe?" His nose skimmed mine, leaving lingering brushes against the skin.

"Kiss me."

At first, he was gentle, tender. But I wanted more. I was needy and hungry for him. He took the hint when I opened my mouth for him, and his tongue brushed mine. They tangled together, sounds from each of us rang in my ears. That. That was the feeling I'd been searching for. It felt like home. God, I wanted to bask in the feeling forever.

After a few minutes and a few long breaths, his hand reached up and drew the hair from my forehead. I took advantage of the movement and pulled his upper body over mine. It felt so grounding having his weight on me, I wanted more. "Madden, please," I whimpered. He cupped my face in his hands, resting his weight on his elbows. "I need you. Please."

"You have me. Joe, God, you have me. Anything, baby."

I groaned as his words settled over me like a weighted blanket.

"I—I need." I was lost.

"What do you need? Tell me." He answered, his lips on my neck, chasing my Adam's apple when I swallowed.

"I-I-I don't know. I don't know. I've never done anything like this, but I want to. I want more. I need more. Please, Madden." Christ, I didn't even care that I was pleading for something I couldn't even describe. I was lost again, in that forest, waiting for Madden to take my hand and lead the way.

"Can I touch you, Joe?" He asked, his lips sliding along my collarbone. I couldn't stop the moan that poured out of my mouth.

"Oh, God, yes. Please. Touch me. Touch me." Maybe later I'd be humiliated but I couldn't think of anything but his hands on me. Touching my skin. Igniting me from the outside in, like no one had ever done before. And I trusted Madden. I knew he'd never take too much. I knew he'd keep me safe. In this moment, I couldn't think. I couldn't see or hear or breathe. All I had was my sense of touch. Like I was hyper aware of every inch of skin his lips kissed, his hands stroked, his hair tickled, his breath warmed.

"Can I take your shirt off, Joe? Nothing else, just your shirt?"

I nodded, unable to form an audible response. He lifted his entire body from mine, then sat up, taking his shirt off and throwing it somewhere behind him. I chuckled, knowing that he was compulsive about his clothing and having it neatly folded or put in the dirty clothes basket. It was a heady feeling knowing he was so into this moment with me that he didn't think twice about anything else. Pulling me up, he reached for the hem of my shirt and drew it over my head, then tossed it in the general vicinity of his. Pushing my shoulders down, he stayed seated and I felt myself turn the shade of ripe strawberries at his gaze. I couldn't watch him watching me, so I turned my head.

"No. Look at me," he said, gripping my chin with his fingertips. "You are so beautiful, Joe. I knew you would be. Just look at you." His gaze was heated, his eyes almost pure black as he ran a hand lightly down my neck to my chest. I shuddered at the feel of it. Goose bumps prickled over my arms and ribs. He snickered, and his hand made its way to my left nipple and circled it once. Twice. Then his soft fingertips trailed to the right side, stopping to linger on the inked numbers and letters he found there. "The only thing you've ever cared about." The words from his lips sounded reverent, like a prayer. His tongue circling my nipple caught me by surprise and my chest surged up off the bed.

"Oh, my God!" I yelled, embarrassed, yet my body didn't get the memo. It arched and reached, searching out more of that blissful feeling. We had been here before, but this felt so much deeper, more real. Because I'd given him permission and he was taking. And this time I was sure what I wanted.

Madden chuckled again, then his entire mouth took in the tan bud as he sucked and licked, torturing me in ways I'd never known existed. My eyes were closed in ecstasy and my hands were fisted at my sides. That wouldn't do. I needed to touch him, too. Wanted him to feel what I was feeling. I'd never touched anyone before like this, and I needed to reciprocate. One hand on his back, I fingered the lines of his rib cage, the bones wrapping around his body, protecting the vital parts of him. The parts that kept him breathing, walking, and pumping blood into his veins. He felt solid underneath. His shoulders were lined with strength and power. His arms corded with long, lean muscles. Jesus. It was surreal. Like I existed in another, braver body. But I wanted it to be me so badly.

I tried to pull him fully on top of me, to feel his weight, but also, to feel if he was as turned on as I was. I madly needed to know if it was just me. Being so fully inexperienced, the thought of me being hard as a tree trunk was embarrassing enough, but if it was confirmed that it was just me, I might've died a slow, painful death.

When I started wrapping my legs around his, he got the memo. Using his legs, he widened mine and fit himself neatly between them. I counted to three, my hands roaming his back muscles once again. When I hit three, I bucked my hips, searching for the answer I was dying to know.

"Holy fuck, Joe. Oh, shit." Madden's mouth was back on mine, his forearms framing my face. Honestly, I could have died happily right then, but then he moved. His hips thrust against me and I felt his hardness brush against mine through our clothes. It was the most magnificent feeling I'd ever experienced. Fuck dying. I needed more. I chased his tongue with mine, then went on the offense. Brushing my lips against his jaw. Taking small bites as I made my way down his neck to his shoulder. I found a spot and licked and sucked, then thrust my hips up again, seeking out that sweet sensation once more.

Madden levered himself up, taking his weight off my body and then rolled off me completely. I was mortified and scared that I'd done something wrong. Throwing my arm over my face, I rolled away from him. "I'm sorry," I whispered, tears stinging behind my eyes. His warm hand gripped my arm, pulling it away from my face. I turned further into the pillow, even more embarrassed.

"Hey, no. None of that. No hiding. Let me see your face, Joe." Shaking my head, my body lay still, facing away from him like an old sock that had been cast away. "Joe, please," he implored, using more force to flip me onto my back. "Oh, shit. You're crying? Joe, baby." Hands were on my face, thumbs wiping at the tears. "Did you think I was rejecting you?" he soothed, his voice low, almost cooing. I nodded, trying to look away. I didn't get far before he pulled my gaze back to him. "Joe, no. I'd never reject you. I stopped because I was getting so turned on and this was new for you. I didn't want to do anything you would regret. I didn't want to go too far. I'm sorry, Joe."

My gaze roamed his face. I could tell he wasn't lying. His

mouth was swollen and red. He had marks on his collarbones from my teeth and my tongue. And then he smiled this radiant smile at me that made him look like he'd stolen a car and gotten away with it. He was protecting me. Because that was what he did. I sighed and closed my eyes.

How did I get here? This gorgeous, talented, nice, safe man wanted me in his bed. And he *wanted me* wanted me. It was dizzying to consider.

"Tell me what's going on in your head? You're killing me here." He was still smiling, but one eyebrow was raised in question.

"I, uh. I just." Deep breath. "S-s-s-o, I promised myself awhile ago that I was g-g-going to tell you what I'm thinking and feeling more. Because I can trust you. I d-d-do trust you." I paused for a minute, trying to regain my bearings in my head. "I've never had feelings for a person before beyond just youseemlikeaniceperson kind of feelings. But now I do. For you, I mean. More than that. But I don't know what the label is. Or what it means. And I really, really liked what we just did a lot and I'd totally be on board for more of that if it was something you liked as well. But if you didn't, then that's okay too. I mean, I don't—,"

"Stop. Joe, stop." I stopped. "I really, really like you a lot. More than a lot. And I loved what we just did. I didn't want to stop. But I also want to enjoy this, and I want you to enjoy this, so I want to take the time with you so both you and I can remember this. I want to remember the morning that you woke up in my bed and we made out. And you let me touch you above the waist. And you touched me, too." He smiled down at me. "I want to be able to go to work today and think about how good you felt under me. How warm you were. How soft your skin was against my lips, against my chest. The way you took what you wanted." He looked away.

"What? Tell me."

"Fuck, Joe. My cock is leaking just thinking about you bucking up into me." My face flamed and he bent his head down, resting his forehead against my chest. "Sorry," he said. "Too much?"

"No. This is just—deeper? Yeah, deeper. Like, yesterday I would have turned into a giant ball of ash and blown away if you had said that to me. But today? Now? God, Madden. It's like the entire back wall and roof flew from the house and I can see an entire world that never existed before. There are birds and trees, lakes and other houses, other people. But mostly, there's you."

He lifted his head again and looked into my eyes. And then he kissed me.

~

"WILL you be here when I get back from work?" We'd lazily eaten frozen waffles with lots of syrup for breakfast and Madden was going to be working an extra-long shift today to cover for Adam. He'd been gracious enough to stay last night at the hospital when I'd needed Madden, so it was only fair. "I'm on from noon to four AM. It's going to kill me, but I can't say I regret the reason I'm doing it." He winked and I immediately flushed a brilliant shade of watermelon.

"If you're sure you aren't sick of me here, then yes." Taking our dishes to the sink, I flipped on the chrome sprayer and started washing the sticky congealed syrup away. I felt Madden's gaze on me the entire time, but I didn't say anything and neither did he. Once I'd turned the water off, he was at my back, his arms wrapped tightly around my waist.

"I've never been this happy, Joe."

~

THE CAFÉ WAS extra crowded today, as if everything was happening all at once. Schools were out for finals and testing, and we'd gotten quite a few business meetings happening in the recent weeks, which was great for business, but kept me running back and forth like a dog at a tennis match. I was just about to take another handful of plastic bags of garbage to the dumpster when Sloan rushed back into the kitchen and grabbed them out of my hands. "You've got someone out front asking for you," he said with a wink.

Confusion etched in my face, I pushed through the door and scanned the room. Standing at the end of the counter were Madden and Adam, both in scrubs, to-go coffees in hand. My heart leaped in my chest when we made eye contact and I quickly moved around the counter to stand next to them. And then it was awkward. Do I touch him? Does he touch me? Did I want him to? Did I want Adam to know? Did he want that? Instinctively, I balled my hands into fists and shoved them into my pockets, my face heating up. Before I could ask what they were doing there, Madden's arms were around me, his lips sealing over my forehead. I melted into the embrace, my eyes closing, lungs taking in the sweet musky scent of him. "I've missed you today," he whispered in my ear before leaning back. His hand traced down my arm until he pulled out my hand, interlaced his fingers with mine, immediately calming the bees buzzing in my stomach.

"I can't get Mads to talk about anything but you, so I dragged him over here for a quick coffee run. It's really good to see you again, Joe." Adam's eyes darted to our joined hands, he smiled.

"Oh, I—," I mumbled, stumbling over my words. I felt a reassuring squeeze to my hand and a smile formed on my lips. "It's n-nice to see you again, too, A-A-Adam," I croaked out finally.

"Hey, Adam, can you give me just a minute, please?"

Madden's eyes darted to Adam once, but his gaze was directed towards me. Adam nodded, smiled my way, then wandered off towards the door. I couldn't take my eyes from Madden. His gaze bored into me. "I did something, and I don't want you to be upset, okay?" Madden removed his hand from his pocket and thrust something at me. I looked down at the object in my hand, then back at his face.

"What are you—."

"Please just take it," he pleaded. He let my other hand drop and put his fingers in his hair, leaving a few wayward strands to flop onto his forehead. He looked so tired already.

"I can't take it. I don't need your phone, Madden. What are you doing?" I questioned, thrusting it back into his hand. He just pushed it back into mine.

"After last night, I can't do this again. You scared me, Joe. Please, can we talk about this later?" He looked behind me, towards where Adam was on his phone by the door.

"So, what, you just went out and bought me a phone?" I couldn't stop staring at it. I had no idea how upset I should be. I wasn't this person. No one gave me things. Especially not expensive things. I couldn't accept it. No way. When I looked back at his face, his features had twisted into a grimace.

"No, it's an old phone that I had in a drawer. I just added another line to my plan. It's not a big deal."

"The fact that you are all jumpy right now and can't look at me means it is a big deal and you know it." I huffed out a breath. "Why are you doing this?"

"Look, I just want you to have a way to contact me, or to call the police in an emergency, or if I need to talk to you—," his body suddenly pushed forward into me, which caused the phone to fall to the ground. The woman with a child on her hip apologized to Madden for her son knocking into him as she made her way towards the restrooms at the back of the café. "I have to get back to work and so do you. Can we please talk about this later?" His voice was stern as he bent to retrieve the phone, brushing it off as he slipped it into my hand again. Before I could respond he leaned forward, kissed my cheek, then said, "Please, just— let's talk later. Have a good shift." And then he squeezed my arm and walked over to Adam. I watched as he went, unsure of what I was feeling. Adam caught my gaze, saluted, then closed the door after them.

25

Madden

"Dude, he didn't look happy when we left. What the hell did you do to him in there?" Adam walked fast, trying to keep up with me as I darted from the café back to work. Fuck. That had not gone well. After what happened to Joe last night, I panicked. I'd been worried about him since day one, but I also hated not being able to get in contact with him like I would if he'd had a phone. I never knew where he was if he wasn't working. I almost went into panic mode if I walk into the café and he wasn't the first person I saw. And yeah, I know that sounded somewhat stalkerish, but if Joe had been anyone else I'd met, we'd have exchanged numbers and multiple text messages by now, so I didn't think I was being unreasonable. Or, at least, that was how I was justifying it in my head.

"I didn't do anything. I would never hurt him, Adam. Come on." My strides were gaining momentum until I felt Adam's hand wrench my arm back. "Hey, man. What the fuck?" I reared back on him and he raised his hands in surrender.

"Madden, man, calm down. What the hell is going on with you?" We both stopped on the sidewalk, then stepped closer to the street to get out of the way of the pedestrian traffic huffing at us as they passed by.

"Look, Joe was assaulted last night, which is why I left."

Adam squeezed my arm and said, "Yeah, I know that. I took your shift for you so you could be with him. Remember?"

"Right. And thanks again for that."

Waving me off he said, "You told me this morning that he was fine, though, right? He seemed okay just now. Well, until I left you alone with him," he smirked.

"He's fine now. I just wanted to be able to make sure he was safe. That I could know he was safe, so I grabbed an old phone and added another line to my cell plan." I shrugged, then added, "I didn't really think it would be such a big deal, you know? It's just a dumb phone, but it would give me peace of mind and hopefully make him feel safer."

"You are a dumb fuck."

Ready to punch him, I reared back.

"Whoa. Dude, chill. Listen to me." Dropping my arm, I took a breath in, calming my nerves. Adam laughed at my obvious anxiety and said, "You told me he's basically on his own, right?" I nodded. "Been that way for a very long time, yeah?"

"Yeah," I confirmed, voice low.

"And this is his first actual job, right? You said it was the first time he's had a bank account?" All I could do was keep nodding like a bobble head. "So, he's probably pretty proud of himself. And he should be. He's making something for himself. And he's got you now, too."

"He does," I agreed forcibly, my jaw tight.

"So, I'm willing to bet this is all new and overwhelming and he's feeling pretty good about it all, and then you show up and basically tell him he's got nothing, and what he's done isn't good enough, that he isn't safe."

"What? No!" I shook my head. Shit. Is that what I'd done? "No," I repeated. Oh, dammit. Adam was right. I'd offered him to stay at my apartment and he barely accepts that. He'd told me he felt like he was taking advantage. Then I started thinking. The way he always washed the dishes and put my clothes away after doing the laundry, he was earning his way. Paying me back. How did I not see this? Of course, he'd hate the idea that I was handing him a phone and a plan and didn't even discuss it with him.

I looked up at Adam and he was grinning at me. "Seriously? You think this is funny?"

"I do! You're cute when you're worried."

"Oh, shut the fuck up, asshole. Let's get back to work so I can figure out what I am going to do about the phone."

"This is awesome. Madden all cute, cuddly and worried."

After tripping him as I entered the automatic sliding doors of the ED I laughed and said, "You're like a cute little foal just learning how to walk."

MY SHIFT HAD BEEN EXTREMELY busy with trauma after trauma racing through the doors and a paperwork mix-up. It was an epic fail due to one of the first years' overlooking two patient files with the same last name and first initial. It was frustrating as hell listening to the family yelling at us as well as at each other. But, after that was sorted I took a quick minute to run to the break room for a quick soda and I sent a text to Joe.

{M}: **Hey, Joe, it's Madden**

Falling into the smooshed leather couch I waited for a response. Amy, a nurse I knew from the OB ward, walked in and went straight for the vending machine. After dropping in some change, she pushed a couple of buttons and picked up a can of Sprite that fell into the bin with a loud clang. Noticing me as she turned back towards the door, she waived her soda-free hand at me and said, "Hey, we are out of this on our floor, so I ran down here. It's good to see you, Madden. Have a good night," then made her way out into the hallway.

I checked my phone for a response but there was nothing. Was he still upset with me? All I wanted to do was help, but the more I thought about it, the more I ended up thinking I was stupid. I should have talked to him about it but deep down I knew he'd never accept something like that from me. I would have been surprised if he did, in fact. Joe was anything but prideful, yet I could understand trying to make something of himself. And I was damn proud of him for getting the job at the café and getting his life on track to have a future. I couldn't really relate, though. I'd grown up in an upper middle-class home with parents who were devoted to their family. My dad had a good job while my mom stayed home and took care of Anna and me. We never wanted for anything. We took yearly family vacations to theme parks and cabins with lakes. I played baseball as a kid and I don't remember my father ever missing a game. Obviously, it wasn't perfect, but it was full of wonderful memories. My mother used to read us stories before bed at night. She'd lie down on top of the covers of my bed and read me books about aliens and little green men, of wizards and magic. Hairy monsters and greedy children. And she'd do the best voices. She had this evil voice that was dark and menacing, then she'd start this low, full-bellied laugh that turned into a sinister cackle that used to give me goose bumps. My dad would always come in and save the day. He'd tuck my stuffed Snoopy dog in with me and kiss me on the forehead, always calling me Joe Cool. I had gone through a Peanuts phase where I'd only watched Charlie Brown and Linus getting up to no good, and Snoopy saving the day, with Woodstock always pinwheeling about behind him. After that, the nickname Joe Cool stuck for a few years.

I'd had the unconditional love of my parents and family until I was eighteen, a legal adult. And then I had opportunity. College, nursing school, Anna and her support, then her family. It was so hard to imagine the life that Joe had. He literally had no one he could count on. No one he could trust. Fuck, he didn't even have food on a regular basis. But was it so horrible of me to want to give him the things that I had taken for granted most of my life? Like shelter, safety, food and clothing? I wanted to provide those things for him. I wanted to be the person that he could trust, that he knew he could count on. I wanted to be his unconditional person.

I checked my phone again, despite knowing I'd not received a text. I needed to get back out on the floor, so I leaned forward and typed out another quick text, hoping for a response that I probably didn't deserve.

{M}: **I'm sorry, Joe. Please let me know we are okay.**

BY THE TIME my shift was over, I was worried I'd really fucked up. I had no new messages. Nothing from Joe. Was he really that upset with me? I was tired, cranky, and felt like I'd been put into a trash compactor. All I wanted to do was get home and see him.

Starting up my car, I pulled my seatbelt on and clicked the buckle into place. My eyes burned as I pulled out of staff parking onto the main road. It was after four in the morning, so there was little traffic, but the roads weren't empty. Realizing I had a death grip on the wheel, I tried to relax.

That I hadn't heard back from Joe worried me to no end. When I had asked him last night if he knew who attacked him, he visibly stiffened and paused before responding. I had sensed fear in his hesitation, and didn't want to make it worse. I'd planned to ask him about it later.

Pulling open the outer door to the complex, I felt like I'd been wearing concrete shoes. My steps were heavy, and each thud echoed loudly in the open expanse. The elevator pinged on my floor and I stepped out, suddenly nervous.

After setting down my bag and hanging my jacket up on the rack by the door, I made my way over to the lump of Joe, smashed once again into the corner of my couch.

"Hey," I said, placing my hand over his neck. "I'm so glad you're here, Joe."

After a couple of slow blinks, his face went from happy to see me to troubled.

"I need to shower, but why don't you get into bed? You'll be more comfortable." I held my hand out to him, helping him up. He nodded and slowly made his way down the hall, me trailing him as I turned off the lights.

ONCE I'D SHOWERED and gotten ready for bed, I could feel the exhaustion of my long day settle in. All I wanted was to hold Joe and sleep forever. I made my way over and slid into bed, tentatively wrapping my body against his. I had just begun to let my muscles relax when he spoke.

"I got your messages. I didn't ignore you." His voice was shaky and thin, like wet paper.

"Okay. So then—why? You didn't respond." I rested my face in his neck and breathed in, becoming addicted to his smell.

He gently shook his head. So, I waited. I knew Joe. It would either be a one-word answer, or an avalanche of words strung together that I'd have to unpack after. When he spoke, he didn't let me down.

"God, Madden. I held that thing in my hand like it was the

most important piece of plastic in the world. I was so afraid to drop it again, or to lose it. I... I've never had a phone. Ever. And then when it buzzed in my hand, I saw the messages on the screen, but when I touched the screen, it needed a password. I had no idea how to respond to you. And then you sent more. And then you were worried. And I couldn't do anything, Madden. I didn't know what to do. I'm so sorry I'm an idiot. Just take the phone back and I'll go."

I realized that I let him talk and I'd said nothing. I took a second to process what he'd said. He'd gotten my messages but didn't know how to respond. This entire time he was worried about *me*. How I would feel about it. Worried *for* me. Oh, fuck.

I put my hand on his shoulder and tugged. "C'mere," I said, turning him to face me. I cradled him against me, tucking his head under my chin. My poor, sweet boy.

"Hey, baby," I whispered. "I'm sorry I forced the phone on you and then left. I should have made sure you knew how to use it. That was my fault. I didn't even think about the password. I don't want you to worry about it anymore, okay?" I looked down at him and he nodded, then rested his head against my chest again. I felt him shudder and sigh, his body letting loose the tension he'd been holding like a tight spring uncoiling.

"Joe." My lips were pressed to his hair, and I took a deep breath, losing myself in his smell. "I've been falling for you for awhile now." We both lay in silence for a minute, just listening to each other's breaths. And then I said, "Tonight I landed. Crashed, actually." He didn't say anything, and that was okay. I'd finally put it out there, the words floating in a cloud of letters above us. The moment was there, and I was content. A few minutes later, his breaths were deep, and I thought he'd fallen asleep, but he pulled away and looked up at me, a quizzical look across his features.

"Tell me. Say the words so I know for sure what you are

saying." His eyes were half-lidded, and he looked so young and vulnerable.

I hesitated, blinking twice. Cupping his face in my hands, I looked straight into his beautiful ocean eyes and said, "Joe, I love you." And then I kissed him. He kissed me back, but my cheeks rapidly became wet. He was crying. "Joe," his name was barely a sigh from my mouth.

"How do you know? How can you be sure?" His voice cracked, and so did my heart.

"Oh, baby. I know because I would do anything for you. I can't stop thinking about you. I want you safe and happy. When you aren't with me, I feel numb. Like I've lost something vital."

Tears streaked down his face. I brushed them away with my thumbs, but soon there were too many. "You are the only person who has ever said that to me, Madden." I felt my own eyes well up and overflow. My beautiful, innocent, brave boy. It broke my heart to hear those words, yet I was so glad that I'd told him that I loved him. I meant it. Every word. And I was going to do my best to make sure he knew it.

26

Joe

Waking up next to Madden had become my favorite thing in the world. As I lay next to him, taking in the deep red of his lips, the subtle growth of whiskers around his jaw begging to be touched, I felt sewn up. As if raw from recent stitches, but mending.

My life had completely taken an about-face in the last few months and I still couldn't believe this was real. Madden loved me. That's what he said. To me! My heart started hammering in my chest, pounding in my ears. My breath was labored. Was I dying? As I fought to breathe, I closed my eyes and saw Devin. He'd found me again. How was this possible? I had nothing, yet he had chased me around the western United States for years. It was time for me to get moving again, but how could I? Not now. Not when I'd found a place to call home.

Taking some deep breaths, I let myself dwell on Madden's features. His long throat, the way his lips part when he's about to kiss me. The taste of him. The way he looked down at me yesterday.

Thinking back to the previous morning had my skin blazing and my dick hard. Being underneath Madden, feeling his weight on me was like heaven. It was something I'd never dreamed of wanting. Being held down by another person had always induced fear. Enough to cause a full-on anxiety attack just thinking about it. But yesterday, I'd relished in the sensation of it. The solid weight of Madden protecting me. Caring for me. Loving me. It was wondrous to be on the receiving end of something so powerful. And then feeling his long, hard cock against mine under our clothing was something I'd never forget.

I took a minute to search his face, then placed a kiss square on his red lips. I felt his smile and leaned back.

"Hey, there. What time is it?" He asked, looking at me softly. As if I was exactly what he was hoping to see when his eyes opened.

"I don't know. Late. Or early, I guess."

"Think you can sleep just a bit longer?"

Could I? His strong arms pulled me against him and before I knew it, I was gone.

I woke up to a delicious feeling in my bones. Heat lapped at my neck like flames that were quickly doused with water. Wait. What? I popped my eyes open to see the top of Madden's head moving over me, his hair splayed out on the side where he'd obviously not moved most of the night. He was biting and sucking my neck, a long sensual trail down my chest. I moaned as he popped my left nipple into his mouth and sucked before tonguing the bud, laving it over and over until he grinned and moved that magical mouth lower. Next, his tongue was in my belly button, twisting and lapping at the hole, kissing and sucking with abandon. With a force I couldn't help, my hips bucked up and he peered up at me with a mischievous grin. Then his face was buried in my belly, his tongue now darting under the waistband of my boxer briefs. Holy, shit. I thought I'd been a sunburned tomato before, but I was blood red now. Shame crept into my thoughts. As much as I loved every tingle of desire that was bursting and lighting up my body, I was embarrassed and felt debased.

What the hell was I thinking? This perfect man wanted someone that didn't exist. He deserved a man who was confident and real. Who had a family and a past to be proud of. Someone who could meet his family and friends without having a panic attack and locking themselves away from the world. Someone who could love him and know what that meant. And that wasn't me.

With a strength I didn't know I had, I pulled myself up from the bed and I ran.

I fucking ran faster than I ever had before. I ignored Madden's cry of worry.

I only stopped to grab my shoes and jacket from the door. I didn't stop to put them on. I couldn't. I fled the scene of the crime like the villain I was. The one that I'd turned into. I was a shadow, not real. I was the little boy in the cartoon I'd seen in the hospital waiting room all those years ago waiting for my mother, sitting alone for hours. It felt like days. It probably was. And after a while, a family was there. A real family. A mom and a dad and a boy and a girl. I hadn't seen the boy, but the mom and dad and girl were there waiting. I remembered the mom telling the girl that her brother would be fine. Just a broken arm. He'd have a neat cast that they could all draw and write on. And then she told her to watch the show. I'd never forget that night. I sat there, watching the tiny television up on the ledge in the corner of the room. The picture was wavy, but it was about a boy and a dragon and the boy met his alter ego, a paper version of himself. And I remember the words vividly in my mind. "Jackie Draper, meet Jackie Paper."

I ran down past the parking lot and down a narrow alley before I stopped and knelt to put my shoes on. I had taken my socks off, so it was difficult to slip them on, but I managed. And I kept thinking about that night in the Chicago hospital. I had pretended that they were my family. That I was the boy that they were waiting to take home. To tell me that everything would be fine. And when I grabbed their hand, they'd squeeze mine even tighter.

I stood there, in the alley, like a scarecrow. I was Jackie Paper. Well, Joe Paper. I was the 2-dimensional version of a person. I'd been that all my life, but I didn't want that anymore. I took a few steps, not looking back. I wondered what it would take for me to be 3D. Or 4D. Or even HD. I needed to go, and I needed to think, figure a way to get what I wanted.

As I walked, my boots chafing against my bare skin, I thought about how much my life had changed since I'd met Madden. I had friends now, something to look forward to. A job, a paycheck. I'd been to the zoo. I'd seen families. I'd eaten foods that I'd never thought I'd try. My entire world had opened in such a short amount of time. Fucking hell. I even had someone who told me he loved me, and was trying to show me not even 30 minutes before.

I felt the tears forming as my throat clenched and I couldn't hold them in. I was flayed open and raw around the edges like a gunshot victim. It wouldn't surprise me if I was bleeding internally. But what would it take? If I really had these things— these both tangible and intangible things in my life now—did that mean that I was a real person? What was keeping me a black and white version of myself? How much more would it take to become Technicolor?

As I made my way through the busy streets back to the gym,

I thought about the family at the hospital all those years ago. I thought about how worried they were for their son. And when the doctor announced he could leave how envious I was at the way they looked at him when he walked out into the waiting room. His family enveloped him into a hug so big you couldn't tell one person's arm from another. It was a tangle of limbs and it brought tears to my eyes. I watched them as they gathered their belongings from the orange plastic hospital chairs. And the boy looked at me and smiled. I tucked my knees up under my chin on the chair, abandoned and alone. A little while later, that same boy came back with his father. He looked at me, right in my eyes. And he handed me a stuffed bunny. He said that he had saved money and wanted me to have something to keep me company, so he bought it for me at the gift shop. And then he left. And I had Bunny.

27

Madden

I had never really considered myself a complete and total moron. I was a college graduate. I'd become a nurse. I was one of the top nurses in the state for fuck's sake. But I let my dick get in the way with Joe again, and I'd worried I'd lost him for good. The morning played over and over in my mind like a broken record. One second, he was moaning and writhing beneath me and the next he was out the door. I ping-ponged between guilt and anger all day. Guilt that I'd read his signals so very wrong and gone farther than he was comfortable with. And I was not okay with that. Then anger warred with the guilt over taking advantage of Joe and Joe just literally running away from me. Jesus, I felt like I'd earned enough trust from him that I didn't deserve to be treated like I'd done something that crossed a line. He didn't even try to stop me. He didn't say anything.

I was beyond the point of knowing what to do. I felt like

part of my body was on autopilot, the other part dead to the world. After spending considerably too much time contemplating my life, I got up and showered, then threw my sheets and clothing into the laundry. As much as I wanted to sleep with the scent of Joe surrounding me, I also hated the thought of lying in sheets that smelled of him without having him tucked in close to me. The feel of his warm, soft, pliable body against mine. Hearing his lungs fill and exhale. I'd never slept next to another man and felt like we fit together so well, like matching Lego pieces. My chest stung at the thought.

After getting the laundry going, I stepped into the kitchen for a quick bowl of cereal. Figuring I'd feed Batman and Robin first, I walked past the table and saw the phone sitting there. That damn phone. I was almost positive it was mocking me, yet I couldn't bring myself to touch it. It was a physical reminder of how the last twenty-four hours had gone so wrong. I found myself sitting at the table, head in my hands, staring at the piece of plastic. Were Joe and I just too many worlds away to make this work? I would never be able to put my feet in his theoretical shoes and walk a mile. I would never fully understand the pain he suffered, the sheer loneliness that he'd been resigned to. But was that really what he needed? Someone who'd been there, done that? Or someone who wanted to give him every experience that he'd never known? Because that I could do. And I'd wanted to so badly. I felt his loss in my bones, like the elderly felt oncoming rain. I ached. I needed him. He'd walked into my life, into my apartment and into my heart. But I had no direction. There was no next step. So, I stared dumbly at the cell phone on my table until it was time to leave for work. With some trepidation in my step, I made myself get on with the day.

❧

"ADAM, I need you to grab the coffees today, man. I can't go in there." Work was slammed and Adam had a well-needed break coming up. There was no way I was going to the café today. I just couldn't bring myself to see Joe until I knew what I wanted and how I felt about everything. I was in love with him, yes. But having him run out on me like that really did a number on my ego, and I felt battered and bruised. And sending Adam would at least give me the presence of mind to know that Joe was okay. That he was safe. My mind was telling me that we both needed this space. My heart felt like an icepick was resting gently against it, just waiting for one wrong beat to puncture a hole and destroy the entire thing. But yeah, I wasn't being dramatic. Nope. Never.

"What? No way, man. You go and I'll cover for you. Go see your man." Adam winked and then did an exaggerated eyebrow lift until finally, he read something in my face that told him the ice pick was dangerously close now. It wouldn't take much. I watched as his smile dropped and he laid a hand on my shoulder. "Shit, what did you do now?" I huffed out a laugh that had no mirth.

"Fuck, man. I don't know," I answered, shaking my head. "One minute we were absolutely fine and the next he was running out the door. Literally."

"What, did he see you naked?" He laughed, trying to lighten the mood, but when I gave him a side-eye, he winced. "Oh, shit. He saw your cock and ran?"

"Fuck, shhhhhhhhhhhhhhhhh," I whisper yelled at him as I hustled him into a closet. "No, you asshole. We were making out and everything was fine and then he freaked and ran. We both still had pajamas on, so fuck you." I growled, then smacked his chest with the back of my hand.

"Okay, okay," he replied, with a throaty laugh. "Sorry. It's still kind of funny."

I gave him a minute to read the desperation in my eyes. "I

just don't know what to do next, but I can't go in there today. Please just get the coffee, huh?" I tried my best puppy dog look.

"Yeah, okay. But you're buying," he said, smirking as I pulled my wallet out of my scrubs.

FUCK me if I hadn't turned myself into a total pansy in the last twenty minutes. The sliding glass doors of the ED seemed to rarely open unless there was some catastrophic emergency, yet when I sent Adam off to the café, the door was in constant motion. And I was a Jack-in-the-Box popping up to look every damn time. I was also convinced that my watch had somehow stopped, or we'd gotten stuck in some fold in the fabric of time or other chrono related debacle. But no. It was just Adam being Adam. And by that, I meant that he probably had been standing outside waving his hand around to engage the door sensors just to fuck with me. I had it so bad for Joe if this is what I was like after a few hours. I couldn't think of anything else. I ran my hands through my hair, pulling at the ends.

"You okay there, hotshot?" Tina asked me with a wink. Then her face fell. "You look like you're waiting on the grim reaper to show up for you."

I blew out a breath and said, "Yeah, just waiting on Adam to get back here with coffee. Thank you, though." It seemed to pacify her curiosity, because she wandered down the hall towards the break room. Fuck, I needed to figure this thing out with Joe.

"Tell me the truth—did you sit and stare at the door this entire time?" Adam had materialized with two coffees and a paper sack.

"Very funny, now tell me what happened before I lose my mind," I whined, taking my coffee out of his hands.

He leaned against the wall, smirking at me. As I turned to

walk away, he grabbed my arm. "Hey, Mads, come on. I didn't realize you were this crazy over him. I'm sorry, man. Come back here." I gave him the finger, then shrugged, making my way back over.

"Please tell me he's okay?" I said, after a deep inhale.

"Well, when I walked in, he was in the back but he came out to clean something. He saw me and turned a brilliant shade of cherry, which is probably fitting, hmmmm?" Before I could punch him, he continued. "I put on my best smile and asked him how he was, like a good friend would." He paused to take a sip of his coffee, then opened the paper bag and rooted through it like it held some integral clue. Before I could scream, he looked at me and said, "Oh, he seemed okay. I didn't mention you, but he asked if work was busy and I told him it was no worse than any other day. Let's see..." and then he was back to his bag. I ripped it out of his hand. The shocked look on his face just about sent me through the roof. "Jesus, Madden. If you are this upset you should talk to him, not send me over there like some Inspector Gadget. Seriously, I don't know what I'm supposed to be finding out and reporting back, but I swear you're taking me back to 3rd grade and I don't appreciate it. Kim Johnson totally kicked my ass during lunch in 3rd grade. It was horrifying."

With that he turned and headed to the break room and I turned into stone. He was right, of course. I was acting like an idiot, but I was working until tomorrow morning and I couldn't get in touch with Joe. I had tomorrow night off, so maybe he'd be working, and I could stop in. I needed a plan. There was no way I was going to lose him. Not like this. Not when I had just found him.

～

"DOUBLE SHIFTS SUCK DONKEY BALLS. I hate that we got stuck

here again. It's going on eighteen hours for me." Adam yawned and let his head fall back against the wall with a bang. I winced, then ran my hands down my face. I hit exhausted eight hours ago. We both ended up working extra because of the three-car pileup on the freeway that happened just as we were about to clock out. Rain was coming down in sheets, so it was no shock that there were accidents in abundance. One of the other nurses, who was typically reliable, called in sick and then another one got stuck in traffic coming in from a vacation in Seattle, so I said I'd just stay and cover. I still had no idea what I was going to do about Joe, so going home felt like the worst idea ever.

My sandbagging had officially come to an end, though. With everyone stable for now, there was a new shift of nurses on staff and we were officially off-shift. I had so many visions of my bed. A lot of them included Joe, but I tried to wipe those away like a name written in sand. After slapping Adam on the back, I slunk my way to my car and practically fell into the seat. It was already after eight AM and I was feeling it. My phone pinged in my pocket and I spent a full minute trying to wrestle it out from under my seat belt, my shirt, my pants and the steering wheel. I probably looked as though I was in a fight with a bee in my car, and when I finally saw the screen, it showed a missed call from Anna. I'd missed three calls from her last night and then I had a couple of messages asking where I was and when I was getting off. From the way things ended up yesterday I'd say the latter was highly unlikely. I rolled my eyes at my own stupid joke. After pushing the call button, I held the phone to my ear and pressed my forehead to the steering wheel.

"I assume you had to work an extra shift because of the highway accident?" She said in a rush, obviously busy doing something.

"Yeah, I did," I replied through a yawn. I looked at myself in the rearview mirror and cringed. I needed a haircut and about fifteen hours of sleep.

"You headed home now?"

"Yeah, I called you back first, but I'm leaving. What's up? I saw I missed a couple of calls from you."

"Oh, that. Right. Well, I hope you won't be mad." She used her cheery sing-song voice and I tensed.

"Why? Are you okay? Is David?"

"Oh, yeah, everyone is fine. Sorry. Nothing bad like that."

"Fuck, A. Don't do that to me. I can barely even function right now. Have some compassion for your little brother."

She laughed. "It's just... well, I went to your apartment last night because I made this ginormous cake and it was too much for us and so I brought you a container full."

It sounded like there was more to the story, so I waited. All I could hear was her breathing. "Is this some sort of tryout for a new phone sex job?"

"Oh, you perv! No," she laughed. "Just... I left you another surprise, so if you see something else, don't flip out, yeah?"

"What? I'm too tired for this. What are you talking about?" I let out a moan. "You didn't find a cat or dog, or something did you? And leave it at my place?"

She laughed, then squeaked. "Well, no. Not exactly."

"What the hell, Anna?"

"It's nothing like that. Just go home and be surprised. And I'll call you later. Bye!"

"Anna? Anna!" I looked at the screen and she had hung up on me. Unbelievable.

Putting the car in gear, I headed home. By the time I'd parked behind my building I couldn't even remember driving there. Did I stop at red lights? Fuck, I must have. I peeled myself out of the car and made my way inside, up the elevator, into the apartment. Throwing my shoes on the rack, my shirt and pants ended up hanging over the back of the couch, and I grabbed a bottle of water. After washing my hands in the sink, I took my water and made my way to bed.

The apartment was blissfully dark because of the rain, so I felt my way to my magical bed and fell into it. I might have even moaned. I realized quickly that I must have because I heard giggling. In a flash I was upright, hand on the lamp, blinking hard at the sudden stream of light. "What the hell?" I said. I was standing in my boxer briefs with my hand shielding my eyes. I'm sure any sort of intruder would have balked at my vigor.

"Hey, Madden," whispered a tiny voice belonging to the love of my life. I immediately felt every muscle in my body go slack and I wanted to cry. I realized that I hadn't really breathed since he ran out more than a full day ago. Instead, I'd been in suspended motion. Life continued, but I didn't participate. All I wanted to do was bury my face in his neck and breathe him in.

"Joe. What are you—?" I asked, then remembered the phone call. "Anna let you in?" He nodded. "Were you waiting in the hallway?" Another nod. I answered with one of my own, then crept back into bed, propped up against my pillows. He was sitting on the other side and I could tell he was unsure of what to do. I lifted my arm as he swiftly found his spot against my body, head against my chest. It just felt so right, which made me let out a long sigh of contentment. "How long have you been here?" As soon as I asked, he tensed like he'd done something wrong, then answered, "Since ten o'clock last night."

"What? Are you serious?" I had to think again what time it was now. "You've been here all night alone?" This time he flinched, and I realized how that sounded. "No, I didn't mean it like that. I'm so glad you're here. I didn't realize how glad, to be honest. I spent all day and night worried about you. About what happened, you leaving." I shook my head, trying to get my thoughts organized through the haze of my tired brain. "I don't know what—"

Sitting up, Joe turned to look at me and said, "I'm so sorry,

Madden. And I know I keep saying that, but I don't know how to do this. I don't know how to react the right way. What I'm supposed to do or say or—,"

"Hey, hey, no." I cupped his face. "I don't want you to apologize. Joe. Baby. I want to tell you something and I want you to listen to me because it's important, okay?" My thumb traced his perfect pink bottom lip and his tongue crept out to lick it. I shuddered and moaned at the contact, my dick filling from that one, single touch. "Fuck," I inhaled, dropping my hand from his face. We needed to talk. He didn't need me pressuring him and I couldn't handle him running away again. This wasn't going to work. I was too close to him. Pulling the blankets off, I stood, pacing the room. God, I was exhausted. After my hand went through my hair a few times, I stopped and let my gaze roam over Joe.

Sitting upright on my bed, I could see he was tense. That wasn't what I'd wanted, but I needed to say this.

"Okay, so I think I just need to get some things out in the open and then I want you to talk to me, too. But I feel like we really need to get on the same page here, Joe, if this is going to work." His lip quivered and it was all I could do not to pull him into my arms. "Baby, none of this is bad. I promise. It's just communicating, okay?" I waited a beat until he nodded, his lips drawing into a straight line and his shoulders pitched back, steeling himself. "I know you worry about your reactions, but you shouldn't. You are a human being with feelings, Joe. You are *allowed* feelings. No one should have ever taken that away from you or made you feel like it was wrong." I took a breath and shook my head. "Everyone reacts differently to situations and there is not one damn thing wrong with that. Not one. Okay?"

He watched me intently, but I could see he was skeptical, even hesitant. And that wouldn't do. "You've been through a lot. You've lived an entire life, like I have, but differently. We are going to react in dissimilar ways to situations and that's okay. We'd be bored if we were the same. You keep me guessing and I love that about you. But, Joe," I said reverently, then lowered myself to the edge of the bed. "You can't keep running away from situations if this is going to work. If this is going to go somewhere. We have to talk about things." Grabbing his hand, I squeezed it once, then said, "You have to tell me what bothers you or frightens you and what doesn't feel good. If I go too fast, or even too slow. If you hate something I cook. Or wear. Or watch." I couldn't help but crack a smile. "I want you, Joe. You. Not someone who agrees with me or wants to gauge my reactions so he can imitate them. I want *you*," I said, punctuating the word. I felt his hand tremble and looked down at it in mine. I whispered, "I want you so badly."

Joe didn't move or speak at all. When I looked up, he was biting his lip to keep from crying and I knew he was worried. He had no reason to be and I couldn't help myself. I crawled over and pulled him into my lap, burying my face in his neck like I'd been dreaming about. He was warm, soft and smelled sweet like honey and something uniquely Joe. After a minute he shivered, and I pulled the covers up over our legs.

Letting out a shaky breath, he said, "I get so tired, Madden. Tired of feeling alone. Not just lonely, but like I'm the only one. I don't ever know if what I'm doing is right or if it's stupid. It never really bothered me before because it was just me, on my own. But now... Now I'm not on my own. I have things. I mean, a few things, but things just the same. And people, too."

His beautiful blue eyes caught me in their gaze, and I smiled, encouraging him to keep talking.

"I want to be normal. And before you say something about there being no normal, yeah, Madden there is. There is the baseline of knowing what to do when you walk into a situation. I don't have the practice or experience that other people do. I want to believe I'll get there. I have to believe that, and I'm starting to. You've helped me see that. But. But, it means I feel stupid or unworthy or sad when everyone else seems to know what to do or think or say and I have no clue."

I nodded, because yeah, I could understand that. It made sense to me and anyone would feel self-conscious if put into a situation like that. But if every situation was different, I could see how it would mean walking on eggshells through life. And then dealing with people getting mad at that reaction. I didn't even know what to say, how to make it better. My heart ached at how much Joe felt every day and how many experiences he dealt with that caused this kind of response.

"You didn't do anything wrong yesterday." Before I could argue he shook his head at me. "No, you didn't. If you were taking things too far or too fast, I could have told you and I know you would have stopped. I know that, Madden. I trust you." His mouth turned up at the edges and I realized he was smiling at me. I leaned forward but hesitated. He met my lips with his and we kissed softly for a minute. It wasn't deep and it wasn't sloppy, but it was *something*. It was a promise. I pulled back and smiled at him, then kissed his forehead for good measure.

"Tell me why you ran, then, baby." *Before my heart breaks.*

His eyes tracked the ceiling before looking at me again. "I don't understand why you want me. Why you said you loved me. What you are doing with me. You could have anyone. Men without enough baggage to need a forklift. Without enough issues to own a magazine. I don't want to be the person that people talk about when they meet us. You know. Those, 'Why is he with him? He could do so much better' looks. I've seen them all my life. I can't—"

"Hey. Shush. I won't listen to you talking about the man I love like that. And yeah, I heard you say *loved* like it was past tense. It's not. I love you. And baby, what you just said is so crazy I can't even take it seriously."

"No, it isn't. It's—"

"Joe, please. I love you because you are smart, creative, and funny, and you keep me on my toes. You make me smile, and you make me want to be a good man. To show you everything in the world there is to see. You make me *feel*, Joe. No one else has ever done that. You are beautiful, sweet, and kind. You light up my world when I see you happy. The look you get when you see something new? God. It's like you radiate pure joy. And you make me feel like I have done something right, Joe. Like if I matter to you, I've accomplished something in my life. And I want that. I want that so much."

Joe rested his head on my chest and said, "I want that, too. You matter to me. You are the only love I've ever known."

"Let's not talk anymore. I think we've said all the important bits now. I've been up for over twenty-four hours and I'm starting to get cloudy." I turned and started throwing excess pillows off the bed, but Joe was just looking at me like I was a math problem he couldn't solve. "What's the matter?"

"I don't know how to do the close touching stuff. I don't know how or when. I'm never sure what's right."

I had to think of what he was saying through the haze in my head. "Okay, I get that. How about this... I will probably never, ever, ever not want to be touched by you. So, if you feel like holding my hand, do it. If you want to rest against me, go for it. If you want kisses, kiss me. Joe, I don't think I could ever get enough of you."

"Yeah, okay. This is one of those things that I'm going to have to trust you on. So, you have to tell me if you aren't comfortable. And I'm not sure about how I feel, so I don't know what to say right now. But I promise to tell you if it's too much."

"Hey, baby?" I asked, looking down at him. He was now tucked up against me again, his forehead against my chin.

"Yeah?"

"I love you." And then we slept.

28

Joe

Knowing that Madden had a very long day and night, I left him in his bed to sleep. I'd stayed up waiting for him as long as I could, but had fallen asleep somewhere around four in the morning, so I was able to sleep for a few more hours after we'd had our talk. Now that it was early afternoon, I needed to get up and do something. I was anxious. Jittery. I felt alive for once. I was so proud of myself, for once. I'd talked to Madden. Really talked. Shared my fears and worries, and I'd listened. My heart was at full capacity as I fell asleep in his arms, safe.

When I woke up, I felt his hardness against my back as he held me close and it was all I could do to hold in my moan. I wanted him so badly, in every way. I'd waited long enough. I trusted him, I knew I did. It wasn't about that. It was more that my brain held me back when it came to sex. It told me it was filthy because of Devin. Because of my father. All my life sex had been dirty. Something you take from someone else to give yourself pleasure. To make your problems lessen, even for a little while. It was a selfish act. That was all I knew. On the streets it was a desperate act. For food, money, drugs, for safety even. Or it was stolen.

I shuddered in the kitchen, thinking of the times I'd seen people being taken, used, then discarded. Only to go back again and again, hoping for something I didn't understand.

I took a long pull on my water bottle and set it back down on the table. My thoughts kept drifting to Madden last night. The way he looked at me before we kissed. The way his green eyes turned black with heat. How his mouth felt on my body just a few days ago. This was different than anything I'd known before. Madden was different. It didn't feel like him taking, when he looked at me like I was a light in the darkness. It didn't sound like taking when he said he wanted to matter to me. And I hoped it wouldn't feel like taking if I was giving myself to him. And I was desperate to do so. I palmed my ready cock under the table just thinking about Madden in his warm bed right now. His eyes closed, mouth soft. Smelling musky, warm and safe.

I wondered if he wouldn't want me because I had no experience. If he'd feel bad about it. Shaking my head, I let out a huff of breath. I didn't want that, for him to feel bad. Because that felt like taking, not giving. And I wanted to give this to him, myself. I had nothing else. I couldn't give him anything like he'd given me. Friends, safety, a place to sleep, food. I couldn't give him anything in return but myself. I could only hope that it was something he'd want.

My mind wandered to the fish and I sat watching them darting through the water in freedom, searching for the flakes of food I'd sprinkled over the surface. I thought about what Madden said last night. How I had different experiences and how it affected the way I saw things. And it did. I wasn't comforted by things. By people. I had to comfort myself. I didn't want embraces, conversations and smiles. I never wanted to be seen. But I sure as hell wanted Madden to see me. I wanted his comforting touches, his embraces, his soft breath in my hair and against my neck. I had my mind made up and I wanted this. I wanted everything with him.

AFTER A WHILE I decided to get dressed and run out for food. I didn't know what Madden would feel like eating, but I knew what he liked from the café, so I grabbed my clothes and my shoes and headed out. The rain had stopped and was now a light trickle that felt cold against my skin. I was grateful for the jacket I'd bought and thought about what I should be buying for myself now. Now that I had a bit of money. I should just save it. I had already purchased a few more clothing items and I should probably start saving as much as I could. Not that I was spending recklessly. I didn't even think I could. I needed to figure out what I was doing now, though. Now that I had a steady income. It might not be much, compared to some, but it was more than I'd ever had in my life. It was also enough on a regular basis that I hoped I'd be able to start saving for rent on an apartment. God, to have a place to live. That was something I'd dreamed about for years, and for the first time, it felt tangible. Like I could see the possibility ahead. It turned my chest warm, and I wondered to myself as I pulled the door to the café open, if I could possibly make Madden proud of me. If he'd feel the burn of pride in his gut if I accomplished something I'd never seen in my future. That single thought brought a smile to my face.

"Hey, sweetheart, you've got two days off. What on Earth are you doing here?" Lulu was like a grandmother to me. Or a fairy godmother. Yeah, that fit better. She'd been the one to first give me a break and I wasn't sure how I could ever thank her enough. I owed everything to her.

"I missed you, Lulu," I said bashfully. She scoffed, tossing her hand in the air, a dismissive gesture.

"Pfffft. You are too young and energetic to be sitting around thinking of me. Now, what brings you in, Joe? Everything okay?" Her eyes turned soft and she looked a bit worried.

"Oh, yeah, it's great actually. I was hanging out with Madden and thought I'd grab a couple of sandwiches, cookies and coffee to go for us." I could feel my face heat up and I tried to ignore the embarrassment.

"Well, that's real nice of you. Real nice. Just tell me what you both want, and I'll get them sorted and bagged for you." The smile on her face was devilish.

I HAD to wait a couple of minutes for someone to leave the building and let me in before I could make my way up to Madden's apartment. I'd left the door to his place unlocked so that I didn't have to wake him if he was still asleep and I didn't have a key of any kind to get back in. I'd only been gone about thirty minutes, so I figured it would be safe and he'd still be sleeping but as soon as I shut the door, I heard his hurried footsteps crashing down the hallway. He appeared a second later, hair disheveled in a pair of pajama bottoms and no shirt. He looked good enough to lick all over. When my eyes finally made their way from his abs to his face, I was taken aback to find a scowl there. I crossed the room to the table and set the bag and tray of coffee cups down.

"What's wrong?" I asked, my head tilted.

His hand immediately went to tug at his hair as he clenched his eyes shut. After a few breaths, he said, "You went to get coffee?" His eyes were still closed, and I could tell he was breathing heavy.

"I did. Are you okay?" I wondered aloud.

"Shit, Joe. I'm sorry," he answered, eyes focused on me again.

"Sorry? For what? What's going on?" My hands were fisted against the back of the kitchen chair and I was keenly aware that my heart was beating out of my chest. Before I could let my throat close, I said, "You're scaring me. Just tell me what's going on." I heard the tremor in my voice and saw his face drop the minute he registered the sound.

He shook his head and stepped towards me, but I flinched before I could take it back. "Joe. Baby. I woke up and you were gone. There was no note." A forced smile appeared on his face and I stepped back from the chair, retreating from where he was closing the gap between us. "I'm sorry I freaked out. I thought you left again. I was out of my mind." He turned to face the table, taking in the coffee and brown paper sack before he looked at me again. "I'm sorry I thought the worst. That you walked out again. I'm sorry that I hurt you." And he was. I knew he was.

"I should have left a note," I said numbly. "I've never done this. I told you I'm no good at this." I dared a look at him and his face was covered in what looked like something I wasn't sure I'd ever seen directed at me. It looked like...love. I took the few steps between us at a rush and buried my face in his warm, hard chest, my hands fisting the worn cotton of his pajama pants. He wrapped his strong arms around me and kissed my hair over and over.

"Please don't ever leave me." His words were so soft, I felt them in his chest more than heard them. I wondered if he'd even meant to speak them at all.

～

AFTER OUR LATE AFTERNOON BREAKFAST, I washed up the dishes while Madden showered. He hadn't mentioned any plans, and I knew he didn't have to work again until tomorrow. I was soaping up juice glasses when I felt a desire pooling in my groin thinking about Madden in the shower. His body covered in soap bubbles. Streams of water brushing them slowly down his heated skin. Would they pop or would they trace smooth, clean pathways over each ridge and indent of his muscles on their descent down his lithe body? With a clang, the glass hit the ceramic bottom of the sink, but thankfully didn't crack or shatter. Fuck me, I wanted to see Madden wet and soapy.

Abandoning the dishes, I made my way down the hallway, telling myself I could do this. I wanted this. I really did. The only fear that was left was not knowing what Madden's response would be. But, like he'd said earlier, there was no way I could predict that, so I continued into the bedroom, taking off one piece of clothing at a time until I was desperately needy and naked. My swollen shaft was aching in need like I'd never known before. It scared me how much my body wanted, *needed* him. My breath hitched as I took in the sight before me. Water rivulets created veins and pathways down the obscured glass walls. Madden's tight body on display just feet away. I took a deep, steeling breath and forced my legs forward, one foot after the other. When my hand met the latch, Madden turned and gasped. "What are you—," was all he said before I pulled the door opened and pushed my way inside the space.

"Oh, God." Two words were all I let him get out before I claimed his wet mouth with mine. My hands found purchase on his chest, fingers trembling as I traced his nipples with my thumbs. He pulled back to look into my eyes, a questioning look. He must have found the answer there because his hands framed my face and took what he wanted from my lips. He sucked, bit, and licked over every inch of my mouth. I thought I knew what kissing Madden was. Turns out I had no idea. My knees became weak as he backed me into the wall.

I needed more, but his hands were still on my face and in my hair. "Madden, please," I moaned.

"What, baby? Anything. Just tell me what you need." His hands fell to my shoulders as he sucked along my jaw, placing kisses over bite marks to soothe the burning skin.

"I-I-I neeeeeed." I couldn't even get words out. "Touch," I panted. "Me."

I didn't think I'd ever heard a sound like that come out of a human being. It was equal parts whimper and groan and it was delicious. My cock was leaking steadily, mixing with the water pouring over us. I'd never felt so needy in my life. "Madden, please." I was whining now. I'd turned into a child. A needy, whiny child.

Suddenly, the water turned off and Madden's lips were gone. Before I could protest, he had the door open and had me by the hand, leading me out onto the bath rug. He pulled two towels off the rack and wrapped one around his waist. The other, he used to gently dry the water from my hair, face, shoulders, then further down until he was kneeling at my feet, towel caressing my hipbones. My face was tomato red and hot as I watched him work, his own face a breath away from my hard cock. He stopped his ministrations with the towel only to look up at me, a plea in his eyes. Before I knew it, his lips were pressing kisses on the delicate head, tongue licking around the crown. I fell back against the shower door, having never felt anything this perfect before. My gaze was transfixed on his mouth, the way his tongue kept jutting out to touch me. And then he opened wide and took me into his hot, wet heat with a groan. Before I even understood what was happening, my hips were bucking and my hands were in his hair, tugging him closer, pushing him away, holding on for dear life. I felt his hands on the backs of my thighs, gently kneading the muscles there. I couldn't think, couldn't breathe. And then it was all too much. "Oh, God, stop. Please don't stop. You have to stop. I'm going to come." Madden's cheeks hollowed out and he sucked with even more pressure, his tongue lapping at the underside of the crown. Everything tensed, and I let go. I let go into his mouth, my eyes shut tight, hands balled into fists, and I screamed.

When I finally caught my breath and opened my eyes, Madden was licking my spent cock, then his lips. They were wet and sinful. "Oh, my God, Madden. You swallowed my cum." He just smirked at me and winked. "Is... I mean... are you... is that okay?" I may have gone into shock.

"Uh, yeah," he said, looking proud and not at all humiliated like I would have been. "Yeah, it is. It's you, baby. It's delicious."

I felt flames licking up my body starting in my knees. I reached out to him and he stood, taking my mouth with his, the taste of my seed on his tongue. It was a heady feeling, knowing that we'd shared something so intimate. So personal, so me, as he said, with him. After a few lingering kisses, I looked down at him. I licked my lips. He was seven inches of thick, fully erect, velvet-covered steel and I wanted to touch him, but didn't know how. He must have felt my hesitation because he gently whispered, "Joe, you don't have to do anything."

Well, fuck. Wasn't that just like Madden? To be selfless and amazing? To give and not want anything in return? No way was I letting him get away with that. I tentatively touched my fingertips to his shaft. It felt so different than my own. He was thicker, but it was so hot and wet, precum dribbling from the slit. I didn't think I was ready for what he'd given me, but I wanted to make him feel good. I wrapped my fingers around him and gently squeezed. The needy moans that came from deep in his throat were enough to give me the confidence to continue. Whispering into his neck I asked, "What do you like?" He shook his head, incapable of words. I was on my own. I tried a few different techniques that I liked on myself. I twisted my hand on the upstroke. I thumbed the slit. Alternated between fast and then slow rhythms up and down, up and down. His wanton murmurs urged me on and before I knew it, his dick was pulsing in my hand, white ribbons of come shooting onto his abs and belly.

Before I could think, I found myself bringing my hand to my mouth, licking the come from my fingers. It tasted different than I'd thought. Not bad at all. As soon as I realized what I'd done, shame gripped me like a vice. I tried to turn away, but Madden wouldn't let me go. "No, baby. Don't. Look at me." He waited, so I shifted back, knowing he was right. I shouldn't be embarrassed, I'd done nothing wrong. In fact, I felt like I'd done everything right. "There you are." His eyes were wonderous as his face lit up. "Joe. I don't even know what to say. You fulfilled quite a few of my fantasies right there."

This time when my face flamed fuchsia, I was proud. I'd given something to Madden that he'd needed. For the first time ever, I'd given myself to someone and they didn't turn their back on me. Didn't hate me for it. Didn't lock me away, scream at me, kick me until I swore I'd never do it again. This was something wholly different. This was something real. I just had to figure out how to hold on to it because I didn't ever want this to end.

29

___

Madden

Nothing in my life had ever felt more right. I felt like I'd discovered a new constellation. Or a mathematical equation to solve for happiness. I was floating on a cloud, my heart taking up too much space in my chest. I grazed my ribs with my hand to ensure none of them were cracking from the pressure.

Epic. That was the word that kept rolling around in my head on an infinite loop. From the minute Joe opened that shower door I was a dead man. Dead to myself because he now owned me. I didn't think I'd ever forget what he looked like standing there, his stance tentative and unsure as hell. But my boy had his mind made up and he went for it. I was not expecting anything that happened, and under normal circumstances I probably would have at least made a bit of an effort to pump the brakes, but fuck. Joe standing there, water pouring down his pale skin, puckering his nipples. That was a sight that is etched in platinum and soldered into my memory for eternity. He gave himself to me. As we lay in bed, my head shook in remembrance, and I placed a kiss to his sleeping face. All I could do was go over and over the sequence of passion in my mind.

As I knelt before him in that bathroom, I felt awed. My boy was trusting me with himself and he needed me in that moment. I wanted to give him everything. I had never expected anything in return. But isn't that my Joe? Always a surprise. And I'd been worried that he would flip out after. That maybe he'd try to run again, but not Joe. He kissed me until our butts were numb from sitting on the bathroom floor. Then he took me into my room, laid me out on my bed and crawled into the space he'd created just for him. And that, too, felt so right.

I honestly felt in my bones that I was in love with him weeks ago, but this... holy mother of balls. This was so much more than anything I had ever fathomed feeling. I didn't know something like this existed in this life. That I could care so deeply about another human being that I would literally give my beating heart to him if he needed it. Hell, I'd give it to him if he simply *asked* me for it.

And so here I was, contemplating harvesting my essential organs for the man who fit perfectly into my side, fit perfectly into my apartment, my life. My heart.

I kissed his head again and rubbed my lips on his damp hair. "I love you, Joe," I murmured, my lips against his scalp. "And I am never going to let you go." Tugging him closer to me, I breathed in his scent as I replayed the past hour again in my head before finally falling asleep.

～

I WOKE up in the dark. I was facing the bathroom, so I had turned over in my sleep. That's when I realized that Joe's warm, hard body was pressed up against my back, his hot erection against my ass. All I wanted to do was push back against him. My body was thrumming at the thought. I eased my hips back with the slightest of movements, but I heard Joe's breath catch. I bit my lip and wondered if he was awake, but I didn't want to move. So, there I was, body stiff with tension, cock stiff with arousal, listening intently and holding my breath. All I could hear was my heart pounding against my ribcage, each beat drumming faster than the last. And then it happened. Holy fuck. Joe thrust his hips against my ass, and I moaned. Within seconds his hand wrapped around my waist as he pumped his hips against me, breath panting against my neck. I couldn't take it anymore.

"Oh, baby, please." My voice sounded raw even to myself. "Tell me what you want, and you can have it." And I meant every word.

"I'm n-n-not sure. I just want," he said, moving against me. "I just want you. God, this feels so good. You feel so good." Then his hand reached around and palmed my hard-on and my eyes screwed shut as I whimpered.

"Joe! Oh, shit. Joe. Fuck me. Please, will you fuck me?" I was out of my mind and I needed him in me. But as soon as the words flew out of my mouth and landed in his ears, all movement stopped. His hand went to my hip, and his hips stalled.

"Um," he croaked. "You know I've never—,"

I flipped over and cut him off with a kiss. "I know, baby, but if you want to, I would love to feel you push that long, hard, beautiful dick into my ass and light me up like a Christmas tree." I didn't want to push him, but I'd also wanted this so badly. And yes, I was typically the one in control. The one to take care of my man, but I'd bottomed before and enjoyed it. And lying here, next to Joe, I wanted him so badly that I'd let him do anything to me. But not at the cost of his comfort. I wanted him to want this. And if he wasn't ready, there was no way I was going to push him.

"Joe, look at me." I waited until his eyes rose from my chest to my face. "I want you to know that you run the show. We don't have to do anything at all, and I won't be mad, sad, angry, disappointed, or anything else you can think of. I love you, and I will wait forever for you to be ready to move forward. But if you want to do anything, anything at all, I'm on board for that, too." I gave him a smirk and raised my eyebrows up and down. At least that garnered me a laugh. Joe shoved at my shoulder, then bent over and kissed it. He trailed his tongue down my chest to my nipple and licked around it and then sucked, tugging it deep into his mouth. I gasped at the pleasure and I could see a smile in his eyes.

He threw his right leg over me, straddling my body then pinned my hands above my head on the pillows. "Stay." Oh, God. That one fucking word had me losing my mind as he slid his hands down my arms slowly, lightly torturing me with his touch. My back arched as I pressed my dick up against his ass, needing friction. He stopped moving and rested his hands against my pecs, looking down at me with a questioning gaze, his teeth pulling at his bottom lip. "Madden, I want to make love to you, but I don't know how." My eyes closed as I tried to hold back tears. He was so perfect. So gentle, kind, and innocent. And he wanted me. *Me.*

I drew in a shaky breath and tried to sit up, but his warm hands forced me back down. With a wry smile on his beautiful face, he said, "No. You stay there and tell me what to do. How to make it good." And just those words had my cock pulsing and precum leaking onto my thigh. I nodded, my eyes closing as I tried to get my brain to function. Right. Prep. It had been a while.

"In the top drawer there," I said, pointing to the bedside table. "There's a bottle of lube and condoms." I waited as he leaned over, his knee on my chest as he reached. He held up the supplies and shook them in his hands, a naughty grin on his face. "Okay, I need to flip over so you can—,"

"No!" He said, adamantly. "Sorry. I can't. I need to see you. I need to make sure you're okay. And that I'm okay. Please? Can it work this way?" The fear and frustration clear on his face cracked into my heart. Just knowing how much this meant to him was everything to me, because it meant that much to me as well. This wasn't fucking around. This wasn't a one-time deal. This was real, and it was Joe. So, yeah, I'd do whatever he wanted.

"Absolutely," I replied, sitting up to kiss him. "Okay, so you have to scoot down between my legs and you're going to have to open me up." He kissed me again, then kissed his way down my body, nipping at my skin here and there. It thrilled me to know he was still feeling this after the last few minutes of uncertainty. I know my dick had gone a bit soft worrying about him, but his ministrations on his journey down the bed had me back in full form in no time.

"Pour some lube onto your fingers and rub it over my hole." I was hesitant to gauge his reaction, but there was nothing but heat in his eyes, which was such a hot look on my boy. I closed my eyes when I felt his fingers tentatively brushing over my hole, then tracing around it in circular motions. I opened my mouth to tell him to push a finger in when I felt the ring of muscle breached, then his finger wiggling inside of me. My legs fell farther apart on the mattress as I bit my lip at the feel of him inside me. Then, his finger was gone. I heard the familiar snick of the lube bottle and then he was pressing two fingers inside me, twisting and turning them gently at first as he watched my face for a reaction. "You already feel so good, Joe. I can't wait to have you inside me." He smiled up at me then and it caught my breath.

"How do I find your prostate, Madden? I want to know

where it is." His eyebrows were scrunched together as his fingers plunged slowly in and out of my body.

"Ah, um, if you bend your fingers a bit, you'll feel a, oh shit, yeah. There. Oh, God." His finger was gently rubbing back and forth over the spongy lump and I groaned in pleasure. "Fuck, baby. Can you see my dick leaking right now? I need you inside me. Fuck." I felt his fingers pull out and as much as I wanted to protest, I wanted his cock inside me more. "Yeah, okay, grab the condom. Do you know how to put it on?" I had no idea if he'd ever had any experience with a condom, but I could tell by the red covering his cheeks that it was a negative. And it only made my balls ache more with need. "Okay, hand it to me and come up here so I can do it."

He kneed up closer to me on the bed and I couldn't resist taking a taste when his crown was mere inches from my face. I licked around the head and felt the salty tang of Joe. A guttural moan sounded from his throat. After rolling the condom up his length I kissed his tip, then told him to apply more lube to my hole and to coat his cock. When he was ready, I winked at him.

"Okay, baby, just go slow. When you get seated fully inside me, I need you to be still for a second while I adjust. I'll tell you, okay?" He nodded, his lip caught between his teeth so hard I was worried he was going to bite into it. "Hey, Joe," I said, rubbing my hands up his arms. "I love you so much. You know that, right?"

With a look of pain, he sat back on his feet and put his head down. In a panic I sat up and put my hand on his cheek, caressing his face. "Hey, baby, tell me what's wrong."

"I want to say it. I want to so badly but I-I-I," he shook his head and took a deep breath. "I've never said it before."

"Joe, I won't push you to do anything you don't feel comfortable with. Don't worry." I was thumbing his jaw when a tear crept out of the corner of his eye. "Joe, please. Don't cry. Do you want to just lie here? We can get back under the covers and just be together."

"No. I want this with you. I really do. I feel it. I'm sorry if I'm ruining everything."

I shook my head. "Don't even think that. This is so much better already than any other sexual experience I've had because it's you. Now tell me what you want."

With a wry smile he wiped his eyes and pushed me back down onto the bed. "Get ready, Madden. I'm going to show you how much you mean to me." My back on the bed, I pulled my knees up to my chest, holding my thighs out, offering myself to Joe. Lining himself up, his tip pressed against my hole, and I felt the pressure as he pushed through, sweat forming on his forehead. He looked like he was trying to do calculus in his head, and I smiled to myself, even as I felt the warm burn of the stretch. "You okay?" he asked, watching his cock head disappear into my body.

"Better than." This was more than sex. This was more intimate, more intense and more real than anything I'd ever experienced before. He looked at my face, his eyes blazing with wonder.

"I can't believe this is happening. You should see how incredible this is. We are like, like, connected, Madden. It's unbelievable." His attention was back on our merging bodies, but I couldn't help myself. I felt my throat tighten at the wave of emotions coursing through me. And just like that, he'd bottomed out and I felt full and tender as my body adjusted. He was still, but I could see how tight he was holding his muscles with the effort not to move.

"Joe, please move. Please. I need you." After a second or two, he rolled his hips a bit, getting a sense of what he was feeling, then pulled halfway out. I whimpered, worried I was losing him, but he quickly thrust back in and started rolling his hips in earnest, pulling moans out of me and echoing them from his chest. "Oh, fuck." I was thrusting back against his thrusts, feeling him deeper and deeper inside my body. After a few minutes, he slowed, almost to a stop, but before I could complain I lifted my legs around his hips, crossing my feet behind his back as he shifted himself, then started coming at me from another angle.

"Oh my God, oh my God, holy balls of gravy I'm going to die. Madden, I think I'm dying." If I wasn't riding a wave of pleasure I would have laughed. With every pass, his head was rubbing my prostate in the most glorious way, sending stars against my eyelids. "I'm getting close. I can't do this. You are so hot and tight and perfect, and I've never felt anything like this before and I just want to explode but I don't want to be selfish or do this wrong and oh my God, please do something or I'll die. I swear I'll die. Maaaaaaadddeennn." He started pumping his hips wildly now and I grabbed onto my cock and pumped once, twice and then I was coming. White heat blasted out of me, showering my chest and streaking my abs. I screamed in silence, my face contorted in pleasure, my eyes squeezed shut. When my ass stopped pulsing around Joe's length, I opened my eyes. He was bucking wildly against me, a feral look on his face and he stuttered to a stop, a heaved moan pouring from his lips as I felt his cock pulsing inside my channel, filling the condom, setting fire to my insides.

I groaned and pulled him down on my chest, not caring about the squish of cum between us. I needed Joe in that moment more than I needed air. I wanted to kiss him, but we were both so out of breath I couldn't do more than breathe hard into his neck and groan in ecstasy.

We lay still until our chests stopped heaving and I felt Joe's deflated cock slip out of me. "Baby, roll over a minute so I can help you with the condom." He did, and I took it off, tied the length and got up off the bed. Joe protested, but it was weak enough I just shushed him and made my way to the bathroom to dispose of the condom and get a wet towel.

Stepping back to the bed I felt a wonderful ache in my ass and wished it would stay that way for days as a reminder of this moment. This perfect moment with Joe.

After wiping us both down, I threw the towel into the dirty clothes basket and got back in bed, pulling Joe to me, his head on my chest. "You okay?" I asked, slowly.

"Mmmmmm. Super okay." I laughed, his head bobbing up and down as a result.

"I love you. Thank you for this. For you. For all of it." I kissed his head three times and ran my hand up and down his arm. His skin pebbled under my touch so I pulled the blanket up higher over him.

We lay silent for a while, both in our own heads. It was a very comfortable silence and it was one I was grateful for. I wished I had more words to explain how I felt right then, how full my heart was.

"Madden?"

"Yeah? You okay?"

"Madden?" This time his voice was softer, more delicate.

"Yes. I'm here. I'm right here, baby." I kissed him on his head again.

"I." He trembled in my arms and I lifted myself onto my elbow to look down at him. His eyes were closed, but he looked content. Sated.

"What is it?"

Once his eyes opened, those twin seas of blue focused on me and he whispered, "Madden, I love you."

30

Joe

I woke up to find myself alone in Madden's bed. His bed that smelled like sex and vanilla and everything I never knew I'd wanted for myself. I had fallen so hard for this selfless man and now I had given the only thing I had left to him. I smiled, thinking about him splayed out underneath me. I'd never have thought he would be willing to submit to me like that. To let me lead. To give me the power. I was flying on the high still. If I lived a thousand years more, I'd never regret last night. It felt like the closest I could imagine being to another person. The more I thought about it, the more my body thrummed with passion and need. I slid my hand under the sheets and flicked the tip of my length with my thumb and then hissed at the sweet torture. God, I felt like Madden had awoken a monster inside of me that couldn't get enough. Ever since the day on the couch we first kissed, my body had been agonizingly sensitive. But only for Madden. Revulsion pulsed through me at the thought of anyone else touching me like he did.

Grabbing his pillow, I pulled it to my face and rolled over onto my side, hugging it to me. His scent was buried in my nose as I let myself drift back to sleep.

~

"HEY, SLEEPING BEAUTY. I MADE BREAKFAST." A low moan rumbled out of me when I felt the bed dip. My face was buried beneath the pillow that I had clutched tightly to my chest, but as my eyes cracked open, I could tell it was late. The sun was bright through the windows and reflected from the mirrors in the bathroom. I'd probably never slept this well in my life. Madden's bed was the biggest bed I'd ever been in, which wasn't really saying much. The only other beds had been the shitty mattress on the floor in my room as a kid and then random single nights at various places. But it was more than just the mattress and I knew it. It had everything to do with the man whose lips were at my neck peppering kisses along my nape. My entire body broke out in goose bumps as my shoulders lifted to my ears in reaction to his touch. "Oh, no. No hiding," he chanted as he pulled the covers completely from me, revealing my naked form. Even though he couldn't see my face, I knew I was a burnt tomato because of the fact my dick was hard and swollen and now he had an eye full. "Fuck, you're gorgeous, Joe. Damn."

I moved the pillow from my face and looked at him. He was kneeling in front of me, his eyes staring at my groin, lips moist and red. He looked like a starving man lusting after his last meal. How was this my life? I whimpered and his gaze shot to mine. A sexy smirk appeared on his face and he asked, "You need some help with that? Breakfast can wait." Before I even answered him, he had me on my back, my swollen head hitting the back of his throat as he swallowed around me.

"Fuck, Madden, holy fuck. I haven't even brushed my teeth and now I'm going to die." I was lost and he laughed around me. My mind was blank at the feel of the hot, wet suction dragging up and down, his tongue lapping the head of my dick. "Wait," I pleaded. "Stop. Seriously, stop." He pulled off, a thin line of spit connecting his lip to my shaft for a moment before he wiped the back of his hand across his mouth.

"Did I hurt you?" He looked confused.

"No. You didn't, but I want more than that. I want us both to feel good. But—," I bit my lip, wondering if talking about things that were once humiliating would ever get easier.

Placing a kiss to my purple, angry cock head he asked, "But what?"

Clearing my throat, I forced myself to ask, "Are you sore?" And then I flinched, simply because I was me.

"Are you asking me if I want to have this long, thick, beautiful monster inside me again, Joe?" The smirk on his face was enough for me to groan out a response. And then I nodded.

A wicked smile took over his face now. "You're going to have to ask me first." Oh, he was mean. And torturous. And irritating. And I loved him with everything in me.

With a serious expression on my face, I sat up and got to my knees on the mattress. I looked ridiculous with my cock jutting straight out like a lust-o-meter pointing directly at Madden. Pulling my shoulders back, I put on the most formal tone I could, and I looked into his eyes.

"Madden, sir. Would you please allow me to use your body for my own amusement by properly filling it with my long, thick, beautiful monster cock until neither of us can remember our own names?" I had no idea where that came from but the look on his face made it worth it. He looked like pure lust.

He had me pushed down on the mattress, his tongue

fucking my mouth in less than three seconds. He was all hands and lips, unable to stay focused on one place too long. It was fine with me, I loved every sexy second of it. And more, I loved the sounds we made. Hot, panting breaths, low moans, lips, and tongues wet against skin. It all had me aching and needy for him.

"Joe, can I ride you?" His face was buried in my armpit, sucking marks over my ribs as I squirmed with need.

"Yes, anything. Just do something soon," I begged.

Grabbing the lube and a condom from the table he gave my cock a long pull before sheathing me. Taking care to make himself ready, he lowered down slowly onto me. Blazing heat surrounded and took me in. I never wanted it to end. His eyes met mine, and neither of us looked away until he was fully seated, his ass cheeks touching my balls. I let out an embarrassing sound, but couldn't have cared less. This was only my second real sexual encounter and I was going to react however I needed to. Plus, I knew Madden would never hurt me for it. I trusted him. When he started lewdly shifting his hips, I gasped and gripped the sheets with my hands. His expression was one of complete and total bliss. Grabbing his hips with my hands I asked, "How does it feel?"

He was panting when he bent and took my lips in a dirty, bruising kiss. Our tongues thrashed and teeth crashed together with a clink. I'd never felt so delicious, so utterly debauched. All I wanted was skin and sweat and his mouth against my body. He lifted up bracing his hands on the headboard, giving him both leverage and a new angle and I could tell his prostate was getting into it now. His eyes rolled back into his head and he bounced up and down obscenely on my hard length. I was getting close to coming but didn't want this to end. I never wanted this to end. In that moment I knew I wanted this with Madden forever, no matter what that meant. I'd give up anything to keep him.

"You want to know how it feels, baby?" he said in between pants, knocking me out of my head and back into the moment. "It feels like my body is full of you. Like you've taken root inside of me and given me life. You're lighting me up from the inside right now, Joe. You are giving me, oh, Goddddd." He groaned and squeezed his eyes shut, taking his length in his hand and jerking himself in time with his thrusts. "You're filling me up and making me whole."

"Madden, I'm losing my mind. I need. I need. Oh, please, fuck, I need." My face tightened as my eyes squeezed shut and I let go.

"That's it, baby, I'm right behind you, oh shit." I felt his ass squeeze my pulsing dick and another last jerk of cum flooded the condom as Madden pulsed creamy white ropes all over my chest.

He slowly eased off me, then fell beside me onto the bed, both of us wet with sweat and panting. "I love you," he said in between breaths. I nodded, feeling emotionally drained and tangled up inside.

Madden got up and got a towel to clean us up and then flopped back down on the bed, but he threw me a look that said 'I know something is going on in your head and I want to talk about it' which, yeah, he was right about. But, instead of asking, he started running his fingers through my hair softly, pulling a sound from me similar to a purr.

⌇

"So, what happens next?" We'd reheated the waffles Madden had made earlier and ate them at the kitchen table wearing only our underwear. It felt freeing, and I couldn't stop my smile, even when asked about it. There was just something special that happened when you let down your walls. I was in a pair of Madden's boxer briefs and nothing else, eating waffles with butter and syrup and I could have beaten the sun in a radiance war. I was comfortable, for the first time in my life, and it hit me like a punch to the face. I probably should have been bolting from the scene. Leaving a Joe shaped hole in the door. Or I should have been horrified, scared, a litany of emotions. But I wasn't. I felt my smile drop as I watched Madden cut a piece of waffle, four squares, each perfectly filled with syrup, then raise his fork to take it into his soft, red mouth. As I looked on, my chest ached and heaved, and my skin tightened. But not like when I was upset. This felt like I had too many feelings trying to break free at once, pulling me apart at the seams. Trying to burst from me.

Madden stopped chewing and his face fell. Concern swam in his eyes as his brows dipped inward. "Joe, what—," but I shook my head, reaching for a smile even through the tears that were threatening to fall. I moved quickly, getting up and seated myself on his lap, arms wrapped around his neck so tightly. This was what I needed to make the tightness in my body release. With my face pressed against his neck I breathed in his familiar, calming scent and my muscles started to relax. His hands were on my back, gently rubbing as I forced myself to pull back and look at him. I smiled and it was purely genuine.

"Sorry, but those were the good kind of tears." My voice sounded flimsy and my mouth was thick with emotion, but I felt calmer than I could ever remember. "I have to tell you a secret," I whispered from my perch on his lap. Well, I was more straddling his lap at this point. My smile never faltered when he brought his hands up to press my hair back from my face. He had an amused look now, as his thumbs wiped away the remnants of tears.

"Go on, then," he answered with a bit of a smile on his lips.

"You are stuck with me now," I blurted, not waiting for a reaction. "I've never felt this safe. So happy, taken care of and loved and just now I realized I feel comfortable for the first time. I want this for as long as you'll let me have it. But not just this," I said, motioning in the air at the apartment. "You. I want to have you. And I know you keep saying you love me. And I feel it too. But it's going to take me a while before it feels okay for me to say it casually. Like you seem to be able to in every perfect situation. But I want to try, Madden. I want to try to make you happy and safe, and loved, too. All of it."

I sucked in a breath and waited. And waited. His eyes were roaming over my face, but there was no answer written there. "Right now, Joe, my heart is so full of awe, heat, and wonder. You have no idea how much those words mean to me. I love you so much and I know it's hard for you, but you told me you loved me and that's enough for now. But knowing that being here with me gives you comfort, I'm not sure I can put words to my feelings. I want you here with me, Joe. I want you to live here with me. Please? I want you to stay. Will you stay?"

I bent down and kissed him, soft at first, then it quickly turned heated. "Yes, I'll stay," I panted against his mouth. "Of course, I'll stay."

We kissed like teenagers for what seemed like hours before I slowly climbed off his lap and onto the floor between his legs. He was so hard from what we'd been doing that his crown was sticking out of the elastic of his briefs enticingly. I licked my sore lips and it pulsed. Holy dinosaur balls. Every time I saw him hard and leaking, I wanted to taste him, but I'd been too scared before. Too burdened by what he would think. But now... Now I wanted and was going to take.

With my hands on his thighs I leaned in and licked the wet pearl from the tip and moaned at the taste on my tongue. Like heaven. Madden's eyes were wide, and he tried to say something, but it was muffled with a curse when I pulled his underwear down below his balls and started lapping my tongue around his sensitive head. His hips lifted slightly, and his underwear slid down to allow me more access as his hands gripped the air, needing purchase on something. I pulled one to my head and rested it there and he immediately stroked my hair and massaged my head. I kept up my ministrations, licking up and down his length, nipping the shaft with my lips curled over my teeth. He hissed and tightened a fist on my head which spurred me into action. I wrapped my lips around his head and sucked until my cheeks were hollowed out. "Oh, fuck, baby. Holy shit that's so good."

I stopped because of the smile that I couldn't shake. Pulling back, I asked, "Really? It's okay?" I'd never done anything like this before and obviously wanted to make it good.

"Better than. Just don't stop. You mouth is so sinful." At that, I wrapped my lips around his length again, applying as much pressure as I could while still licking all around the crown. "Your face is so beautiful right now with your lips around my cock. You look gorgeous kneeling in front of me like this. Oh, Joe."

I was so hard and wet, I knew there was a dark spot on my underwear, but I couldn't concentrate on anything more than Madden in my mouth right then. I moaned and then he moaned, which spurred me into quicker, shorter flicks of my tongue against his base and under the head. I felt him grow unbelievably harder in my mouth before he pushed against my forehead in warning. But I didn't want to pull away. Did I? No. I didn't know if I was up for swallowing, but I wanted to feel him come and taste him in my mouth. I sucked harder, jabbing my tongue into his slit over and over, then sucking as hard as I could. Finally, I felt his cock pulse as jets of warm fluid, filling my mouth. It was more than I'd expected, and I gagged on it, pulling back far enough to swallow, yet kept his still leaking dick in my mouth. Seems I was up for swallowing after all.

It was so worth it. The blissed-out look on Madden's face would keep me content for days. I let him slip from my mouth as he sat back in the chair, both of us panting and sweating from the work. "You didn't have to do that but oh, my God, Joe. That was amazing and I didn't want it to end."

God, I loved him. Loved that I could do something for him that could make him this sated, happy and relaxed. I stood, pushing my hand against my long, trapped cock. "Hey, let me take care of you," he said, hand reaching out to caress me through the wet fabric. It took two gentle strokes and I was coming all over myself, hunching over like Quasimodo in a bell tower. I fell back into my chair, resting my head on the table. "Shit, we're a mess," he laughed, and I couldn't help but laugh back.

"I've never come this much in my life." I was tired and thirsty again, and in desperate need of a shower. I had dried cum all over my body I was sure. But I didn't think I'd ever felt this happy in my life.

AFTER SHOWERING, we stripped the sheets and put on a new set. Before he could protest, I was lying on them, making sheet angels as he laughed at me. That's when I asked him what happens next. "Well, I have a conference I have to go to in Chicago for work. It's a nursing training class taught by a well-respected member of the field and the hospital is paying for my trip. I leave Thursday and get back on Saturday." He sat on the bed next to my flailing limbs and took my hand in his. "I want to go get your stuff from wherever it is and bring it back here today. I want every part of you here. And when I get back from my trip, I want to discuss your plans a bit more." He looked so sure, but I didn't know what he meant.

"Plans? What plans?" I asked, confused.

"I don't really know. Did you want to go to school? Do you want to stay working at the café? Do you want to paint the kitchen? Get new bath mats? This is going to be your home, too, right? That's what we talked about? You staying?"

I nodded vehemently. "Yes, absolutely. Yes. I just hadn't thought about the other stuff yet. Plus, I want to pay for stuff."

Now he nodded. "Okay. So, it sounds like we do have things to discuss. Do you mind waiting until I get back or do you want to do it now?"

I thought about that for a minute. I wasn't sure what I wanted yet. Or needed. "I'm not sure."

"I want to think about it too, so let's both take the few days and come up with questions or ideas and we can go over everything on Saturday. For now, I want to take you out." My face exploded into a huge smile at that. It seemed my life was finally coming together.

31

Madden

Oh, shit. Oh, fuck. Damn. I had no idea if I'd just fucked this all up or not. It was possible that I had completely overstepped and ruined everything. And Joe had trusted me. My head was pounding and my heart felt like it was racing a train. Why did airplanes have to be so loud? What had I done? Why did I ever think that would be a good thing? The woman in the small seat next to me had been side-eyeing me for two hours and all I could think was that my life was over, and I was going to die with her face in my head. Rolling my eyes, I tried to remember to breathe. Maybe Joe would be happy. Okay, yeah, no. Not even a possibility. Why did I have to go and ruin the best thing that had ever happened to me? Ever.

I should have just stayed at the hotel in Chicago. I should never have rented a car. I should never have looked up the coordinates from Joe's tattoo. And I really should have known better than to drive out there. Fuck, I wish I could just pretend the last 24 hours had never happened. Throw the entire trip into a bag, tie it up, drop it into a box, close it and seal it with duct tape and bury it under a mountain. But now I owed him honesty. Otherwise, I'd have to live with this guilt forever. And I only had his feelings in mind. That sounded like a cop-out in my head the minute I said it to myself. I had fucked up and now I had to pay the price. I couldn't lose Joe. I couldn't. End of. I knew my heart wouldn't survive it. A low groan came from somewhere and I opened my eyes, looking around me when I realized it was me.

One more hour of misery and I'd be home. Well, the airport. And then another hour and a half to home. All I wanted to do was crawl into bed with Joe and feel every inch of his warm, soft, sweet skin under my lips and on my tongue. I wanted to show him how much I loved him with my mouth and my hands and my body. How he owned me, heart and soul. And he did. That morning when he told me he loved me...that was a moment I would never forget. The impact of those words made a permanent imprint on my soul. Life had started again. And I needed Joe now. He was the life in me. Made me see and hear, brightened my senses. He just somehow took over my heart and mind and I would do anything to keep him there. And that scared me, too. Because I'd only been on the receiving end of loss. But, even though my parents died, they showed me what love, romance, and partnership was about.

'Please let Joe understand' was my new mantra. The prayer I said in my head every few minutes when my heartbeat kicked into high gear. I would never keep a secret from him, I promised. I'd always ask him before doing anything stupid again.

"Are you alright?" The voice shook me out of my terror. I turned to see the woman six inches away from me, her bushy eyebrows bending at the center of her face. I looked down to see my hands gripping the arm rest so tightly that my fingers were white. Shit. I had to think about letting go of my grip before my hands complied and eased off. Shaking out my fingers I said, "Sorry, just nervous." She nodded, still staring at me like I was a wild monkey on the loose.

Think happy thoughts I told myself. Of rainbows and unicorns and oh my God could I be more gay right now? I might have been completely losing my mind because this wasn't me. At all. I was a confident guy. I didn't take no for an answer. And I would do anything to ensure that Joe knew that I did this out of love for him.

As soon as the wheels touched down, my finger was poised over the airplane mode button on my phone, waiting for the familiar ding to tell me it was okay to use. I waited, foot tapping. Come on dammit. Ding. Thank you, baby Jesus in a manger. All I'd wanted to do was call Joe, but he would be at work tonight. I'd switched the password on the phone I'd given him and showed him how to use it. He was a bit slow with the texting, but I didn't mind. In fact, it brought a smile to my face when I'd watch the three little dots light up the screen, then disappear multiple times before receiving one or two words in answer. The point was, he was now reachable, and I couldn't have managed this trip without speaking to him every night.

The phone finally caught up to real-time and alerted me to four voicemails and seven missed calls, all from Adam and Anna. Shit. I pushed play on the message button and held the phone to my ear only to hear Adam panting into the phone about seeing Joe. Seeing Joe where? The next message was Adam again, talking fast, panicky, saying that Joe was at the hospital. What? There was an incident at work. Another message all garbled. The last message was Adam, in what sounded like a bathroom, his voice echoing the words, "It's bad, Mads. You need to get here right away. They've taken him to X-ray and George thinks one of his arms is broken. But he fought damn hard. And the police caught the guy."

My head was spinning, my heart racing, and I was hours away from Joe. George thinks an arm is broken. They caught the guy. What guy? Why do phones have to fail in an emergency like this? And why is no one getting off the plane? Shit. Joe. My heart.

The second my Vans touched the dingy gray carpet of the gate I was on my phone. Adam picked up on the third ring, just as all the blood in my body raced to my ears. "Mads, you're back. Thank fuck. When will you get here? We need you, man. He needs you." The urgency in Adam's voice did nothing to calm the pounding in my head.

"I just got off the plane. I need to get my car and I'm on my way but I'm still two hours out. What the fuck happened, Adam? Is he okay?" My voice broke and I felt like I was going to lose my mind. I had no control and no idea what Joe was dealing with.

"Apparently, a few weeks ago some fucker attacked him in the alley behind the café."

Weaving through crowds of people, my bag weighing heavily on my shoulder, my phone clutched to my ear in the other hand, I looked like a hot mess, but I couldn't have cared less. I needed to get to my boy. The words Adam was breathing into my ear had me seeing red. "Yeah, I know. So, this guy came back? Tell me what happened." I sucked in a breath. "Tell me how he is, Adam. Don't bullshit me."

"Physically, he's not good. He's got two black eyes, bruises all over his face, jaw, neck and chest. His arms are scratched up and one is broken. A couple of ribs look broken as well, but I can't tell for sure."

"What do you mean you can't tell for sure? What did the X-ray show?"

"Well, that's the problem." His voice sounded hesitant, off somehow.

"Just fucking tell me, Adam." I wasn't in the mood for games. This was my Joe.

"Okay, okay, shit." He sucked a breath through his teeth before continuing. "You know how he is. He won't let anyone near him. We can't get an X-ray. He won't let us touch him at all, even to set his arm. Dr. Johannes wants to get a Psych eval done."

"No fucking way. No one is talking to him. Fuck, Adam. You've got to talk to him. You have to—,"

"I know. I know. But Madden, he's not... He's not himself. I think he needs a sedative." Before I could cut him off for his ridiculous words he spoke again. "Just listen to me. He's curled into a ball in the corner of the room, Madden. He won't let anyone near him. His arm is bad. His shoulder may even be dislocated. We need to treat him before the swelling prevents us and we have to wait. You know it's for his own good. He needs to be checked out, Madden. He needs medical attention."

Fuck, fuck, fuck. I could see Joe in my head, bleeding and hurt, curled into himself. My heart ached and my eyes burned. I had just made it to my car and threw my bag in the back. Pushing the heels of my hands into my eye sockets, I moaned. Fuuuuuuuck. "I'm in my car. I'll be there as soon as I can, but I need you to take care of him, Adam. He is my heart, okay? I don't know what I'd do without him."

"I know, Madden. Dude. I *know*, but he needs to let us do our jobs. Tell me what to do. What would you do?"

I could let the panic take over or I could take a deep breath and help my boy. "Okay, the last time this happened I crawled over to him slowly. Make sure he knows it's you, Adam. It calms him when I rub circles on his back."

"Will he let me touch him?"

I squeezed the bridge of my nose with my thumb and fore-finger and thought for a minute. "Honestly, I'm not sure. I need to be there, Adam. I can't believe this is happening." I was starting to lose it. The sound of grating from the rough edge of the lane caught me by surprise as I swerved back between the lines of the freeway. Shit.

"Madden, I'm going to hang up. You need to concentrate on getting here and driving safely, okay?" I could hear him talking to someone else, his voice muffled. "Hey, dude, I'm going to see if I can talk to Joe. I'll call you in a little bit, okay? Be safe." Before I could say anything, the line went dead.

Taking a few deep breaths, I drove. And drove. It felt like days went by before I made it into town. I was fifteen minutes from the hospital and still hadn't heard back from Adam. I'd called every twenty minutes or so, but he never answered, and I knew I just had to get there. Joe had to be fine, and then he could kill me for what I'd done in Chicago.

RUNNING DOWN THE WHITE, ammonia scented hallway, I couldn't even remember parking or getting out of the car. I saw the hospital and then I was inside, and by the time I'd made it to the nurse's reception area, Adam was walking towards me, his hands up and out like he wasn't sure if I needed a hug or I was going to punch him. Honestly, I was probably somewhere in the middle at this point.

"Where is he?" I half-yelled. I wasn't going to wait any longer to see Joe. My skin was crawling as if I had hives from the adrenaline.

"Hang on a sec, man. Let's talk first." Adam tried to usher me into the waiting room but there was no way I was having that. I pushed him aside as forcefully as I could without outright assaulting my friend. "Madden, man, come on. Don't do this. You need to know what happened." I looked down at the hand that was wrapped around my bicep and gritted my teeth. My jaw ached in answer.

"What I *need* is to see Joe!" What in the actual fuck?

"Madden, if you see him right now without knowing what he's been through, you're likely to traumatize him with your reaction. Just sit the hell down and listen to me." Adam had always been a good friend to me. I'd never call him soft-spoken, but he wasn't loud, and he didn't get mad very easily. This was a new side of him, and it was making me nervous and uneasy. So, I sat. Or I fell, really, into those stupid plastic chairs where the doctors either ruin lives or give good news. Give hope. Hope. I wasn't sure if I remembered what that word meant right now.

"You're right. I'm sorry. I just need to see him. He's... Well, he's my *person*. I can't..." I trailed off when my throat tightened. Adam drew my hand between his and squeezed. As much as I was grateful for the comfort, I needed him to tell me whatever it was before I lost control.

"Okay, so after I spoke with you, I did what you suggested. He let me get close, but wouldn't let me touch him. He just kept rocking and whispering 'don't touch me' repeatedly." I winced as he closed his eyes. "I told him you were on your way, that we needed to check him out. He was so upset, he was shaking his head, saying your name over and over. It scared the shit out of me, man. Fuck." He gazed at the ceiling, as if trying to force the memory from his mind. I squeezed his hand impatiently. "Sorry, man. This is hard to say," he said through a grimace. "So, it took a while, but I just kept talking to him about you and telling him that you were on your way. Eventually, he calmed down enough that he could listen and process what I was saying. I couldn't get him up onto a bed, but he let me check him over if I told him where I was going to touch him and got his permission first. So, I did as thorough an eval as I could." He took another deep breath.

This wasn't going to be good, was it? "Just tell me," I whispered.

His cheeks filled, then he let out a puff of air. "His left arm is broken, as is his left wrist. He has multiple broken ribs and a fractured collar bone." Adam shook his head as I took in the news. "That's all I could see from where he was. He'd settled enough that I was able to ask him if he wanted some meds and he did. I gave him a sedative, Madden." His eyes met mine, and I blinked, then and squeezed his hand, asking him to continue. "With that, he let me take him up to X-ray. I held his hand the entire time, and he was fine." He looked me in the eyes as he said it, reassuring me. I could only nod. "We found a small fracture in his right eye socket." My heart couldn't take any more. I looked to the ceiling before I lost it completely. Oh, God. I heard a sob and turned to Adam who was staring at me with wide eyes and a lost expression. Right, the sob had come from me, I realized, when tears started falling onto my shirt. My boy was broken. No, not broken. He could be fixed, and he'd be fine.

As much as I'd known about trauma, which was decidedly not enough, I knew Joe would be thinking back to what he suffered as a child, to his monster father and his perverted friends. It scared the shit out of me to think that an assault so horrific as this could possibly cause lasting effects. More scars, both physically and mentally. God, how much could one single person take? I wanted to shout at the world. No one deserved this, but especially not Joe. He was the kindest, most thoughtful, most loving soul I'd ever known.

"We had to do a rape kit."

The statement immediately made my stomach churn and I raced for the bathroom a few doors down. I'd barely made it to the toilet before I was retching into it. My entire body heaved as saliva poured out of my mouth, my nose, tears streamed down my face. I didn't even realize I was shaking my head until Adam put his hand to the back of my neck.

"It was negative, Madden. He wasn't raped. But we had to check. And I was there the entire time. I held his hand and rubbed his back and told him that you were on your way." Adam's voice broke and I turned to look at him. He was crying. I turned on the water and washed my mouth out in the sink, then my face. When I'd dried off, I pulled Adam to me and hugged him fiercely. Knowing Joe wasn't alone during this ordeal meant everything. I wanted to tell Adam. I felt as though I owed him a debt that I could never repay. He just slapped me on the back a few times and wiped his own face. "He's family to me now, too, you know," he said with a sad smile.

"Thank you," I rasped through my sore, tired throat. "Take me to see him, please, Adam. I just need to see him."

The look on his face told me there was something else and I wasn't going to like it. I watched as his face turned ashen and pained and I had to sit back down.

Leaning over, my face in my hands, I whispered, "Jesus Christ, Adam. Just tell me. I... What else?"

"I don't know how—"

"Just tell me," I pleaded.

"You can't see him, Mads. I'm sorry. He made me promise that I wouldn't let you see him. That was the only way I could get him to agree to the sedative and X-ray. I'm so sorry."

My chest felt like it was going to explode, and my ears were ringing. Surely, I hadn't heard him correctly. Joe didn't mean that. There's no way. "You must have misunderstood him. There's no way he wouldn't want to see me."

Adam rested his hand on my knee and squeezed. I was at a complete loss. What had I done? I turned to face Adam, to find an answer, but his face was almost as broken as mine. I had to get out of there before I did something I'd regret, like punch Adam in the face and lose my job. Standing, Adam jumped up and took a step away from me. He must have read my mind. Putting my hands up, palms facing him, I whispered, "You take care of him Adam. Just, promise me."

His head nodded frantically as he said, "Yes. I will. I promise I will." I stared at him for a moment before turning and walking back outside.

I almost fell onto the concrete bench as I put my head down and tried to catch my breath. Had I just lost Joe?

32

Joe

I let out another groan and tried not to clench my jaw. Everything hurt. Every movement, every breath. I never thought the simple act of blinking could hurt. Basically, my left side was broken. And my right eye. And my heart. All I had wanted was Madden. It was so hard to let Adam help me. My entire being protested it. Eventually the pain took over and I couldn't take any more. Curling into a ball when everything was broken didn't help. And after Adam said he wouldn't touch me without telling me exactly where and exactly how first, I let out a breath and nodded. I knew it was the only thing I could do. And if it would get me to Madden, I'd do it. I'd do anything. And then I remembered Devin.

Groan. Clench. Wince. Trying to bend a finger on my left hand, a tear fell instantly from the jolt of pain that radiated through my wrist and my arm. I needed Madden. There was a part of me that wanted to just close my eyes and sleep, to make the time pass, but as soon as I did, I'd see Venom, and then Devin. Pure anger and hate radiated from their presence in my mind, sending shivers racking through my body. Which then caused tremendous amounts of pain, starting the entire cycle over again.

Closing my eyes, I tried to picture Madden's apartment. And then I remembered Batman and Robin. Perfect. I saw them flying through the water in their tank, chasing one another, diving for food. I visualized the elegant way their fins pushed and pulled the water from their shimmery scales, and it was exactly the relaxing vision I needed. I let myself relax, feeling the flow. Finally, at a place where I could control the pain, I heard a voice and my eyes shot open.

Adam stood in the doorway, his face pale, eyes pained. "What happened?" I asked him as he moved further into the room. His steps seemed somehow heavy and slow and it made me feel nauseous. I watched him slump into the chair next to my bed and he looked like he'd just been through hell. Looking up at the ceiling, he scraped one hand down his face, over the stubble that had grown throughout the day.

"I, uh. I just talked with Madden. He left a minute or two ago." There was a long pause before he continued. "I don't understand what you're doing, Joe. He cares about you so much. This is breaking him. Why are you doing this?"

I tried, in vain, to rub my fingers on something to calm myself. Moving them felt like someone was shoving nails into the bones. I winced at the pain, closing my eyes, but heard Adam walk up next to the bed. After a few seconds, he asked how much pain I was in, but I couldn't answer. I had nothing to say.

After charting something into his iPad, he headed towards the door, but not before turning back and, voice low, pleading, "I don't understand any of this, Joe. You need him and he needs you. I can see how much he cares about you. I've never seen that in him before you." He let out a frustrated breath, then continued as I listened in silence. "You are difficult to get to know, Joe. I'm sorry, but it's true. You have all these little rules and quirks and some people couldn't handle them. I couldn't handle them, man." He laughed, but there was no humor in it.

I desperately wanted to rub my fingers over Madden's t-shirt. I needed it. I blinked a couple of times, remembering that Adam was still talking to me.

"Look, Madden is a really nice guy and, somehow he gets you. He likes trying to open you up and show you things. He's my brother and this is hurting him. *You* are hurting him, and he doesn't deserve that. Why are you doing this? What does he have to do with anything that happened to you? Can't you see he's in love with you? He just wants to protect—"

"That's the problem! He wants to protect me, but he can't. And I can't let him get hurt because of me. I can't let my past ruin his life!"

Adam's shoulders sank and he walked to the bedside, leaning on his left leg, his arm on the mattress. I didn't want to know what he was going to say. I'd already said too much to him. This wasn't fair. I just needed to get out of this bed, this room, continue like I had each and every other time Devin had found me. *This was no different than any of the other times*, I kept saying to myself. *Madden doesn't make this any different.*

"Joe. Look, I don't know much about your past, but it's obvious something traumatic happened to you. Is that who this Devin guy is? The one that hurt you in the alley tonight at work? Because you don't have to worry about him. The police arrested him and have him in custody. He's not going to hurt you again, or Madden. So, if that's what's—"

I shook my head, wincing at the pain, willing the tears not to fall. "There's more." God, was I really going to tell Adam this? Madden didn't even know. No one knew. I'd never said it out loud because then it wasn't true. If I told Adam, I felt like my entire past would end up in this room, devouring my life once again.

The face that Adam was making was so gentle and understanding now, that I didn't know how to feel. Did I trust him? Madden surely did. And I trusted Madden.

"I... I was abused as a kid. My... my father used to h-h-have his work friends come over and..." I trailed off, looking down at my lap. "The worst was this guy Devin. He took things from me that I didn't even know I had."

"Shit, Joe. I'm sorry. And he's the guy? From tonight?" I nodded. "Is he the same guy from a few weeks ago?" I nodded again, wiping a solitary tear from my face with my good hand. When I looked up at him, his eyes were narrowed in a look of confusion. "So, this is over then, yeah? Why are you worried about Madden?"

"Because no one knows the real story," I answered in a whisper. Adam reached for my good hand, then pulled back at the last second, remembering. I needed the contact in that moment for strength, so I grabbed his before he could fully pull away. The shock on his face barely registered before I started my story.

I told him about my father, Venom, and how he'd verbally and physically abused me and my mother from the time I was small. I told him about them calling me Bird for as long as I could remember, and not ever knowing my real first name had been Bernard until I'd run away. I had enough foresight to take any paperwork and pictures I could find. That was the reason I kept up a gym membership. I needed a place where I could lock up my 'valuables' where they wouldn't be stolen or damaged.

When my mother got sick, we took a trip to the city (Chicago) and she met with a doctor who told her that she had cancer and it was too late to help her. After that trip, my father wanted nothing to do with her, she was officially worthless to him. After she died, the yelling, spitting, hitting, and drinking got worse. That was when he started inviting his friends over for drinking and cards; in reality, cards were just to keep them busy while they waited their turn for me. That happened once. Then Devin started handing Venom a case of beer each week, and he was the only one who came over.

My body was thrumming with fear and helplessness as I relayed my story to Adam. It didn't make me feel any better. If anything, I felt even more numb to the experience, like I'd packed it all away so well that retelling it now was like talking about someone else entirely.

Adam let go of my hand, just long enough to pull the chair over to my good side, then grabbed it right back up in his. I might have even smiled.

"When I finally realized I couldn't stay anymore, I left. I took everything I had, which wasn't much, and threw it in my backpack. Instead of walking to school, I walked west. And just kept walking. I lived on streets, in alleys, slept on benches. I always had the feeling that I was being watched or followed. And if I stayed in one place for a while, Devin would find me. And when he found me, Venom would be right behind him. I kept moving. Eventually, he'd find me, and I'd move again.

"What does your father have to do with this now, though? You think he's going to find out that Devin found you and come after you? Why?"

I let out a huff of breath that hit me right in the broken ribs. I took another, slower intake of air, then said, "If he doesn't have me to sell, he doesn't have anything."

"Christ, Joe. I don't even know what to say, but you need to talk to Madden about this. I know he won't want you leaving. He won't want you on your own again at all. And he'll take care of you. We can figure out what to do about your father."

Shaking my head vigorously in denial, I held in a breath at the pain it caused. When I opened my eyes, Adam was watching me with sorrow etched in his features. I knew that look well. I had come to despise it. Pity usually followed.

"Thank you for all you've done for me, Adam, but you should just go. I can't do this right now. I need to be alone. Please? I just want you to go." I closed my eyes and pulled my hand away, cradling it to my chest.

I heard his slow exhale, then the screech of the chair against the tile flooring of my room. I didn't breathe again until he was gone.

ADAM WAS in and out of my room the entire next day. Yes, he was one of the nurses, but he wasn't *my* nurse. I both hated and loved him for it. I had spent my life alone and was used to it, but somehow, in the last few months, I hadn't been alone at all. It was kind of comforting to know that he was around. That he at least, knew me. What I could or couldn't handle from the other nurses. Anything that involved me being poked or prodded was done by Adam.

After spending all day in bed thinking about it, I realized that he never once pushed me to tell him anything about myself, but I did it anyway. And I would again. He was someone that I considered a friend. And that was surreal.

Adam peered through the doorway after lunch, and kept looking at me like he had something to say. I was exhausted, achy, and wanted to sleep, so I asked him what he wanted.

"Madden is here. He's on shift and has been asking about you, Joe. He doesn't understand what he's done wrong. He's... Well, he's a wreck."

I felt my muscles tighten in response. "It's better to do this now. You don't know the man who is probably on his way here. You don't understand."

"No, you're right. I don't understand. But it's not fair to keep him in the dark, Joe. You owe him more than this. It isn't right what you're doing. Keeping him from helping you. He loves you. You love him, I know you do. You know he'd do anything for you, but you not allowing him to see you? Don't you see how wrong that is?"

I knew how upset he was when his hands fisted in his hair, and he let out an exaggerated roar. "I've seen him, Joe. He's breaking apart over this. Not only does he not understand, but your pushing him away is telling him how little you actually care. And I can't imagine that's true. Now, I'm going to work, but just think about what I said." And without another glance, he was gone.

33

Madden

The last seventy-two hours were replaying through my mind on a constant loop as I finished up my shift. It was both calming and frustrating as fuck to know I was so close to Joe, yet I couldn't see him. To be fair, I had gone and done something behind his back, something that could potentially change his life, but still. Was he really going to just run away again, just like he had previously? Even after I told him I loved him? Didn't he think I at least deserved a goodbye?

The truth was, I wasn't ready to let him go. This isn't how I'd seen this relationship play out. Quite the opposite, in fact. I'd seen us making a life together, being a family. I'd seen us traveling and seeing the world, hand in hand. This wasn't how our story ended. Not like this, in a hospital.

Walking to my car, my body grew weary and tired, everything around me a soundless blur. When I pulled my keys out to hit the unlock button, a hand grabbed my forearm and I whipped around to find Adam, looking more tired than I'd ever seen him.

"Hey, Mads." Running his hand through his hair was something he only did when he was either very upset or very tired. He was too vain to mess up his perfectly coiffed hair otherwise. Knowing this, I stopped and focused on him. "I've spoken to him. A lot, actually. I think he's starting to trust me." He looked at something over my shoulder, then made eye contact. "He's doing this because he doesn't want you involved in some sort of twisted abuse played out by his father. I'm trying to get him to talk to you, but he's afraid you'll get hurt." He paused again, allowing me to think about his words. "I think he's going to leave again."

I shook my head. "No," I said. "No, he can't. That's stupid. I found something out in Chicago, and I need to talk to him. He doesn't understand. He doesn't have to keep running."

"I... I don't understand. What are you—" I cut his words off, because I had an idea.

"Adam, do you think you could get him to see me one last time? Tell him I just need to give him something."

"I can try, but I doubt he'll listen."

"Then you have to make him, Adam. You have to try. I need this. Please." My voice sounded high and needy, but I didn't care anymore. I didn't care about anything anymore. Getting Joe back was the only thing that mattered.

"I'll see what I can do, but you know how he is. He just kind of shuts down his emotions when he wants to. Oh, I was going to ask you. He seems very fidgety all the time. Is that normal for him? He told me he's not on meds, so it's not likely a withdrawal symptom."

"It's his stimming. He rubs his fingers on soft cotton, like the hem of a t-shirt or a soft blanket. He probably doesn't have anything." I unlocked my car and walked over to the trunk, lifting the lid and pulling out my gym bag. I had a t-shirt that was clean, so I handed it to Adam. "Here, give him this. It will help him feel more stable."

Adam nodded, then slapped my shoulder. "I can't promise anything, but I'll ask him again, man."

"Thanks, Adam. I don't know what I'd do without you."

I SHOWED up for work two days later after two nights alone in my bed, tossing and searching the sheets for Joe's warm, soft body to hold on to. I'd wake up and remember. My house reminded me of what I'd lost, my shower reminded me of what I'd had.

I'd brought the small box that I'd hand-carried from Chicago with me, stowing it safely in my locker until I had some time to see Joe. I wasn't going to ask for permission. I needed to talk to him, and he was going to have to see me.

I forced myself to focus on my patients for the next six hours. The hospital was busy due to a driver that was texting on the freeway. Four separate ambulances were sent to us and most of the patients came through me one way or another.

When I finally had a break, I grabbed the worn box and made my way down the echoing hallways to Joe's room. The door was closed, so I waited a beat, then slowly opened it, peaking inside. My hand automatically drew to my mouth as I took in the sight before me.

Joe's face and neck were mottled with blue and black bruising that continued under the neckline of the hospital gown. His lip was split and all I could see of his left side was covered in fiberglass casts. I had to catch my breath, fortunate that he was asleep to look him over as I had.

Remembering the box in my hands, I tentatively stepped around the bed to where the chair was and set it down. When I turned, two gorgeous blue eyes (okay, one and a half) were staring back at me, glazing over with tears threatening to fall. I rushed over to him and panicked, not knowing where to touch him. Dammit, I just wanted to comfort my boy.

Joe raised his right hand to his face to wipe the tears, but I got there first, cleaning the marks on his cheeks with my thumbs. "I love you so much, Joe. Please don't push me away." His body heaved with sobs as I held on to his right side where I could, kissing his hair, cheek and neck. It felt unreal, touching him again after so many days without.

When he leaned back, I wiped more tears from his face and looked him slowly up and down, taking in the changes, the bruises, my t-shirt that he was holding onto with white knuckles. That made me smile wide enough to show molars.

"Joe, I'm sorry. I am so sorry for just showing up here when you asked that I not, but I had to see you. I couldn't stay away."

I watched as Joe nodded, eyes sparkling again. My eyes trailed over his body, taking in his bruises, his cuts, the bandages. I couldn't believe how broken he looked.

Then Joe, being Joe, always trying to make me laugh, said, "It's just a flesh wound."

In that moment, I would have given him anything in the world. Still, I knew my coming here, bringing this box, sharing my trip with him, was going to make him hate me.

"I didn't want you to see me like this, b-b-but also, I don't want Venom to..." he trailed off, eyes on the ceiling. "Ven—, I mean, my f-f-father wasn't a good man. I told you part of it already, but I didn't tell you everything. And now, I just don't know what I would do if he knew about you. Madden, you don't know what a horrible person he is."

"Joe, I need to tell you something, it's about my trip to Chicago." I pulled the chair over to the bed, setting the box on the blanket near his foot. His gaze never left mine, which I knew was forced. He rarely made eye contact with me unless it was important, which, I suppose this was. I knew he was trying, and, for that, I had a bit of heat rising in my neck. My palms were sweating because I didn't know how this was going to go, and I had this one chance.

"When I was in Chicago, I went to see the coordinates from your tattoo. I just wanted to know you better, Joe. I just wanted to feel closer to you, or something. As soon as I pulled up to the address, I knew it was wrong. I knew I shouldn't have gone there without your permission. Without telling you, even. My intention was to bring you something that would make you remember something good."

"There was nothing good, Madden. There was nothing you could find there anymore that could bring me anything worth remembering." I looked at his pale face, now wrecked and battered, and I wondered if he would care about what was in the box. "Just say it, Madden. Please? Let's get this over with."

With a long breath, I told him about driving to the coordinates I'd memorized from his skin; how they led me down a long, narrow dirt road with trailers lining both sides. I had parked the rental car and sat against the curb in a grassy area with trees lining two properties. I wasn't sure what I had been looking for, but it wasn't that.

After a couple of minutes, a blonde woman in a track suit walked over to the car and asked if I'd needed something. Her eyes had this softness to them. Her whole face, really. She seemed weighted down by her life and somehow sad. I wasn't sure what to say, but I told her that a friend of mine used to live around there and I was in the area. One thing led to another and she'd told me that she remembered Joe and worried every day since he'd left. Then she had invited me over for lemonade and asked about Joe and where he was. She sounded like she had really cared about him and where he'd ended up.

I explained that she'd really cared about him and was able to hold on to some things for him, just in case. Pointing to the box, I told him it was what she'd given me for him.

"Do you want to open it, Joe?"

He shook his head and quietly answered, "No, I want to hear the rest first. I can tell you're holding something back, Madden. I just need you to tell me because I can't keep wondering what it is. Just tell me."

Resting my hand on his leg, I gave it a squeeze. "Fair enough. She told me about your father. She said she didn't know what he was into, but he had a lot of shady looking men showing up at night and when he wasn't drunk, well... he was always drunk." I paused, applying light pressure to Joe's thigh, willing myself the courage to tell him the rest. He nodded, so I continued. "No one knows what happened, but he wasn't seen for a few days. Apparently, someone had come looking for him and they found him dead in his chair with dozens of bottles of alcohol in the house."

"What does that mean? What are you saying? Just tell me."

"Joe," I whispered, reaching for his hand. It was cold, but I held on. "He's dead. He's gone." My voice cracked, because I didn't know how he'd take the news. This man was his only living relative that he knew of. Even if he hated him, there was still the sting of loss. His face was smooth and open. I could tell that he was processing the information and I would wait. I would stay here as long as it took for him to realize what I'd said. And how it would ultimately affect him.

After a few long minutes, he mumbled something I couldn't make out, but I didn't miss the tear that silently rolled down his cheek.

"What did you say?" I asked him, lifting my hand to his cheek.

"I said it's over. It's over." It was almost a whisper the second time, then a smile broke out on his face.

"Joe, I don't—" I started to say, shaking my head in confusion.

"He can't come after me now, right? It's over? He's dead. That's what you said, right? He died?"

"Well, yes. But, what do you mean, 'he can't come after you'?"

"He sent Devin after me to find me, then he was coming. Devin was just looking for me for my... for him." He paused, but I knew he wasn't done talking, so I waited. "Is it really over, Madden?"

His face broke my heart when he looked up at me, his eyes shiny and wet. I reached over and pulled him to me, his head against my chest. "It's over, baby." I kissed his hair and pressed my cheek to his head. He nodded against me and I found myself rubbing his back, like I always seemed to do. It felt natural and warmed me beneath my skin.

Eventually nurses came in and checked on Joe, then left us alone again. Neither of us spoke, but Joe looked tired. He'd had quite an exhausting, even harrowing couple of days. I pulled back, my intention to give him space to lie down and sleep, but he fisted his hand into my shirt and whimpered.

"Baby, you need to sleep. I'm not going anywhere unless you ask me. I know we have more to talk about," I said, running my hand through his hair, "but you need to rest and heal. We can deal with the rest of it later."

Shaking his head in protest, he said, "No. I thought you were going to be in danger from Venom. I thought he would hurt you and I couldn't handle you being hurt. I didn't want to be apart from you. Please don't go. Please say you forgive me for pushing you away. I just—"

He'd had too much. This was more than he could handle at once. This room, with its beeping, wires, and bleached smell. This hospital where I worked and now basically lived. The man who had abused him years ago and followed him now. And the death of his father. It was all too much, and he needed to process, and I knew it. I wasn't going to make him talk through it all with me. Not now. Maybe not for a while.

"I'm not going to leave, Joe. I need you to rest, though. You have to trust me." His eyes spoke volumes when I peered into them. He trusted me, I knew he did. It was everything else that he didn't trust. Everyone and everything else had let him down. He'd never felt protected before and, more than anything, right now, he needed to feel safe.

I slowly sat him up and guided him to shift down in the bed as I got in behind him, my legs wrapped around the outside of his own. I pulled him back gently by his good shoulder until his head rested below my chin. And he was safe. I was wrapped around him, like a cloak of security. Within minutes he was asleep. Minutes later, so was I.

34

Joe

One flap at a time, I pulled the box open. What I saw lying beneath the battered cardboard took my breath away. The tears instantly returned, as did my hammering heart. Lifting a dirty, haggard, and worn Bunny from the box, I leaned against the bed and sobbed. His fur felt lush against my chin as I held him close. His poor body was missing so much stuffing he was more like a rag, but in that moment Bunny was perfect. Terror filled my bones as I thought about the last time I'd held him in my hands. The last day that I was a boy. The day that Venom decided I was useless, stupid, and needed to be a real man. I remembered clearly how mad he was at seeing me with Bunny tucked close in my bed. And how much of a beating I'd taken for it.

After the fog in my brain lifted, one of the nurses came in, checked my vitals, checked my eye, my arm, my wrist, and poked around at my ribs. I felt like a voodoo doll under scrutiny. Once she was done with her extensive bodily search, she told me the doctor would be coming around in the morning to sign my discharge papers. I was at a crossroads, as cliché as that was. I knew what my life had been, what it could be, with Madden. I wanted it. I wanted more. And that need that coursed through me scared me silly. I'd never felt more adult and loved, yet utterly alone than I did in that moment. I sat in my stupid gown, on a thin mattress, in the hospital and thought of Madden. Because of course I did. All of this was because of him. I had a job, well, that wasn't really because of him, but seeing him in the café had motivated me to do my best. To want more for myself. To be *worthy* of more for myself.

The door opened and a tall, dark, gorgeous Madden stepped in from the shadows. He'd never looked so good. His green scrubs accentuated his eyes and made them shine. And that smile, holy fuckballs. It did things to my insides.

"Hey, baby. I missed you today, but I get to take you home in the morning. I have the next two days off, too." Setting a vase with flowers I hadn't even noticed down on the windowsill, he said, "Those are from the café, again. I think that's a daily delivery now."

My eyes darted to the three other vases, all holding arrangements in varying degrees of health. Seeing them made me smile.

"Look, Joe, we need to talk about me going to Chicago and bringing back that box." Madden's eyes darted towards the chair where the box had been, quickly turning to me when he noticed it was missing.

I pointed at the bed, silently asking him to sit. "Madden, you did me a favor by going there."

His head jerked up at my words. "What?"

"I figured something out, Madden. And I never would have known if you hadn't gone back there. I owe you so much."

He stood up. "Okay, what?" His face was a mask of confusion.

I lifted the worn, threadbare Bunny from my pillow and held it up to my cheek.

"You're Joe," I said, a huge smile transforming my face. "You're Joe and you saved me. And you were there for me every day for my entire life, Madden. You."

"I'm pretty sure you're Joe. And I'm still completely lost."

I gestured at the bed again, and he moved to sit down at the edge.

"Okay, so the first time I met you in the café I knew you. Well, I thought I'd known you from somewhere. You had this familiar look about you, but not really. I don't know how to explain it. But, do you remember being in a hospital in Chicago when you were a kid? You had broken your arm."

I waited, watching as his eyes roamed the ceiling, then back down at me. "Yeah. But, how did you know that?"

I picked up Bunny and handed him to Madden. Taking him in his hands, a smile formed on the left side of his lips. "This was in the box?" He asked. I nodded. He looked at Bunny again, then I could see when it dawned on him. "This is Bunny?" he asked, staring at the greying material. "This is Bunny, right? The one thing..."

"Yeah," I said, wiping my eyes with the back of my hand. "Yeah, that's Bunny. The *only* thing I'd ever loved." I focused on his face. "Until recently."

"Joe." His voice was the softest I'd ever heard it. I felt it in my bones. His gaze moved from my face to Bunny, then he placed a kiss on Bunny's head, right between his floppy ears. When he pulled him away, his eyes were still focused on the animal. "Thank you for being there for Joe."

If that didn't deserve a swoon, I didn't know what would. I had no words, and we sat there for endless moments, just looking at each other.

"I don't understand why you said I'm Joe. I'm missing something. And how did you know about me breaking my arm?" He'd set Bunny down next to me on the pillow where he'd been previously resting.

"You don't understand," I said, shaking my head, then remembering why that was a bad idea. "Do you remember that day? In the hospital?" He nodded. "I was there, Madden. It was me. In the waiting room. I was there when your Mom, Dad, and sis—well, Anna, were waiting."

He stared at me. "I don't—" He said, and I smiled.

"Just think," I said. "You left with your family, but a few minutes later you came back. And you brought me something."

He looked at the doll lying next to me again. And then it clicked. "Oh, my God. That was you? Oh, my God. Joe. I bought you Bunny?"

I nodded and he was up and kissing my lips, my hair, my eyes, then stepped back, his gaze on Bunny.

"I don't even understand how this is possible. I'm trying to remember everything. I wish I had... Well, I don't know what. God, Joe. You were so small and scared and alone."

"Do you see, Madden? You saved me. That day, you gave me what I needed to endure it all. You've been saving me my entire life. You are the most unselfish person I've ever met, Madden, and I love you with all my heart. Even if it isn't worth much, it's yours."

"It's worth more than anything else in the world, Joe." His face was so full of joy. Taking a seat on the bed again, he said, "Wait. You said earlier that I was Joe. What did you mean by that?"

I smiled. "I had always hated being called Bird. It wasn't a name, it's an animal. I have never understood why they would name me after an animal. So, as soon as I left, I changed my name to Joe because I thought the person who'd given me Bunny was named Joe. For some reason, that was the name I had always remembered your father calling you. I had no idea how wrong I was. I must have misheard him."

"You gave yourself the name that you thought was mine?" His face was confused.

"Your parents loved you. That was obvious. I had watched them and your sister. They were so different than what I had. And they were so happy. Then you walked out with your cast and your parents smiled so proudly at you. I was jealous, but I looked at you and wanted your life. I wanted that for myself. I spent years wishing my real family would come and find me. And I always pictured *your* parents." I smiled sheepishly. "Is that totally weird? You know, considering."

Madden laughed, but it was choked. "No, it's not weird. Although, you probably didn't hear my dad wrong. He used to call me Joe Cool. Because I used to go around the house with a bowl on my head and pretend to fly a plane like Snoopy."

I smiled. "The infamous Red Baron. That's one reference I actually understand."

We were both quiet for a long time, lost in thought. We both jumped when the nurse pushed through the door, then smiled at Madden. He looked at me, sadness in his eyes.

"I should go. You look tired and you need to rest." I nodded, belying my urge to pull him onto the bed and never let go. "I'm going to go home, feed your fish and get the apartment ready for tomorrow when you come home. And we can plan everything we talked about."

I nodded solemnly. When he lifted his hand to cup my face, I tried to smile, but it was weak. I didn't want to be without him now. Not even for a minute. I needed him and wanted my life to start right now, not tomorrow.

"Joe, I know, baby. I don't want to go, but you need to rest and I'm going to do the same. I will be here first thing to bring you home. I promise."

I closed my eyes and nodded, feeling every bit as tired as he'd described.

His lips against mine should have made me jump, but instead made me moan.

"I love you, Joe. More than I ever thought was possible."

As he made his way through the door I whispered, "I love you, too."

EPILOGUE

6 WEEKS LATER

Joe

"Don't worry, I ordered pineapple on a quarter of the pizza only. The rest of it is full of manly toppings just for you." After placing the pizza on the kitchen table, I pulled out some plates and napkins and served up dinner while Madden picked a movie on Netflix. Handing him his while he sat back on the couch, I climbed over his outstretched legs and curled up into place on his left side, my back resting against his body, his arm stretched around me.

"Thank you, baby," he said, kissing the top of my head. "You ready to start?" he asked, humor in his voice. When I nodded, he pushed the button on the remote and Dumb and Dumber started. Before I even knew what was happening Madden was already laughing, my body shaking as I chewed my mouthful of bacon and pineapple. I smiled to myself, thinking of how lucky I was to have the life I had. How lucky I'd been to get away from Chicago and find my way here. To this city. To this man.

While Madden turned the lights out after the movie, I got into the shower and gave myself a pep talk. I wanted this so badly, I was ready. Even if I turned into a burnt tomato, I wasn't going to allow myself to back out of this. It was too important to me.

Madden was at the sink brushing his teeth when I was done and as I walked past him, I slapped his ass. "Hey! If you want to bring a bit of kink into the bedroom, I'm not going to turn you down." His words were laced with humor and I rolled my eyes. Maybe at some point I'd be a bit more open to other things. I trusted Madden more than anything. He'd spent our entire relationship taking it slow, at my pace. I'd hoped tonight would show him that I wasn't stalled in one place. I was moving forward every day.

When he turned off the bedroom light, I was already in bed, under the covers, Bunny on my pillow on the far side of the bed, Phantom curled up in a heap by my nightstand. Under the soft glow of the bedside lamp, I could tell Madden thought we were just going to sleep. He took his clothes off, replacing them with a t-shirt and light pajama shorts, then lifted the covers. And exposed me in my fully naked, fully erect state.

"Holy shit, Joe." I laughed at how wide his eyes were. "Should I take everything off?" He asked, unsure. I nodded and laughed again at his excited stare.

He stripped quickly, then got into bed, crawling over to get on top of me, but I shook my head. "No." His forehead creased as he took in the word. "No, I want to be on top tonight," I said, rolling him over and straddling his body. I set my hands on his firm, slightly hairy pecs and leaned down to taste his mouth. Mint toothpaste mixed with Madden's signature vanilla flavor. My body craved it.

After kissing him for a few minutes, I bit his lower lip, then traveled down his chin to his throat. There was something about his Adam's apple I just couldn't get enough of. My tongue lapped, then I softly bit the hard nub, caressing it again after. I continued exploring south, sucking his tanned nipple into my mouth, teasing it with my teeth, then let it go with a pop as he moaned deep. Savoring every inch of his warm, taught chest, I licked and sucked and nipped a path to his hard cock, jutting up beautifully from the trimmed nest of black hair at the base. Sitting my ass on his knees, I bent down and ran my nose along his length, saliva flooding my mouth as I made my way to his tip.

"Oh, fuck, Joe. Baby, please. Please suck me." I smiled deviously at him, relishing in the knowledge that he had no idea what I was planning on giving him tonight.

I ran my tongue around his crown, taking my time with the underneath, then loosely nipping at his slit. I smiled when his hips bucked up and he groaned. He made me feel like I was powerful. Like I had something worthy inside of me. And in moments like this, when it was just the two of us, alone, I felt like a part of me owned him. And damn if that didn't make my own cock jump against my stomach.

"Hand me the lube, Madden." Reaching into the drawer of the night stand, he pulled out the bottle of lube and a foil packet and handed them to me. I stared at the condom between his fingers. We'd both been tested when I'd moved in and we were both clean. I finally brought up the topic of sex without condoms a week ago with Madden, who seemed to worry when my entire face, neck, shoulders and chest turned the color of a ripe raspberry. We didn't make any decisions then, but I knew he wanted to go without when I felt ready. If I felt ready.

I looked down at him, his eyes wary as he watched me vacillate between using one or not. Keeping my eyes locked on his, I threw the condom over my shoulder and smiled. His eyes grew wide as he said, "Oh, fuck" and then grinned. Taking the lube, I poured a generous amount onto my fingers, then bent over, taking his long length into my throat. While Madden was busy moaning, I inched my lubed finger into my asshole, trying to prepare myself for the surprise I wanted to give my boyfriend.

It hurt. Not the worst pain, ever, but it was an uncomfortable pressure. I'd been used to far worse when I had been around Devin, but I wasn't going to let that ruin what I wanted with Madden. He would never knowingly hurt me. I trusted him. I knew I wanted this, with Madden, and I'd tried to start prepping myself two days ago. I'd gotten up to three fingers in my hole in the shower this morning, so I knew I could do this. Because it was Madden. And I wanted to belong to him. I wanted him to know that I was his and no one else's. I was giving myself to him in every way, and this was the last piece I had to give. He'd already taken my heart.

I lapped at his heavy, full balls while I added a second finger in my ass, scissoring as much as I could in this position.

"Hey, come up here and kiss me, baby." Smiling, I pulled out of myself and off him, then crawled up his body to press my lips to his. The kiss was savage and needy. He pulled me into his mouth, tasting me like it was the first time. My cock twitched at the thought of him tasting himself on my lips and a needy moan escaped me. "What are you doing back there with your hand, baby?" He asked me, his hands grabbing my ass cheeks and spreading them. His eyes went to mine as I felt his finger slowly sliding across my cheek to my hole. Once he felt the slickness his eyes rolled back into his head and he hissed through his teeth. "Fuck, Joe. Fuck. Is this happening?"

I bit my bottom lip and nodded, but he shook his head. "Words, Joe. I need words or this stops here." Of course.

"Madden. I want to feel you inside me. I want your bare cock in my body. I want to feel how much you love me and need me and want me until you can't take it anymore, and then I want to feel your hot cum fill me up and mark me as yours. Because I belong to you." Holy shit, somehow I'd said that.

Madden's hand wrapped around my nape as he pulled me

down and ravaged my mouth. His tongue fucked my mouth like it was the last time, and he had to make it count. All I wanted was to feel him deep inside me, feel his thick length fill me up. Goose bumps traveled from my arms to my legs, and I whimpered. "Please, babe."

Both of us froze. I'd never used an endearment before and I hadn't even planned to now, but it just came out. And it felt... right. I smiled and Madden kissed a line from my lips to my ear and he whispered, "I love you. Hearing you call me babe is going to make me come before I even get inside you." I shivered and thrust my hips into him.

"I need you inside me now, babe. Please. I'm begging."

"Fuck, Joe."

I sat up and said, "Can I ride you?" He nodded furiously as I lifted onto my knees while he grabbed the lube. After slicking his cock and my hole generously, he tapped my hip and held his length at the base. I took a deep breath and looked at the love, lust, and heat on his face and knew he'd take care of me. I knew I'd never need anyone else as long as I had Madden. And I'd do anything to keep him.

I adjusted myself over him so that the tip of his fat cock breached my opening and I took a deep breath, the sting burning my eyes.

"Hey," Madden said, softly, hand brushing my cheek. "Take your time and go slow. If you push out while moving down it'll be easier." I nodded, my face pressing into his hand. As I took his advice, he pierced my body, inch by tantalizingly hot inch. I panted, feeling both pleasure and pain consume me. Finally, after long minutes, his balls touched my ass, and I let out the breath I'd been holding. "You okay, baby?" he asked me, rubbing his hands up and down my arms. I looked into his eyes and knew he was trying his hardest not to move. His teeth were clenched, and I couldn't help myself. I let out a burst of laughter. The movement of my body sent his cock unbelievably further into me and it felt like he was rearranging my insides. Making room for him inside of me. A perfect fit for always. I groaned from deep in my chest as the flickers of pain turned into bursts of pleasure. Hesitantly, I rolled my hips and gasped at the overwhelming sensation of his dick rubbing that spot inside of me that no one had ever touched before. I looked down to see my hard cock dribble precum onto his abs. A burst of lust ripped through me.

"Madden, please. Move, please. Make me feel good." I croaked out the words through rough pants of breath, feeling sweat trickle down my spine.

"I'll give you anything you want, Joe. Always," he replied, then flattened his feet against the mattress, ramming his hips up into me in a quick, deep rhythm that had my dick bouncing off of him, my wetness painting trails against his skin.

His fingers had my hips in a vice grip, all I could do was throw my head back and take everything he gave. I'd never felt so cherished. So loved. My entire life I'd thought that being in this position, giving myself to someone so wholly and completely would make me feel used and out of control. Like, with each thrust they were taking a piece of me that I could never get back. And I didn't know if that was true with a hookup or not, but with Madden... God. It was the opposite. With every heartbeat I knew we were adding layers to our relationship. Building a bond that grew stronger with each touch. Each caress. I wanted to give myself to him like this because I knew that if I was his, he'd always catch me. He'd take care of me and love me. Because it was the same for me. He was mine, just as I was his. And I'd do everything to make him feel good.

Just when I thought I couldn't take anymore, Madden's hand tightened around my length and he jerked me in time with his thrusts. "Holy, shit, I am going to die," I announced, slamming my eyes shut and gripping his shoulders tightly. "Oh, God, oh, God, I'm dying, shit." I trailed off with more gibberish, and Madden said, "Come for me, baby," and I did. I howled my release as his cock pumped into me. I spurted trails of hot, wet come up his chest as he rammed into my ass, and when I felt his cock thicken impossibly, I felt it. Wet heat coating my insides, burning me from the inside out. Claiming me as his. Giving me his very essence.

"I love you so much," I said into the sweat-filled air, falling forward onto his chest. I didn't care that my mess was between our bodies. It felt good in the moment.

"I love you too, Joe. Thank you," he responded, fast whooshes of breath in my hair.

We lay there, infused together until his cock softened enough to fall out of me. I felt the trickle of fluid making its way down my balls onto Madden. "Oh, fuck that's so hot," he said, and I laughed. "You are so beautiful lying here all debauched like this. I just might get used to it."

"Well, I'm not going anywhere, babe. You are officially stuck with me." I kissed his chest and sighed contentedly. I was sore, spent, and sticky, but I wouldn't change one single thing.

"All I want is you here with me. To stay." And then he rolled me over and kissed me deeply. And then he made good use of the slicked, stretched state of my hole until we let our pleasure consume us.

THE END

ACKNOWLEDGMENTS

Anyone who knows me at all, knows I'm not a crier. As I sit here writing this page, I'm close. So many people have given their time, love, and encouragement in support of me. All things I've never had before, and it's meant the world. I wish I could list every single person by name, but I'm afraid I'd take up half of this book. So, I'll do my best with this page. Here goes...

Nero Seal, you believed in me before anyone else. You saw talent where I saw flaws. You pushed me to write, but also to give Joe and Madden the story they deserve. I can't thank you enough for that. I love you!

Perin, you talked me through all my doubts and fears, giving me a safe space to wallow and grow. You told me to write my own story, and I did. I hope I did them justice.

Emma Jaye, you gave me more time and professional opinions than I deserved, and I'm especially grateful for your feedback. As are Joe and Madden.

Tida, NJ, Elli, Tessie, and **AJ**, I don't know how I would have survived without you guys. Thanks for being there, for giving me so much support. For guiding me and forcing me to believe I could do it. You're amazing and I'm so glad to have you in my corner.

Claire Castle, you are the nicest, most real person I know. You give without question and your heart is so big. I have loved getting to know you and the boys you've dreamed up. Your friendship has meant more to me than you know. Love you!

Teresa and **Christopher**, you read my words first and didn't hate them. You didn't give up when I told you to, and you made me feel loved. I'm so thankful to have you in my life. I love Team Trash Panda. **Bahar** and **Chase**, I love each of you, and I know how lucky I am to call you friends.

Clyde, I have learned so much from you. You are so giving, loving, and supportive. You've taught me something new every single day. You're a brilliant writer, mentor, comedian, and friend. Your opinions and advice have given me structure and direction when I was sorely lacking in both. Your words have touched me, your friendship has lifted me, and your support has given me hope. I love you so much.

To the Twitter **#WritingCommunity**, I wish I could write each of you words to express how much I appreciate the family I have in you. Everyday you brighten the darkness and remind me that a family doesn't have to be blood. I have never felt so emboldened and worthy of happiness in my life. You've shined a light in my little corner of the universe, giving my lonely, untethered astronaut reason to smile, write poems, share pics of hot men (and Ruby Rose—**TT and Mario**), and take off my space suit and belong. I love you all so much. **Rory, Crow, Kota, Travis, Kennnnnnnnn, Cameron, Halo, Torsten, Genius, Celyn,** and **Ethan**, you have shown me the way and lit up the path. I'm more myself with you than I've been IRL with my family. **Mary,** for polishing my words. **Dean Cole,** you are mad brilliant, a beautiful person, a stellar writer, and a very genuine friend. Thank you for the beautiful boys on my cover, and for always being so nice. I love you all.

AUTHOR NOTE

Thank you so much for reading about Joe and Madden. They've lived in my head for a while now and I'm thrilled to have this opportunity to share them with you.

Book reviews are the lifeblood to success as a writer. I'd appreciate you sharing your thoughts, even a sentence, on Amazon, GoodReads, and/or Bookbub.

ABOUT THE AUTHOR

Ash Knight is a voracious reader, lover of pancakes, and believes that love is love. Ash is a sucker for a good love story with a happily ever after. This is Ash's first novel. You can find Ash on <u>FB</u> and <u>Twitter</u> or writing her next story of men finding happiness together.